Praise for *Starship Maui*

"It feels like I've travelled to Maui and back having been so immersed in the world of these chapters. Thank you for the beauty and the life lessons embedded in the book."

— Elaina Ellis, *Literary Editor*

"Your natural gifts as a storyteller blend seamlessly with your artist's eye for detail. The beauty of the landscape unveils itself gradually and thoroughly with an understated richness. Yes, it was a time of sex, drugs, and rock n' roll but those also served as portals to a quest for consciousness and understanding, an authentic striving."

— Jim Hinton, *Singer-Songwriter, Music Historian, Professor*

"*Starship Maui* is a delightful sojourn into a bygone era of 1970's Maui life! This glorious glimpse into an idyllic Hawaiian nature paradise is perfectly painted in soft pastels by artist/writer Richard Dux Missler. "Jon" tells us of his adventures as a young man in his early twenties, living his ideals as he unwittingly rubs elbows with luminaries of the time, as well as the very special ordinary people he meets. All, including his dog Kolohe, are equally part of his journey of evolution. I especially enjoyed the intermittent chapters that return us to "present-day Jon" reminiscing as he writes, with his colorful spell-checker, Raoul. What a character! This is such a fun ride that I can't wait to board *Starship Maui II*."

— Elizabeth B. Jenkins, *International Bestselling Author*

"I had the pleasure of reading *Starship Maui* and enjoyed it tremendously. There's an endearing mischievousness to Mr. Missler's narrative. His love for Maui comes through clearly, as does his general love of life and people. The relationship between Jon and his dogs was wonderfully expressed. The book is pleasingly genuine. Rich with metaphor (but without being overladen) and gentle lessons on life's seemingly unending contradictions. One of my favorite lines from the book was, 'Life is school.' Indeed."

— D. W. Ulsterman, Bestselling Author

"*Starship Maui* transports you to a realm where the raw pulse of nature and the human spirit converge—like an unfiltered groove that awakens every sense. Jon's 1974 adventure on Maui, with its spontaneous exploration, wild encounters, and a deep yearning for connection, feels like a soulful journey of self-discovery, inviting you to embrace life's unpredictable beauty."

— Brian Park-Siart, *Owner — Aku Bone Media*

"Missler opens his book with Jon thumbing a ride on the road to Hāna, a perfect metaphor for the era of which he writes. I felt as if I was travelling that road along with him. What he gives us, as readers, is a glimpse into a world when life was simpler and more carefree. *Starship Maui* rekindled so many of my own memories from that time period when I too had begun to explore and engage in the adventure of life."

— Paul Espinoza, Singer-Songwriter, Touring, and recording artist

Other works by Dux Missler

Magic Maui Coloring Book
1978

Hawai'i Fun Activity Book
Petroglyph Press, 1985

STARSHIP MAUI
A Journey Through Life on Maui in the '70s

A NOVEL
BOOK I

RICHARD DUX MISSLER

Starship Maui is autobiographical fiction. Any resemblance to persons living
or dead may not be merely coincidental. That being said—names and details
have been changed to protect privacy, characters created, dialogue invented or
reimagined. Some events have been repositioned in time to fit the format of the
novel. My apologies for anything I have gotten wrong or misrepresented.

Library of Congress Control Number: 2024922240

ISBN: 979-8-9900621-2-2 (Paperback)
ISBN: 979-8-9900621-3-9 (eBook)

Edited by Elaina Ellis
Layout and design by Book House Publishing
Book jacket © 2024 by Bob Paltrow Design
Photograph of author by Patricia Missler

Printed in the USA by Village Books

CORNER HOUSE PUBLISHING
books@cornerhousepublishing.com

"And think not you can guide the course of love.
For love, if it finds you worthy,
shall guide your course."

Kahlil Gibran

CONTENTS

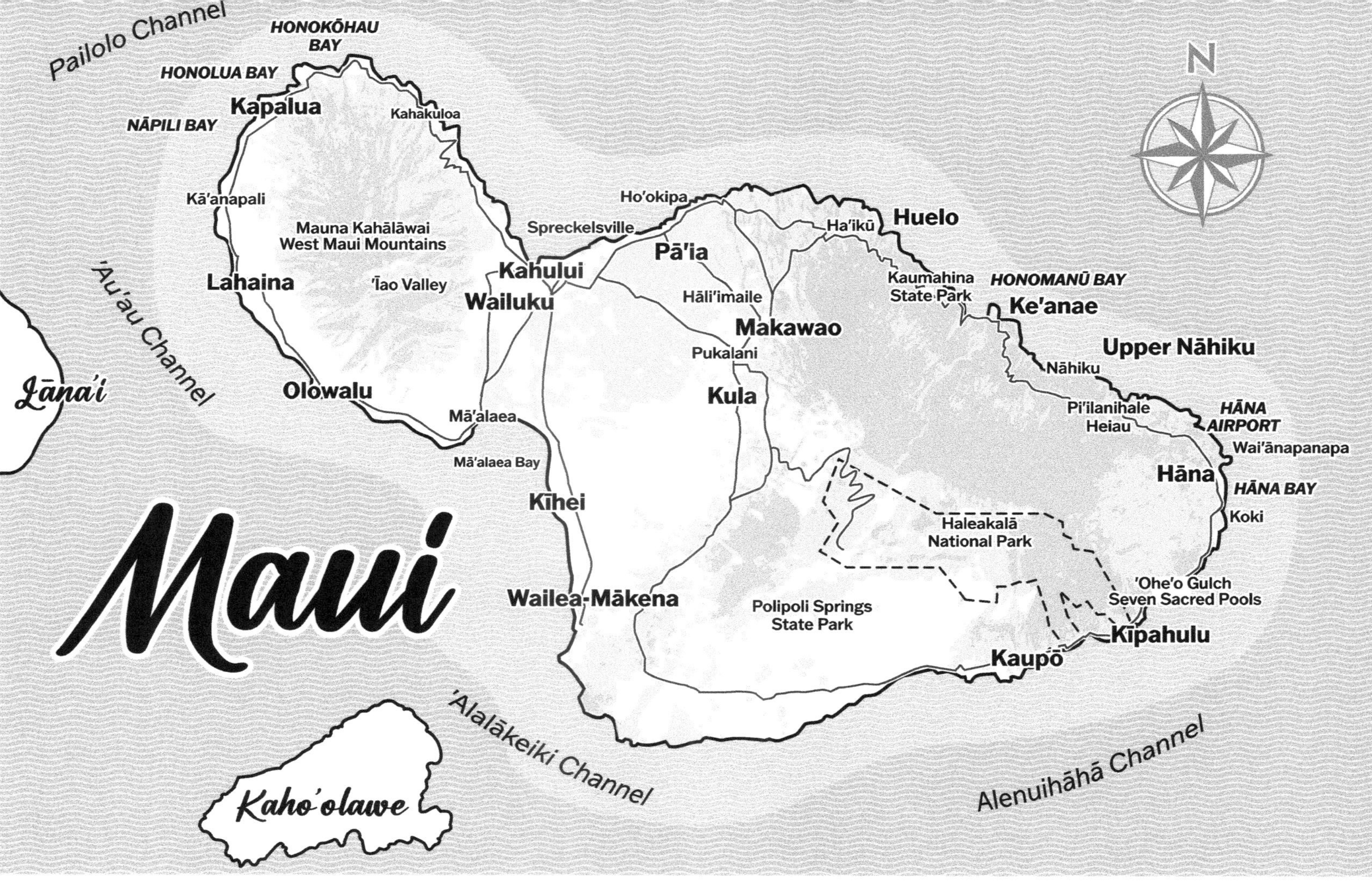

N
Pailolo Channel
HONOKŌHAU BAY
HONOLUA BAY
NĀPILI BAY
Kapalua
Kahakuloa
Kā'anapali
Mauna Kahālāwai
West Maui Mountains
'Īao Valley
Lahaina
Olowalu
'Au'au Channel
Lāna'i
Maui
Kaho'olawe
Sprecklesville
Ho'okipa
Kahului
Wailuku
Pā'ia
Hāli'imaile
Pukalani
Makawao
Kula
Mā'alaea
Mā'alaea Bay
Kīhei
Wailea-Mākena
'Alalākeiki Channel
Ha'ikū
Huelo
Kaumahina State Park
HONOMANŪ BAY
Ke'anae
Upper Nāhiku
Nāhiku
Pi'ilanihale Heiau
HĀNA AIRPORT
Wai'ānapanapa
HĀNA BAY
Hāna
Koki
'Ohe'o Gulch
Seven Sacred Pools
Kīpahulu
Kaupō
Haleakalā National Park
Polipoli Springs State Park
Alenuihāhā Channel

FOREWORD

I JUMPED AT THE OPPORTUNITY TO WRITE a foreword for my good friend's novel. We go back a long way, old what's-his-name and me.

I first met Jon in Hāna, in the 1970s. Back then he lived on a property owned by a collective including my college roommate. It was truly a tropical paradise, except for those damn mosquitos.

Starship Maui is "autobiographical fiction." That's what Jon's calling it, anyway, after our research into genres and subgenres and what-not. It's based on real-life events but not bound by the facts. I love that. Facts aren't everything. And I am honored to have been part of the process. Proofreading, mostly. The dude cannot spell. Would you believe he wrote the whole manuscript longhand?

The book is fabulous. I'm not just saying that because I'm one of the characters. I wouldn't do that. Okay, maybe I would do that, but trust me, it's a good read. Jon has captured a flavor of the times. Not the flavor I was tasting, mind you. While I was working a 9-to-5 office gig in the city, Jon was working on his tan. I don't hold it against him. Bastard.

By the mid-seventies we had seen it all. Political assassinations, a man on the moon, the summer of love, and the Kent State massacre. The country was deeply divided over the Vietnam War. Marginalized groups of our society fought hard for civil rights and equality. There were riots, peace marches, protests, protest songs, draft card burnings, and bra burnings (which I fully supported). The sexual revolution was going strong. Everyone was on the pill. This was before sex could kill you. Casual sex was sometimes just that, casual. Fueled by idealism, cannabis, LSD, and rock-n-roll, the counterculture was widespread. Many "dropped out," seeking alternative lifestyles. With only his backpack and a one-way ticket, Jon heeded the call. He arrived to the party early—he was on Maui before the hordes of tourists, yuppies, and the rich-and-famous, including Oprah. I don't think he had a plan. He was winging it.

But I'll tell you right now, the whole story can't fit in one book. I'm not supposed to tell you this yet, but Jon is working on a second installment. So, let's call this Book I, in which he sets the table and hands out the pūpūs (appetizers). If you're still hungry when you finish, well, perhaps Book II will deliver the meat and potatoes. Or in this case, the tofu and potatoes.

Don't let the hype about the era scare you. This is a charming tale with all the trimmings. Some might even say it's a hero's journey, a boy's attempt to find out what it means to be a man. A love story between the self and the universe.

Let's hitch a ride. Enjoy.

Sincerely,
Raoul Lovejoy

P. S. I read somewhere that women read more than men do. Hello, readers. Did I mention that I am single?

AUTHOR'S NOTE

A s I first stepped off the airplane on Maui, I had no idea what lay ahead. My life would never be the same. Weeks earlier I had graduated from high school. It was the summer of 1969, and I had just turned eighteen. I was recruited by the Maui Pineapple Company for a summer job, along with several of my good friends. We were a ragtag mix of kids from the suburbs of San Diego. Leaving behind a world of sidewalks and 7-Elevens, we were transported to the pineapple fields of Maui. For the first time in our lives, we were on our own. Many great adventures were shared that summer.

Starship Maui takes place five years later. I sojourned to Maui a few times before staying for good. Maui welcomed me with open arms. I felt blessed to be living in Hāna—my dream.

I became caretaker of an old plantation house on twenty-five acres of luxuriant jungle. In exchange for caretaking, I lived there rent free. There was no electricity and only an outhouse. Without a car, my thumb and my legs were my means of transportation. It was a simple life.

My meager savings continued to dwindle until I was flat broke. When I harvested my first crop of "Maui Wowie," things were looking up. That reminds me of a story. Have you heard this one?

I wrote this book because I felt compelled to preserve a seventies slice-of-life, Maui style. Experiences, places, and most importantly, people—the interesting and sometimes off-the-wall characters I met in that time and place. The seventies were wild and wooly. Drugs, sex, and rock-n-roll. Not necessarily in that order, but yeah, usually in that order.

Starship Maui portrays a unique moment in time. Of course, all moments in time are unique. Everything changes. It's the nature of our world. What once was, is no more. Time moves on. Places and people change and disappear altogether.

Reality is colored by our own personal perceptions. This is my version of the tale.

This is the way I remember it.

—Richard Dux Missler

1 | ROAD TO HĀNA

"HARD TO SAY WHEN IT ALL BEGAN. I mean, a long, long time ago, there wasn't even an Earth at all."

Jon looked at Kolohe as though he expected a response. Kolohe gave Jon one of his sideways glances, cocking his head and perking one ear up. Then the dog continued about his business, sniffing the roadside, and leaving his messages here and there.

Jon set his duffle bag down and eased his daypack off his shoulders. He turned the duffle bag so that the narrow end was facing traffic.

"What I mean, Kolohe, is that we're all made of stardust. What's the world coming to when a well-behaved dog, such as yourself, gets a ticket for not being on a leash? On Maui? In 1974? Who would believe it?"

Kolohe was pretending not to listen.

"You even water the road signs. A civil servant." He grinned at his own humor.

As a car approached, he stuck out his thumb. It continued without stopping.

Jon crouched beside his pack and extracted a carob candy bar. *Town runs have their good points.* Kolohe appeared by his side, sniffing the morsel as Jon unwrapped it. He gave Kolohe a corner of the candy bar and petted his head.

"You're a good dog, even if you are a rascal. Go on now," he said, waving him off.

Jon stared at the road sign ahead of them.

NARROW WINDING ROAD
NEXT 30 MILES

"Time to get a ride."

Looking past the sign, his eyes followed the lines of the deep valleys as they rose into sharp ridges, and disappeared into the clouds. He turned towards the ocean. A rain squall was pulling across the sparkling blue water. The falling rain formed a moving curtain. Ahead of the rain, the sky was clear. Fluffy white clouds reflected on the ocean's surface.

Two more cars passed. Jon let out a sigh, but Kolohe was happily stalking a mongoose. Jon took a hairbrush from his pack and began to brush his hair, which hung below his shoulders in thick waves; the tropical sun had bleached the top layer a golden brown. He tied it back in a ponytail and ran the brush through his beard.

Kolohe came to sit beside him, and both looked back to the horizon.

A rainbow had formed out over the ocean.

That's a good sign.

A yellow Datsun pulled over, a middle-aged couple smiling at him from inside.

"Hi, thanks for stopping." As Jon opened the door, Kolohe burst past him and jumped into the back seat.

"Is he friendly?" the man asked.

Kolohe stretched towards the front seat, licking the woman.

"He sure is!" the woman remarked, before Jon could apologize for his dog's behavior.

"Get back Ko. You be good now. He gets excited. Loves a car ride."

The car rounded the first of many curves. The surface of the road was a patchwork of asphalt, and in many spots, it was so narrow that when two cars approached one another, one was forced to pull over to let the other one pass. Ferns grew in a thick carpet alongside the road. Guava trees stretched out above the ferns, and yellow guavas lay along the edge of the road in various states of decay. Every inch of soil was covered with living greenery. The multitude of plants and trees were competing for space, and in places, cast the road in shadow. Large banyan trees towered high above. Their roots below groped over one another in a tangled mass. In the canopy, silver-green leaves of the kukui nut trees stood out in contrast to darker shades of green.

The woman turned in her seat, watching Kolohe hang his head out the window.

"We miss our dogs. We had to leave them home in Kansas. I'm Donna, by the way. And this is my husband, Jack."

Kolohe brought his head in to give her hand a lick. She scratched him under the chin.

"That's a good boy. He is a boy, isn't he?" she asked.

"Uh huh," Jon replied. "I'm Jon and his name is Kolohe or just Ko for short. Kolohe is Hawaiian for rascal."

"Oh, are you a rascal?" Donna said, talking baby talk.

Jack glanced back at Kolohe.

"He looks like the old Our Gang kid's dog. They had a white dog with spots that looked just like this one. Gee, maybe that was before your time."

"I remember watching that show when I was a kid. I see the resemblance."

Jack nodded, then turned his attention back to the winding road.

"This road get any better?"

"Hard to believe this is a highway, isn't it? There are some spots where the driving is easier, but for the most part, this is it. The Hāna Highway."

"You live out there?"

"Yes. A little ways before Hāna. This road goes right by my house. It's kind of like my driveway." *Landscaping by God.*

"Is there much to see in Hāna?"

"Well, there's Hāna Bay, and ah . . . a great view from the cross on the hill. There's a little road that goes up to the cross." Jon paused, considering. "Actually, there's not much to it. Two stores, a gas station, post office, oh, and a movie theater. People rush out to Hāna, thinking there's going to be something there, but getting there is really the thing. The drive to the Seven Pools, out past the town, is incredibly beautiful. There are waterfalls right next to the road. The road does get a little narrower though."

Jack frowned into the rearview mirror. "How can it get narrower?"

Jon laughed and shrugged. They all sat in silence for a moment, then he pointed out the window. "This whole hillside coming up is bamboo, a bamboo forest."

"Will you look at that," Donna exclaimed.

"You own your own place out here?" Jack asked.

"No. I'm a caretaker. There are five different owners. It's what they call a *hui*. It's a group of people who buy land together because none of them could afford it by themselves. I live in the house, on the property. They're still making the money to pay for the place, so in the meantime I get to enjoy it."

"How big is it?"

"Three bedrooms . . . Oh, the land? Twenty-five acres."

"Twenty-five acres. That's a good-sized parcel."

"There's a stream that runs along one border, and I can hike to the ocean."

"Do the owners live back in the States?"

"He means the mainland. You keep doing that," his wife scolded.

The banter reminded Jon of his mother. He missed her spunky spirit. She lived across the ocean, over two thousand miles away, in the Bay Area.

"Most of them are here on Maui. Two live on the other side of the island, in Nāpili. That's out past Lahaina. And, let's see, one is on the mainland selling puka shells or something. One is in South America, and I'm not sure where the other one is. I haven't even met them all."

"Is it an investment for them?"

"I'm not sure. I think they eventually want to move out, build houses, and stuff. It's just hard to make a living out here. Not much in the way of jobs."

"What do you do?" Jack asked. "Do you work? How do you make money?"

Okay Dad . . . what's this, the third degree? Too many questions.

Jon focused on the mountain apple trees, whose branches were filled with scarlet blossoms.

When hitchhiking one never knew who would be stopping. The encounters were generally brief; at the end everyone said goodbye and continued with their lives. Jon was reserved and private. He didn't often reveal his personal story to others, especially to strangers. He felt like he was being put on the spot.

He sighed, supposing it wouldn't kill him to share a little more with Jack and Donna. *Let the interrogation continue.*

"I do artwork, oil paintings, and paint a few signs here and there. I also make jewelry. Puka shell necklaces with silver and turquoise beads. I do sell a painting every blue moon. I don't have to pay any rent so that helps. And there's also a lot of fruit growing around where I live, so if I do get hungry . . . ."

"It sounds like you're doing your own thing. Good for you," Donna said. Her voice was warm and nurturing, and Jon softened in response. "But it must get lonely out here. Do you live by yourself?"

"Uh huh. Well, Kolohe and me. It can get lonely. When I first moved out here, I wasn't sure if I liked it, you know, with all the rain and mosquitoes. But I'm getting used to it. I like it."

"Thank goodness you have sweet Kolohe for company."

"Actually I'm caretaking him too. One of the owners had too many dogs, so they farmed him out to the country." Jon looked out the window. He was eager to steer the conversation to something less personal. "Check out the bark on these trees coming up on the left. They're called rainbow eucalyptus. See the colors running up and down the trunks?"

"My yes."

The road continued to twist and turn its way to Hāna. In and out of valleys and around ridges; alternating between deep jungle lushness and breathtaking ocean vistas. Where the road curved farthest into the valleys it crossed a bridge over a stream and more often than not, just below a lovely waterfall. Around the ridges the terrain was steep. Cliffs dropped sharply to the ocean on one side of the road and rose into a vertical wall on the other side.

"Oooh, what's that there?"

"That's Ke'anae Peninsula."

"Mind if we stop for a picture? Maybe your pup needs a break?"

"Sure. Ko will like that."

The three stood at the overlook.

"Gosh, that's beautiful." Jack had just taken a couple of pictures and had his camera hanging around his neck.

The bluff dropped several hundred feet and the peninsula hung suspended below them. Ocean waves crashed on the jagged shoreline, the white spray contrasting sharply against black lava. Coconut palms grew in clusters. Their fronds were dancing with the trade winds. The interior of the peninsula was a study in green, an intriguing patchwork of taro fields. The taro was grown in water, in the manner of rice paddies. The fields, or *loʻi*, were fed by a good-sized stream that ran through the area, from above. After a heavy rain, small waterfalls appeared along the cliffs. A few houses were scattered on the peninsula. There were two old churches. That such a small community would have two churches testified to an earlier history. The church closest to the water was large and made with big round stones.

"Honey, get a picture of Ko."

"The dog . . . ? Yeah, okay."

Kolohe was across the road getting a drink from a small stream. Jon clapped his hands. Ko came running. Jon sat on the rock wall with Kolohe at his side; Keʻanae Peninsula stretched out beyond them.

Rain began to fall . . . big drops. Jon looked to the darkening sky. "Big drops around here don't always mean a passing shower. We'd better get going."

As they drove off, the rain began to pound. Jon had to roll up the windows. Ko paced back and forth until Jon cracked the window, just enough for Kolohe's nose to stick out. After a long sniff of wet air, the dog settled down next to Jon, resting his head on his caretaker's arm.

"What do you think, dear? This rain is wild—should we really go all the way out to Hāna?" Donna asked her husband.

Gee and she seemed so nice. Jon looked at Kolohe, raised his eyebrows and twisted his mouth into a funny shape. *They wouldn't let us out in this downpour, would they? That would be inhumane.* He thought about his garden. *The snails will be having a feast. The rain always brings them out. Better check the green beans when I get home.*

"Let's keep going," Jack answered. We've come this far."

They drove through an area where large leaf philodendrons were completely covering the trunks of the trees.

Donna turned to Jon. "Those vines, ah, what's their name?"

"Philodendrons."

"Yes, that's it. We have those. I mean, I see them in the nurseries. They don't get this big back home."

"They like it here."

The rain had stopped.

"My house is just around this next corner. There's a place to pull over on the right. You two have a good time on the island. Thanks so much for the ride."

"You bet. Good luck."

"Goodbye Ko. Bye now."

Jon saw a white pickup truck parked across from the house. "We've got company, buddy," he said to Kolohe. But the dog had already bolted out the door.

2 | HUI

A walkway sloped to the front door of the old plantation house. The door was centered on the face of the house and a small, peaked roof covered the front step. It was a style reminiscent of a church; the porch roof echoed the shape of the main roof. Someone had covered the house in wood shingles, but that was some time ago. The shingles were now a multitude of colors, faded squares enlivened by mosses, molds, and lichens. Blues, greens, yellows, and oranges, all splotched with white. It was a storybook house.

Through the screen on the top half of the front door, Jon could see Ruffus, a large cream-colored lab.

"Hey Ruffus."

As soon as the door was open, Kolohe and Ruffus commenced to sniffing each other. They knew one another from Kathleen's place in Nāpili, where Ruffus was leader-of-the-pack.

Jon dropped his backpack and duffle bag inside his room, the first door on the left. He noticed his oil paints and canvas had been removed from the kitchen and placed in his room.

"Hey Kat."

"Jon, how are you?" She gave him a hug. "Good to see you. Were you on the other side?"

"Yep. Up in Hāli'imaile at my friends. Did some laundry in Pā'ia."

"You know when you come to Nāpili you can bring your laundry."

"I know. Thanks. Kind of a long way to haul everything; not that I have much."

"Your friends, are they the ones you had the bike shop in Lahaina with?"

"Mike and Shay. You met them when you brought your bicycle in to have flat tires fixed. Those kiawe thorns were good for business."

"I did. Sweet folks. Jon, do you know there's a giant cane spider up in the corner of your room?"

"I've seen him. He's been there for a while. I don't mess with him, and he doesn't mess with me."

Kathleen smiled. "Can you please catch him and put him outside?"

Kathleen had twenty some years on Jon. She was forty-five, matronly and roundish, but had a girlish southern charm. Her dark hair was twisted into a bun and held with a chopstick. She had gentle eyes, freckles about her nose and cheeks, and an infectious smile. Kathleen was a born optimist, and she was not afraid of responsibility; on the island she served as a den mother for many people. In fact, it was Kathleen who landed Jon his caretaking job. It was amazing that they let him become caretaker at all. He didn't even have a car. Kathleen liked Jon. She had ventured to Maui in the mid-sixties and now co-owned a small clothing store in Lahaina. The shop, Maui Ragtime, specialized in clothing sewn on location, in house. Her partner in the shop, Jenn, was presently traveling in South America. Jenn was one of the hui.

"Kolohe looks so clean. No more of that Nāpili red dirt on him. Does he like having his own place?"

"He does. But did he tell you our big news? He got a ticket today for not being on a leash . . . in Pā'ia."

"What? A ticket? That's ridiculous."

"I know."

"So what? Does he have to go to court now?"

"It's a twenty-five dollar fine."

"What did you do? Did you have to buy a leash?"

"I had a piece of rope I used until we got out of town."

Kat shook her head. "I brought you a big bag of Friskies."

"Thank you. Dog food at Hasegawa's is pricey."

They sat at the small wooden table in the dining room; the only place to sit in the whole house, unless you chose the floor. The living room didn't have a lick of furniture other than a large stringed piano backboard leaning against one wall. The dining room was very small, the layout accommodating interior stairs that led underneath the house.

"Paco is here. He drove into Hāna in his Jeep," Kathleen explained. "And Jerry is down cutting the trail with a machete."

"Good. It needs it. The ferns grow fast."

"I threw some snails out of your garden. I didn't know snails got that big."

"Thank you, I know! The African snails are huge. Their shells are like a seashell. Kind of pretty."

"Looks like you'll be getting some green beans soon."

On the table was a kerosene lamp and a gallon-size glass jar with a burned down candle in it. They didn't provide enough light to read at night, although Jon tried. Nights alone in the house took some getting used to. On several occasions he heard what sounded like someone walking around outside the house. But the land was so dark at night and the terrain so rough, he figured no one could possibly walk out there without a light. Plus Ko didn't bark. Eventually he learned to ignore the unexplained sounds. He learned to ignore—or live with—a lot of things out here. Like the mosquitoes. They didn't bite him much; maybe they passed him over thanks to his mostly vegetarian diet. He found that when they did bite, they didn't do much. Didn't even itch. They were just tiny noisy nuisances.

"Hey, when you mentioned you and Ko had news, I thought you might have seen the headlines. Did you hear? Nixon resigned." Kathleen snickered.

"What? No way. Nixon resigned, wow." Jon held up his hands making two peace signs. "I am not a crook. Amazing."

"I'll bet, out here, you tend to lose track with what's happening in the world."

"Pretty much. First to go is the time," Jon reflected. "Then the day, month, year, and then it's, who's president? So, who is president now?"

"Ford!" Kathleen chuckled.

Through the window Jon saw Jerry, Kathleen's son, coming up the hill from the property. He noisily came up the stairs from under the house.

Whereas the front of the house rested on the ground, the rear was built in a traditional post and pier style, to accommodate the steep slope of the land. It provided a dry workspace underneath along with a screened-in shower, fed via pipe from the nearby stream. Cold water only. From there a short path led to the outhouse.

"Watch your head," Jerry mumbled to himself. The opening for the homemade doorway was very short and had been the cause for much head banging and swearing. Over the top of the door, on the inside, someone had painted, "Watch your head."

"That hill is a motherfucker," Jerry, out of breath, exhorted.

"Jerreeee!" Kathleen protested.

"Oh, sorry Mom. Well, it is," he responded. "I'm sweating like a pig. Ran out of beer. Had to come up. What's for lunch? Hey Jon. Check out these old bottles I found."

Jerry had his shirt off and was obviously comfortable in his own skin. His beer belly hung over his jeans; it was white and pasty, with contrasting patches of dark body hair. He ran his fingers through his shortish brown hair, which was all over the place. Jerry was sporting a two-day old beard. He had a boyish face.

"Do pigs sweat?" he asked to no one in particular.

"Get this, Jerry. Kolohe got a ticket for not being on a leash," Kathleen said, "in Pā'ia."

"What? That's nuts. Hey buddy, some of those papayas you left on the windowsill were beginning to melt. I had to toss them."

"Sorry 'bout that. How's work?"

"It's okay. The Tree House has been busy, which is a good thing. Time goes by faster when we're busy. The kitchen can get crazy. It's fun." Jerry left the dining room in search of something to eat; they could hear him gulping down a glass of water at the sink.

"I'm going to go visit Skip and Kim," Kathleen said. "Jon, would you like to come along?"

It was a short walk, around a few bends in the road and just past the steep dirt driveway leading up to the commune. Yellow ginger grew thick along the roadside and bloomed along with smaller patches of white ginger. Their intoxicating, sweet fragrance hung in the air.

Six feet tall elephant grass framed the entrance to Skip's driveway. Once inside, the yard opened up. Two horses were tied in different spots. An old car smothered in grass and morning glory vines peeked from one corner. Beside the makeshift house was a large shed-style open carport. A fishing boat on a trailer sat underneath. Nailed on the crossbeam, facing the yard, were several marlin tails and marlin bills. Hanging from the beam were plastic fishing floats. The largest one, faded orange, was the size of a basketball. An older green and white VW van sat in the driveway.

Kat stopped to pick a beautiful pink hibiscus flower which she tucked behind her ear. At the house, she knocked and entered—the door was open. Jon followed. The house was a hodgepodge of rooms pieced together, covered in recycled siding but with new corrugated tin roofing.

"Skip, this is Jon."

Skip smiled and extended his hand. "Oh yeah, I've picked you up hitchhiking." Skip's handshake was gentle. Not limp, but a refreshing opposite of the firm handshake. He had a small build, with dark hair and eyes. He was Hawaiian/Chinese with a little Irish thrown in. His skin was a deep brown from years in the sun and on the water.

"Where's Kim and the keikis?" Kathleen asked.

"They went to the other side, to Kim's sisters. Gonna do some sewing and dry out a bit. Been plenty of rain lately, yeah Jon?"

"For real."

"You two want coffee? I just made a pot."

Skip served the coffee in bowls.

"Short on mugs?" Kathleen asked.

"No, no. You want a mug? I just like to drink my coffee in a bowl. I like the way it feels in my hands."

"Thanks, I'm good," she said, nodding. "You have electricity, yeah?"

"Temporary hook up. We've had it two years."

Everyone laughed. "When do you get a permanent hook up?"

"Probably never. No building permit, that's why. The electric company doesn't care. They charge more for a temporary hook up."

Skip pointed to the partially finished interior wall. "Brah, check out this siding. You know what kine wood this?" He spoke with the warm, lilting island dialect Jon had come to recognize as an intrinsic part of life here. He'd absorbed some of the local pidgin himself. It was hard not to.

"Looks like hardwood."

"Pallets brah. Free wood." Skip explained, "I sand and stain them. Probably oak. Takes some time. Plenty nails, but yeah. Kim thought I was crazy when I started the project, but she happy now."

"Have you met Kim, Jon? She's an Olympic swimmer. Beautiful girl," Kathleen said.

Skip smiled proudly. "She can out-swim me."

"Love to meet her," Jon said.

"Skip, how long you stay Hāna?" Kathleen asked.

"'Bout three years. After I got out of the Army, I came home to our family land. I was in the Army two years. I knew I didn't want to be in for four years, so I let myself be drafted. Two years was long enough. I got lucky and spent the whole time in Germany. All of my friends went to Vietnam. Two years in Germany wasn't bad. I got out, came home, and just dropped out. Enough already. Jon you ever in the service?"

"No, never was."

"Eh, good for you. Lucky. Landed in a good house, too." Skip pointed in the direction of their place, and said again, "A good house. Termites aren't gonna eat it."

"Why's that?"

"That's an old house. You ever look on the geological survey map? Your hale is on it. The survey map was printed like in 1950. In the old days, when the lumber came in it was dropped in Hāna Bay and floated to shore. So, the wood that built your house got a nice saltwater bath. Termites hate that."

"Interesting."

"Oh, and there's a good pear tree, on the curve, just this side of your house. On the makai side. You seen it?" Skip asked.

"Pears?"

"Yeah, it's a good one. Buttery. Have to keep an eye on it though. Someone always seems to beat me to them. Just when they're about ready, someone go cocka-roach em."

"I didn't know pears grew in Hawai'i," said Jon.

"No, no, no. Not pears like mainland kine. Avocado. Alligator pears.

These ones are shaped like a pear but with longer necks."

"Avocados."

"Avocados. We call them pears. That one turns dark, kind of purple when they ripen. Thick skin. Ripe when you can just push in a little. If you wait until they're soft, like a regular avocado, pau already . . . too ripe," Skip explained.

Jon nodded. "That's happened to me before." *I like this guy.*

"Most locals won't eat avocados. Pig food."

"Lucky pigs," Kathleen said.

ON THE WALK BACK TO THE house, Kathleen asked Jon to cut some ginger flowers. Jon climbed down the bank of the road into the head-high ginger. The yellow ginger flowers grew in a large cluster atop a solid fibrous stem. Jon pulled out his pocketknife, careful not to drop it into the tangle of plants. He cut two wonderfully fragrant bouquets, and they continued walking.

A line-up of African tulip trees grew along the roadside. Their pale trunks stretched upwards while their large, exaggerated orange blossoms littered the pavement. The house itself came into view, immersed in a sea of green, punctuated by the explosion of bright multicolored impatien flowers that lined the walkway. A clump of banana trees provided privacy to Jon's bedroom window. He had grown familiar with the plants that surrounded the house. Along the far side of the house grew a stand of torch ginger. Their majestic leaves towered overhead, some reaching the roof. The large, shiny, torch-shaped flowers were deep red with yellow edges. They appeared to be carved out of wax, something from another planet. On the Hāna side of the house a footpath led to the lower area. Along the path grew a rare Hawaiian Loulu fan palm, and a large croton bush with colorful leaves. Near the path there was a tall rainbow shower tree, a glossy pomelo tree, and another citrus tree with a mystery fruit that looked like tangerine but was sour like a lemon.

Paco was back from Hāna. His Jeep was parked on the dirt driveway, dwarfed by the large old mango tree it sat under. Below this stately tree was Jon's small garden. It was here where the trail dropped deeper into the property.

Paco and Jerry were sitting at the small dining room table.

"Howzit Jon? I hear Kolohe is a criminal now," Paco said.

"Yeah, how's that. I couldn't believe it."

Paco was Mexican American. He had light olive-colored skin, a medium build, short black hair which he kept combed straight back, and a bushy moustache. He was around Kat's age, but had a totally different personality. He was generally guarded with his feelings, keeping others at a distance, yet able to turn on the charm when it suited him.

"Jon, you want to smoke a joint?" Paco asked.

"Sure."

"The grass I have isn't too good. You got anything?"

Jon shook his head *no*.

"Alright then. Can you roll it?" Paco handed Jon the baggie of weed with rolling papers inside. "Roll a fat one. Hey, I ran into a guy I know, in Hāna. He invited me to a sunrise wedding tomorrow morning at the cross on the hill. You want to go?"

"Sure."

"You know how to get up there?"

"I'll be sleeping," Jerry interjected.

"Yeah, of course," Jon said, ignoring Jerry. "That's one of the spots where people go to look for mushrooms."

Paco raised his eyebrows as if to ask a question.

"They're psilocybin. Pretty mellow." Jon handed Paco the joint.

Kathleen's voice drifted in from the kitchen. "I hear they grow on the dried cow pies."

"Yep, that's right."

"You roll a nice looking joint."

"Years of practice. Mountains on the ends, valley in the middle. Perfect joint. I majored in reefer-ology in college."

"You went to college?"

"I did. Thank God for art."

"My school was the streets of Detroit." Paco frowned momentarily. "You studied art?"

"Junior college. Took a lot of different art classes. I even had a metal sculpture class where I got to do some welding. That was fun. And you're serious about the streets of the Detroit?"

"Yeah, plus I learned some stuff in prison. Did a year in a federal penitentiary for a pound of weed. I was living in LA at the time."

Kathleen joined in, "We were dating when Paco got busted."

"Yeah," Paco said, looking over at Kathleen. "She waited for me."

"When Paco got out, I had yellow ribbons tied on all the trees in the yard. You know, like the song *Tie a Yellow Ribbon Round the Ole Oak Tree*."

"How romantic," Jerry said sarcastically followed by one of his cartoon laughs, a loud over-the-top guffaw.

The evening passed quietly. The soft light of the kerosene lamp and candle led to soft conversations. The boys smoked another joint while Kathleen read in her room by flashlight. A cocoon of rain enveloped the house.

3 | OLD FRIENDS

Raoul looked up from the manuscript.

"Excellent Jon, I like it."

Jon had been studying Raoul's face as he read.

The two old friends were sitting in Anthony's Coffee Shop in Pā'ia. Jon was turned sideways in his chair so he could see out the open door, onto the street. Raoul sat facing Jon, a stack of handwritten pages before him.

"This is a great reunion, Jon. I can't believe I'm back on Maui."

The two hadn't seen each other for many years. They were now in their mid-sixties. Jon's hair and goatee were white. Raoul, what little hair he had, was tied back in a wispy ponytail. The lines of time were etched in their faces.

"You've written a shitload, my friend. Do you know where you're taking this thing? What do you know about word count and genres?"

"Not a clue."

"Of course not. Genres are categories. In fiction there's science fiction, thriller, historical fiction, right? In nonfiction there's memoir, and academic stuff. Trust me. Being a librarian, I know this shit. Different genres have different word counts. The actual number of words; not too long, not too short. It's a real thing. The bottom line is, I think you're writing a decent novel, based on your life. And you might have enough material for two books."

"No way. Seriously? That's crazy."

"It's a good thing. I'm thinking you can have Part One and Part Two."

A beautiful young woman walked in, a Maui local. She passed the men on her way to the counter.

"Hi," Raoul piped up.

She replied with a curt smile.

"Gotta love Maui."

"Yep."

"Ah, now as I was saying." Raoul had his head cranked around, eyeing the girl. He turned back to Jon. "It's good. You set the stage. Maui, the seventies, poor-ass ugly hippy boy."

Jon was thinking, *who is Raoul to talk, with his pathetic ponytail?*

"I didn't say he was ugly."

"Oh yeah, my bad. No, actually, you still look remarkably like yourself."

"Thanks, I think."

"Did you see? She smiled at me. I think she likes me."

"Um-hmm. She would like you to stop staring at her and go back to your rest home, Grandpa."

"That's one thing I never did."

"What's that?"

"Make babies."

"And we appreciate that," Jon quipped with a slight smile.

"Maybe it's not too late . . ." Raoul reflected, gazing up towards the ceiling. "No, I'm too selfish."

Jon sipped his latte.

"When do we go up the mountain?" Raoul asked.

"Two weeks."

"I better get most of my proofreading done before that. Don't know how much I'll be able to do in Haleakalā Crater. I've been walking the hills in the city, getting ready."

"Good. I know San Francisco has some famously steep hills."

"You know, printed books are becoming obsolete. Still, I enjoy having something in my hands."

"I'm sure you do."

The two friends looked at each other and laughed.

"You're not in a hurry are you, Jon?"

"Nope. Just watching the world go by."

"I'm going to read another chapter or two. Oh, one thing—you know the part about the dog looking like the old Our Gang dog? Younger people aren't going to know what that is. That's a certain generation."

"True. Well, it's a period piece. They can Google it."

"Guess so."

"How about this?" Jon addressed an imaginary camera. "For all of you young folks out there . . . the old Our Gang dog was a white, short-haired dog. White with black spots and one big black spot around one eye. Medium-sized dog. Skinny tail," Jon finished, turning back towards Raoul. "There." *Satisfied?*

Raoul leaned forward, "When do I get to the part where I'm having sex with a beautiful, bodacious . . ."

"It is fiction, so I suppose that's *possible,* but . . ." Jon interrupted, his voice trailing off.

"Ouch."

"Patience me laddie. Only the names have been changed . . ."

"To protect the innocent," Raoul completed Jon's sentence.

"To protect the guilty."

Over the years, Pā'ia had become the quintessential quaint town, having retained its charming old storefronts, reminiscent of another era. Freshly painted and maintained, it offered a wonderful mix of art galleries, shops, and restaurants, plus the mother of all healthfood stores—Mana Foods. *If they don't have it, you really don't need it, end of story.* Also gracing this small beach town was a Buddhist Stupa blessed by His Holiness the Dalai Lama himself, in person.

The main road, Hāna Highway, passed through the heart of town and hosted a steady flow of traffic. Residents commuting to and from work, the beach, yoga class, or shopping, alongside tourists from around the world. Older couples were here on their dream vacation, and a younger crowd set on windsurfing at Ho'okipa, catching a swell at Honolua Bay, or challenging their skills in the monster-sized waves of Pe'ahi, aptly called Jaws.

Pā'ia was known as the "hippy capital" of Maui. The colorful array made for some extraordinary people watching. Brazilian women in bikinis walked down the sidewalk, carrying their surfboards and speaking Portuguese. There were clean-cut surfer dudes alongside free-spirited long-haired hipsters, with beards, dreadlocks, and tattoos in abundance. There were older men and women who settled into Maui many years ago and managed to survive and even raise families.

It was easy for Jon to distinguish the tourists from the "locals," but something was missing. One didn't see a lot of brown faces. *Driven off the island by the high cost of living,* Jon mused to himself sadly. *The Hawaiians have all moved to Las Vegas.*

Jon and Raoul's eyes were drawn out the door and across the street. They were watching a young woman whose ample breasts were attempting to escape the confines of her tight tank top as she moved. Her colorful pants had ties crisscrossing up the side to her waistline, with nothing but skin peeking through.

"The ass is always greener on the other side of the street," Raoul remarked.

"Gandhi?"

"Lovejoy."

"Okay, Mr. Raoul Lovejoy." Jon added, "You belch what you eat."

"Gandhi?"

"Actually, Ramakrishna."

"Ramakrishna, don't think I know him."

"Great Indian saint. Known for his pithy sayings."

Raoul looked back to the street, popping the last bite of his breakfast sandwich into his mouth.

"Hopefully I'll be burping up this bacon later," Raoul deadpanned. "It's an honor to be your proofreader, Jon. But here on Maui, I may have a hard time concentrating."

The men had another good laugh.

"Agreed."

4 | SUNRISE WEDDING

Paco woke Jon as planned. They jumped into his Jeep and headed to
Hāna. The dark sky was clear and overflowing with stars. Jon wore his
hiking boots, blue jeans, T-shirt, and long-sleeved flannel shirt. *My finest
wedding attire,* he thought to himself, smiling. The Jeep had no side or
rear windows, so the men were buffeted by the cool morning air.

In Hāna they drove up the narrow one-lane paved road that led to
Fagan's cross on the hill. The large cross was constructed of lava stone. It
was erected in memory of Paul Fagan who established cattle ranching in
Hāna and built the hotel there. They parked off to the side of the road,
along with more than a dozen other vehicles already there. The parking
area adjacent to the cross had been cordoned off for the bride, groom,
and their families.

Paco and Jon joined the crowd gathered at the top of the hill, in
front of the cross. The group formed a large circle to await the sunrise.
Standing quietly in the pre-dawn darkness, time stood still, and the
modern world dropped away. Jon felt transported to ancient times;
together with his tribe, summoned to witness a sacred bonding of two
people in a holy promise of life and love shared. All eyes were on the
eastern sky where an ember of light was growing. The black shadows of
night were giving way to shades of grey and slowly melting into greens

and blues. As a gentle wind rose from the ocean, a magical landscape began to appear all around them. The great Pacific Ocean was cradling Maui in its arms.

Jon became aware of the gentle rise and fall of his breath and of the movement of air in his nostrils. In the stillness of the morning, he could also hear waves breaking in the distance. Picturesque Hāna Bay was sleeping peacefully below, backed by steep red cliffs, and covered with ironwood trees. The surrounding hills were cut from green velvet. Clouds on the horizon began to dance with color. He was so absorbed in the moment, so immersed in the natural world around him, he felt himself not just an observer but an integral part of creation.

Clouds aflame, the entire sky was now alive and awake. The sun's arrival was heralded in yellows, oranges, reds, and a streak of violet that stretched into deep purple. He glanced from the horizon to the circle of friends. A murmur ran through the crowd as the sun climbed above the low-lying clouds to reveal itself.

Attention turned to the bride and groom. The golden hue of a new day lit their faces.

The ceremony was short and sweet. The officiant read from Kahlil Gibran's *The Prophet*, on love and marriage. The bride and groom each recited thoughts and feelings they had written for each other, followed by an exchange of vows and rings.

Jon scanned the crowd, recognizing friends and familiar faces, and taking in the smiles of many others he didn't know. The whole circle had joined hands now, singing the closing song—

> *May the longtime sun*
> *shine upon you,*
> *all love*
> *surround you,*
> *and the pure light*
> *within you,*
> *guide you all your way home.*

JON SPOTTED HIS GOOD FRIEND JOSEPH.

"Paco, this is Joseph."

"Hey man, howzit?"

"Howzit," Joseph replied. "Jon and I go way back."

Joseph had long brown hair, a thick beard, and fine features that framed his light brown eyes. His smooth, graceful hands masked his strength and dexterity; he was a skilled woodworker.

"You've known each other a long time?" Paco asked.

"Since junior high in San Diego."

"Far out." Paco looked distracted.

"And we picked pineapples together out at Honolua in sixty-nine," Joseph added.

"Haole crew," Jon added.

"Hey boys."

Jon turned to see Rainbow and Patchouli, his neighbors who lived at the commune.

"Hey neighbor, hi Patchouli."

"That was beautiful. Almost made me want to get married again," Rainbow exclaimed. "I put on my nicest tie-dye. Wasn't easy. I had to find a shirt without any holes in it."

Patchouli was rolling her eyes, "Yeah, right." She too was adorned in tie-dye and, true to her name, reeked of patchouli oil.

Jon's friends Paulo and Dawn stopped on the way to their car. Their four-year-old daughter, Anna, was wrapped in a crocheted blanket and carrying a stuffed bear.

"My man."

Paulo gave Jon a firm handshake and slapped him hard on the back several times. He was clean-shaven, his thick dark hair in a loose braid. Paulo was Italian, and originally from the Bronx. He was a talented conga drum player and performed in venues around the island.

"Hey Dawn."

Dawn was slender and dark-skinned, with a kind manner that always put Jon at ease. She gave him a quick hug, then continued down the hill, following the kid, who had toddled ahead. Joseph jogged a few yards to catch up to his wife and child, then turned and shouted back to Jon and Paco.

"See you at the reception?" Joseph shouted. "Just down the street at Alicia Bay Laurel's place. You'll see the cars."

From the walkway, Jon could see the small house was packed with people. The crowd spilled onto the front porch. Growing across the length of the porch was a vine with reddish-maroon, crescent-shaped flowers which cascaded in long clusters, and hung like a lace curtain. While Paco slipped into the house, Jon stopped closer to the vine to check out the shape of a flower; it reminded him of a Hawaiian warrior's feathered helmet. He put his nose close to the vine and sniffed, then shrugged.

"I guess when you're this beautiful, you don't have to smell good too."

A woman was standing in the doorway, softly laughing.

"Kind of like me," Jon joked back.

"Uh huh," she laughed. "Kind of like that. It's a jade vine. Also comes in a greenish-blue color. Hey, I don't think we've met. Alicia."

"Nice to meet you, Alicia. I'm Jon. Great little house you have here."

"It's not mine—I'm renting. Just got back from a book tour in Japan. Stopped on Maui, on my way home, and decided to stay."

"You're a writer?"

"Yes. Writer and artist. To tell you the truth, my new book has been wildly successful. I'm as surprised as anyone. It's about living life the natural way."

"That's so cool," Jon said. "I like to write too, but mostly I'm an artist. I draw and paint."

"When's your birthday? What month?" she asked.

"May."

"Taurus?"

"Yep."

"What day?"

"The 14th," Jon replied.

There was a silence as Alicia looked at Jon, a smile spreading over her face.

"That's my birthday!" She gave Jon a tight hug. "My Taurus brother. How old are you, Jon?"

"Ah, twenty-three."

"Okay. I'm a couple years older than you." She winked. "Hey kid, before you leave, come find me. I have something for you."

JOSEPH HAD PARKED HIMSELF ON THE sofa on the front porch. He patted the cushion next to him and Jon took a seat.

"A couple weeks ago I went hiking through the crater with some friends," Joseph started the story, as if they were already mid-conversation. Typical.

"Love the crater. Jeff and I used to hike the crater when we were living in Makawao at the dairy."

"Full moon. Dropped some L and hiked through at night by moonlight," Joseph continued. "It was clear but cold."

"Whoa, the crater is already so unreal, like, even in the daytime and not on acid."

"It was a trip," Joseph raised his eyebrows. "Second time I've done that."

"You one crazy buggah you."

"Hey Jon, I got a new piece of property in Ke'anae Valley. We're building a house."

"Is that down on the peninsula?"

"No. The valley. Mauka of the highway. The dirt road that goes in is by the smaller lookout. The gate is usually open or unlocked. You should come check us out."

Joseph and Jon watched as three young men approached the house.

"Do you know these guys—the boys from Lower Nāhiku?" Jon shook his head.

"Hey guys, this is my friend Jon," Joseph called out. "He lives in Harry, Leanne, and Faith's old house."

"Hi. I'm Mike."

"Jon."

"No need to stand up brah. I'm Pato."

"Scott."

"Welcome to the hood," Mike said.

"Thanks."

Joseph and Jon followed the boys into the house for the champagne toast. It was the only alcohol served at the reception. Observing the guests, Jon felt right at home. They were young, colorful, and free-spirited. After the toast, Joseph introduced Jon to the newlyweds, Reed and Sunshine. Although they didn't know Jon, they were both warm and welcoming. Jon thought to himself that Sunshine was aptly named. She had long blonde hair, sparkling blue eyes, a warm cheerful demeanor, and was radiant on her special day. The two lived on the other side of Hāna, in Kīpahulu.

Rainbow called Jon to the food table. "You gotta try this dip."

"Okay, yeah," Jon nodded. His stomach gave a small growl.

"Man," Rainbow said, mouth full of chips and dip. "Last week we went nuts and tie-dyed everything. Got carried away in the moment. T-shirts, pants, socks . . . even underwear," Rainbow paused. "Yes, I do have some underwear, you know, for special occasions." He laughed.

A young woman approached, her thick curly hair hanging over her shoulders and down her back. She was wearing a deep purple embroidered velvet dress.

"Hi there," she said, looking intensely at Jon.

"Jon, do you know Rachel? She's our neighbor. Rachel and her son Timmy live just down the street, past the colonel's."

"I hear we're neighbors." She was looking Jon up and down. He felt like she wanted to have him for breakfast.

Rainbow moved away with his plate of food just as a tall, broad-shouldered guy in an aloha shirt approached, wedging his way between Jon and Rachel.

"I hear you're living in my old house in Upper Nāhiku," he said to Jon, without introducing himself.

"Guess so."

"You know those metal planters outside the house?" he asked.

"Yeah, I have some marigolds and zinnias growing in them." Jon loved his little garden.

"Those are mine. I paid good money to have them fabricated. A fifty-five-gallon barrel cut lengthwise with legs welded on."

"Okay" Jon eyed this guy warily. *Seriously dude?*

Rachel was watching quietly.

"I'm going to come get them. And the piano backboard, that's mine too." he turned and walked away.

Jon and Rachel looked at each other.

"That's Harry," she said. "Ex-Navy. Black belt in Aikido. That's his fishing boat anchored out in Hāna Bay." Jon nodded, taking it all in. Not every "friend" on the island was so friendly.

Feeling ready to leave the party, Jon sought out Alicia, who gave him a signed copy of her book, *Living On The Earth*. The inscription read: *To my Taurus brother. Peace and Love. Alicia Bay Laurel.* Her generosity was the anecdote he needed after that tense conversation with Harry. Jon found Paco in the crowd, and the two headed out.

"Jon, where did you know that song from?" Paco asked. "The one from the end of the wedding. Heard you singing along."

"The Incredible String Band. I had an album of theirs. That song was on it. My musician friends, Paul and Jim, used to play it. It's apparently an old Celtic poem and Irish blessing."

"You're alright."

Jon's hand was on the Jeep door, about to climb in, when he heard a voice call out from the porch.

"Hey!" Rachel called. "Jon. Stop by and see me sometime."

5 | EMERALD POND

IN THE EARLY MORNING DARKNESS, Jon lay nestled in his sleeping bag. The downpour was providing a multi-layered orchestra. The loud drumming on the tin roof was dampened and echoed by the attic crawlspace. These deeper notes were accompanied by the tap-a-de-tap, tap, tap, tap, tap of drops striking the surrounding plants and trees. A curtain of water falling from the roof added a constant ripping sound like a roaring fire, and below it all was a melodious rift as rain fell into the overflowing jars and buckets that he had set out to catch drinking water.

Kolohe was still curled up on his bed of choice—an old piece of carpet under the house. Kat, Paco, and Jerry had all gone back to the other side of the island, so Jon had the place to himself. He rose and walked to the kitchen looking out towards the ocean. The silky light of dawn was beginning to manifest. The colors of day were awakening and slowly resuming their usual positions. He was pleased to see several large patches of blue sky.

Gingerly, he walked down the sloping pathway to the outhouse, holding a beach towel over his head in a losing effort to stay dry. The outhouse itself was a bit of a curiosity, as it was a two-seater. The seats, side by side, were the subject of much speculation. *The butt of many jokes*, Jon thought to himself. The outhouse was open air, but had a back wall and roof. Everything was damp and wet. He took the toilet paper from its plastic bag and dried one of the seats. He waved his hands around him to ward off the hungry mosquitos. This was not a spot where one was inclined to linger, although the view was amazing. From here the land dropped into a lush jungle. The trees nurtured a dense understory mixed with ferns and mosses. It was an ecosystem hundreds of years in the making, and undisturbed. Bird's nest ferns grew in many of the larger trees. Jon's favorite was a giant bird's nest fern, in the crotch of an old kukui nut tree. The fern had a span of over eight feet and was magnificent.

After feeding Kolohe, Jon enjoyed a papaya and finished the dry roasted peanuts that Kathleen had left. He saved the empty peanut jar to store turpentine for cleaning his paint brushes, then considered what to do next. He pulled out his bamboo flute and took a seat. The forest birds joined in. His playing was random and improvised. Later he might work on a necklace. As he played, he eyed the puka shells that he had set out and organized the night before. He had a stash of shells he'd gathered at Windmills Beach. For now, though, he had some chores to do.

He was thankful that Paco had bought a plastic container at a garage sale in Lahaina; it held ten gallons, sat on the kitchen counter, and had a faucet on one end. Jon began to transfer rainwater from his makeshift catchment system to the kitchen. It was a slow process. He scooped water using a cup, careful not to disturb the layers of sediments from the rusty roof. With the cup he filled a saucepan, carried it upstairs, and poured it into the larger container. He went back and forth many times.

He swept the floor and moved the kerosene lamp from the table. He threw the aging yellow ginger flowers out the kitchen window, as they were spent and attracting tiny gnats.

Once he was satisfied with his housework, he walked downstairs to ask if Ko was up for a hike. Kolohe was always up for a hike, and they could set out from the property. No need to leave home for an adventure. A short distance from the house, the trail dropped through a mix of kukui nut, African tulip, guava, and banana trees.

Kolohe trotted ahead. The downpour had stopped, but the vegetation still dripped and glowed from the morning rain. Thanks to Jerry's work clearing the path, you could now walk without getting your clothes soaking wet. That wouldn't last long as the ferns grew fast, but it made today's hike a pleasure.

Most days Jon found himself out here alone, with just Kolohe for company. But on occasion, folks used this route to get to Ulaino Road. If you were on foot and you knew the way, it was a major shortcut.

As the terrain dropped, the vegetation changed. There were strawberry guava, common guava, and patches of lantana, which seemed out of place in such a wet area. The forest contained many mountain apple trees, with fruit growing along their trunks and branches. The mountain apples were delicate, juicy, and best eaten on the spot.

The path leveled where it came to a bluff. This finger of land had steep drop-offs on three sides, affording a great ocean view. Here sat the remains of a tumbled-down shack. Jon wondered who had lived here. The roof was rusted away and the wood floor was rotten; both had collapsed long ago. The sections of wall that remained were barely standing. Paco had talked about putting up a tarp and camping out in the shack, but it was too far gone for that. The structure was returning to the earth, its time and place fading quickly.

Next to the shack grew fat, tall bamboo, coffee trees, and a leafy bush with unusual flowers. Kathleen had told Jon this was a Japanese lantern hibiscus. He took a moment to inspect the red and purple flowers, each shaped like a miniature intricate papercut lantern.

A large yellow guava hung temptingly nearby. Jon knocked it down with a stick. He sat on the bluff and sliced off the ends of the fruit, cutting it in half with his pocketknife. The pink interior contrasted with the bright yellow exterior. Jon checked for the small fruit fly larva; the worms had a black spot on their heads which made them possible to spot, although their bodies were translucent and resembled guava seeds. Fruit picked from the tree was almost always good, but still, he checked. He had learned the hard way back in his pineapple picking days. He was halfway through a guava he'd found on the ground when one of his friends mentioned, "Hey you know sometimes those guavas have little worms in them." Sure enough, the fruit he was eating contained a bunch of the little fellows. After that incident, he never ate guavas off the ground, and always looked before he ate.

Kolohe came to see what Jon was eating. It only took a couple sniffs to determine it was nothing good. Jon patted him on the head, scratched him behind the ears, and left his hand resting on his back. They took in the view together. The sea was silvery blue beneath a cerulean sky with fluffy white clouds. The trade winds were constant but gentle.

From here the trail was not so obvious and became more interesting. Jon enjoyed the adventure, following the path down a sloping bank to a twelve feet deep channel. The channel was not caused by flowing water but by an ancient lava flow, most likely a lava tube whose roof had collapsed. Spanning this cleft was a natural lava bridge, around four feet wide and ten feet across to the other side. The surface was rough and uneven. Tall trees overshadowed the area, making the rock mossy and wet. One had to tread with care, but it was worth it. The bridge was a portal into a magical realm.

Jon made his way across, but Kolohe refused to use the bridge. The dog had his own way of moving around these parts. Kolohe worked his way back up the hill, along the edge of the channel. He disappeared. Jon waited, and moments later Ko reappeared at his side.

The path then skirted a cliff that dropped straight down a hundred feet. It was a dangerous spot. The terrain sloped towards the drop-off and was often covered with slippery mud. At the bottom of the cliff was a large crystal-clear pool. Deceptively, the clarity of the water made the pool look shallow. During heavy rain, from the adjacent cliff there appeared a roaring waterfall. Generally, the stream seeped underground, only to surface at the base of the sheer rock face. The family who lived below, on Ulaino Road, had run a pipe to the base of the cliff where the constant flow of water kept the end of the pipe submerged and provided running water to their house.

Jon and Ko carefully made their way, as the trail wound over rock, tree roots, and through patches of shampoo ginger. The shampoo ginger was a short plant, two to three feet high. The cones were maroon and shaped like bloated hot dogs—that's what Jon always thought—with small delicate flowers that sprang sporadically. The core of the cone was juicy. When squeezed, it produced a pleasantly-scented, slimy liquid, thus its name—though it was more of a cream rinse or conditioner than a shampoo.

Located just above the spot where the stream crossed Ulaino Road was Blue Pond, a fickle pool that was deep enough to bathe in some days, and completely dry on others. Even though large mango trees covered it in shade, when the water was flowing, Blue Pond was the bluest of blues. The color was intense and other worldly. The blue water set against straight, column-like tree trunks gave it a surreal look. It was a Maxfield Parrish painting come to life.

Today the pond was perfect. A small waterfall projected from a lava ledge directly into the pool.

"We're making a stop."

Jon cut two shampoo ginger cones and set them next to the water. He slipped off his clothes and waded into the pool. The water felt good. Jon dove under and swam to the waterfall and back. He then retrieved his ginger, squeezed the juice out and applied it to his hair. In the deeper water he dunked himself several times to rinse off. Jon sat on the rocks to air-dry, until Kolohe nudged his shoulder with his cold dog nose to show his impatience. "Fair enough," Jon said, and put his clothes back on.

It would be a short walk to the ocean. Ulaino Road was a jeep road that began near the small Hāna airport, passed through rolling pastures, then disappeared into a thick jungle ending at the ocean. Where the stream crossed the road there was a dip which had been concreted. Jon removed his boots, which he had just put back on, to cross. The water was several inches deep. Kolohe didn't like it, but he quickly crossed. He was happy to be on the move again and wagged his tail as he walked.

They passed an old house. Jon had peeked in the windows before. It was neatly kept but generally vacant. A picturesque waterfall some-times ran behind the house, creating a beautiful backdrop. It was another on-again off-again waterfall, usually dry but spectacular when flowing. Before reaching the beach there was one more driveway, a house hidden from view. Stan and Susanne, a young haole couple, were the caretakers. Stan was a baker by trade, and a bit out of place in this remote jungle.

Farther along the road was a good-sized banana patch. *Hey, it's not in anyone's yard,* Jon reasoned. He would check for mature bananas on the way back, knowing he could pick some green and let them fully ripen at home.

Soon the road became a footpath. On the left was a narrow shred of standing water, most likely brackish. Ferns grew out of the rock and hung over the water. Dragonflies flew about, skimming the water's still surface.

At the ocean, the skyline opened dramatically. On one end of the beach, steep cliffs came close to kissing the edge of the sea. At their base was a marshy area with a few taro plants. Someone had inserted a pipe through the bank and a constant stream of water poured from its end. Jon had seen Stan filling water jugs here. Looking up the coast in the other direction, towards Hāna, was a small cove. The beach consisted of large stones and rocks, rounded smooth by waves and time. There was some sand but not much. On this windward side of the island the ocean was often rough. At night, when the waves were big, Jon could hear them exploding on the rocks. It sounded like canons going off in the distance.

Jon and Kolohe walked along the shoreline. Jon was looking for interesting driftwood, preferably something flat that he could paint on. Mixed in with the driftwood were the long, dried leaves of the area's abundant hala trees. Sections of the fruit of the hala were scattered about. These were shaped like candy corn, although much larger and more fibrous; it was not something you would generally try to eat. Jon's eyes scanned the beach, always hoping for treasure. Today he got lucky. He found a flat board, weathered, with rounded edges. He guessed it originally was siding from a shack. The board was perfect for painting on. A little over a foot long, with irregular ends.

In front of the small cove, they turned around. Their true destination was in the other direction. Just past where the trail ended at the beach, tucked away from view, was another special spot. The beach narrowed there, edged in by large boulders. Hala trees, with their pre-historic look, clung to the rocky cliffs. Their nubby cylindrical trunks bent upwards, supported by a multitude of fat, hard, air roots. Up top, the tree resembled pom-poms, but the clusters were made of long sword-shaped leaves with tiny teeth along their edges. It was an important cultural plant in Hawai'i as the leaves were woven into baskets.

Jon stepped and jumped from rock to rock. It was much harder for Kolohe, who looked at Jon like he was out of his mind but followed anyway.

"Hang in there boy. Almost there."

Jon sat on the smooth surface of a boulder. The ocean was fifty feet behind him now, with small waves breaking. An exquisite waterfall danced before him. It was high and wide, with water flowing from rock to rock, along crevices and cascading from many places along the chiseled rock face. To one side, nestled on a ledge, grew some taro and watercress. Near the bottom, where the cliff receded, delicate curtains of water fell into the pool. The sound was soothing and encompassing. The large pool was a lovely green color due to moss growing on the submerged rocks. He had christened this spot Emerald Pond. It was a meditative and healing place.

Jon watched the water as it wove its way down to the pool, melting into reflections of the sky above and the shapes of rocks under the surface. He felt a pang of loneliness. *Wouldn't it be so much better, so much sweeter, to have someone to share this with?*

He glanced over to see Kolohe pouting, brown eyes wide and unblinking.

"You know what I mean."

Jon took off his shirt to feel the warm sun before plunging into the cool water.

6 | BRAIN FOOD

"It's a little sad, this story. Jon in paradise and no one to share it with. By the way, I'm going to be needing some brain food," Raoul proclaimed. "All of this proofreading . . ."

"After all these years, I can't believe you're still toking."

"I can't believe you stopped," Raoul was looking at Jon over the top of his sunglasses.

The two were in Pāʻia relaxing at their boutique inn. Raoul was laying in the sun, on a wooden Adirondack chair. Jon sat in the shade.

"That's one mistress I don't see anymore," Jon reflected.

"Mistress, hell, you were married."

"That's funny. Let's just say we spent a lot of time together. I like to say that I conducted a five-year study and after five years, the results were inconclusive, so the study was extended."

"So, what do you really think?"

"I would say that while it isn't physically addicting, it is psychologically addicting. Plus, smoking probably isn't the best thing for you. If you've ever seen the glass tubing on a water pipe, it gets pretty gunked up."

"True."

"But, hey, medical marijuana, who knew?"

"I did bring my medical marijuana card. I can't believe that Hawaiʻi hasn't legalized recreational marijuana. Back home all I have to do is head down to the local pot shop. You wouldn't believe some of the incredible cannabis they're growing now days."

"I know."

"So how did you stop?"

"That's its own story. Let's save that one."

"When was it?"

"Oh, it's been a while. I was stoned for years. It was a lifestyle. I got married. My son was three. It was time. The further away from it I got, the better it felt."

"Now, back to the situation at hand. Shall we rustle up some good Maui Wowie, bro? Or should I say *brah*, now that I'm in the islands?"

"Better let me do the talking," Jon smirked. "Shouldn't be too hard to find in this neck of the woods. Let's go hang out by Mana Foods. Lots of locals in and out of there."

"They may think we're narcs. Nah, we're too old to be narcs. They could outrun us."

"For real. That's why we'll have to shoot 'um if they try to get away. Actually, that reminds me of a story." They began walking towards Mana Foods. "There was this guy, back in the day, one of the Ke'anae boys. They were renting a house on the road overlooking the peninsula. He started hanging out in the Hāna Ranch Store parking lot trying to sell weed to tourists."

"Where is he when we need him?"

"Yeah, right? Friends told him, *hey, you can't be doing this. It's poor form.* But still, there he was. One day an undercover cop shows up. Haole guy from off-island posing as a tourist."

"Busted."

"Here's the interesting part. After flashing his badge, the cop pulls out his gun. He tells him *you better not run.* My friend—not that I hung out with him much, but we were all family of sorts—he couldn't believe what was happening. He asks him, *What? Are you going to shoot me for a bag of weed?* It was then that he noticed the cop was really nervous. His hand, holding the gun, was shaking. My friend told him, *You need to relax and put that thing away. I'm not going anywhere. Is this your first bust or some-thing?* And it was. True story."

"They sent the rookie."

"Yep."

Jon and Raoul grabbed a couple of coffees and began to loiter in front of Mana Foods, trying to look inconspicuous. With the cosmopolitan mix of people, they were fine.

"We're looking for a little herb," Jon softly spoke to a young blonde girl with dreadlocks heading into the health food store.

She looked him in the eye. "Hmm. Not sure."

Fifteen minutes later, she emerged from the store with her groceries.

"You guys still here? Any luck?"

Jon shook his head, no.

"I'll check with my boyfriend. He might be able to help you out."

"That would be greatly appreciated," Raoul smiled.

"How much you looking for?"

Raoul quickly answered, "A half."

"More like a quarter. He's an expensive date."

"Don't get me in the middle of this," she said, "you guys will have to work it out. Sit tight."

"We'll be here," Raoul said, then turned to Jon. I thought this was an all-expense paid trip."

"Hey, you're lucky I'm willing to indulge you. Weed is definitely beyond food, shelter, and clothing."

"You mean I get some new clothes?"

Jon didn't comment.

After a few minutes the girl's boyfriend came down the street. He was tall and thin, with blonde shoulder-length hair, clean-shaven, with glasses and a baseball cap. They all walked together to his van in the nearby public parking lot. The guy hopped into the back of the van through the open side door. His girlfriend, sitting in the front passenger seat, turned to watch the action. Jon and Raoul sat in the open doorway.

"How much for a quarter ounce?" Raoul blurted out.

"Where you guys from?"

"I live on the Big Island."

"San Francisco. Hey, I do have my medical marijuana card on me."

"Well, alright then. California card?"

"Yeah."

"Oh, sorry man. You gotta have a Hawai'i card."

Raoul's face dropped.

The boyfriend started laughing hard. "I'm just messing with you, man. You don't need no card."

"Had me going there."

"I can let you have a quarter for seventy-five."

"Ohhh."

"Only this time I'm not joking," he grinned. "It's good bud. Check it out."

Jon was impressed. Compact buds with golden reds, greens, oranges, a hint of purple with white and red hairs, all covered in sticky resin that glistened like little diamonds. He handed the zip-lock to Raoul. Pulling out a bud, Raoul pinched it, inhaling the pungent fragrance.

"That's some good shit. Pardon my French. I'm in love. You had me at hello."

"Okay. Yeah, yeah. Don't get carried away," Jon said.

They finished their transaction, shook hands, and strolled back to the inn.

Raoul retreated to his room. He emerged shortly thereafter, glassy eyed and smiling. They sat on the rooftop patio.

"Ah, the pause that refreshes. Thanks Jon."

"Like Ramakrishna used to say, even one hemp smoker recognizes another." Jon handed his phone to Raoul. "Here's a little ditty you might enjoy. It's a '70s piece out of my old journal."

I'm just singing this song
this hash is going song
cuz the hash is going fast
and I'll toke it to the last
but it won't be long
til I'll be singing
a song of long-gone hash.

that was yesterday's song
but yesterday is gone
and so is the hash.

"I like it. It's a poem I can relate to. I've been there. At least everything worked out rather nicely today. With a little help from my friends."

"Except for the seventy-five bucks missing from my wallet."

"You can afford it. What are you, like a millionaire?"

"Something like that. You know, I was never much of a money grubber."

"You pretty much lived on nothing, didn't you?"

"Ate a lot of papayas. But money or no money, people still have their problems. Everyone is lost in their personal drama. That's why meditation is so great. It's a time out. A mini vacation from the world. Very helpful to one's perspective," Jon reflected. "The cool thing about having money is that you can help people out . . . make a difference in someone's life. That's cool."

"You can help me out. Shoot a big chunk of green my way."

"Of course, having money can be a burden too." Jon looked over to Raoul, then away.

"A good problem to have," Raoul noted.

"True, true. It's all mixed up, you know, karma and all that. Sometimes something good will happen to someone and it turns out for the worst. Like successful musicians or movie stars that self-destruct. Or on the other hand, something horrible happens to someone and it turns out for the good. I've seen people on TV who've been through some traumatic physical tragedy, and they say, *I wouldn't change a thing. Now I appreciate every day, every minute. I'm happier and a much better person due to this experience.*"

"So, I'm not getting the loan? Instead, you're going to smack me in the face with a shovel so I can be happier?"

The men laughed.

"I'm just saying. Getting what you want and not getting what you don't want isn't necessarily for the best."

"Yeah, I can see that. But still."

"That's it, the *but still.*"

"There's always a big but, eh?"

"Right. It's the whole thing of will versus surrender. In Hinduism, you exert your will but surrender to God's will as to the outcome. One thing I've always appreciated in the Christian faith is the idea, or concept, that whatever comes to you, good or bad, comes from God. I like that."

"I need another hit."

"Didn't mean to bring you down, man. But hey, the house is on fire, the roof is burning, and the floor is about to collapse. The clock is ticking."

"Now that's cheerful. I guess it's like Jim Morrison said, none of us are getting out of here alive. What's that meditation you do?"

"Mostly zazen. Buddhist tradition."

"What religion are you, then?"

"Guess I'm a religious poi dog."

"Poi dog? What's that? Mixed breed?"

"Yeah. I'm just thankful to have made it this far and to have experienced so much."

"I'm here for the chicks."

"Right. It's all smoke and mirrors, my friend. Real only for a moment."

"Hey, watch this." Raoul stuck his hand into the open bag of chips, lying on the table beside him, palm down. He quickly flipped the bag and pulled his hand out, right side up, with a handful of chips. He looked at Jon. "Crocodile death roll."

"Crocodile death roll," Jon repeated. "Really? You know, we all need someone in our lives to make us look good. You're my guy. You're doing a great job. You make me look real good."

"You've gotten mean in your old age."

"Oh, sorry."

"In your book, does it include the part where your first wife gets abducted by aliens in the crater?"

"What?"

"Later heard to say it was the best sex she ever had."

"The book doesn't cover that time period."

"So, it really did happen?"

"You're deluded, old man. Although that is funny . . . a vicious rumor." Jon was amused at Raoul's creativity. "You'd be freaked out too if you woke up to bright lights and strange looking creatures standing around you, checking you out!"

"Sounds like the last party I was at."

7 | PAPAYAS AND PATRICK

I AM CHOOSING, LEFT, RIGHT, DAY, NIGHT.
Sequestered by wet weather, time passed slowly, one day blending into another. Days slipped by for Jon without seeing another soul. Often he had no idea what day it was, let alone the time. His wristwatch had stopped running a year ago and his pocket watch broke when he crashed his bicycle. Jon concluded that it was okay not to know the time. His journal—a black notebook he'd labeled "Captain's Log"—was open in front of him.

What comes during the day . . . I'm creating. Creating my world—in the context of existence and within the framework of what's already here and ongoing. Our viewpoints and concepts rest upon creation; the structure of creation. Our habitual beliefs formed from childhood. A dream world of layers created by generations and upheld by us all in each moment.

The rain stopped. It was an opportunity to go on a papaya run. Jon grabbed his nylon daypack. When empty it fit into his back pocket.

As always, Kolohe was happy to tag along, especially after several days of rain. The two walked down the highway. Past the small pasture with cows, past the road that climbed up to Rainbow's commune, and past Skip's driveway. A newer, clean, Toyota Corolla was on the side of the road. Jon knew a tourist car when he saw one. An older woman stood next to the car, and another woman sat inside. The car looked uneven, somehow, lilting to one side. They had a flat tire.

Kolohe had already approached the standing woman, offering his head for a pet. The woman looked at Jon with hope in her eyes.

"Can you help us?"

"Um, ah . . ."

"We can't change it. We don't know how." The other woman got out of the car.

"Our friend got a ride to Hāna to call the rental car company, but we don't know if they'll come. You'd be a lifesaver."

"Okay, let me see what we've got." Jon wasn't overly mechanical, but changing a tire, yeah, he could do that. He pulled the jack and spare tire from the trunk. The two women stood watching.

He jacked the car up, removed the flat tire and put on the spare. He lowered the car with the spare tire on. It got flatter and flatter with the weight of the car. The expression on the women's faces turned from grins to frowns. The spare tire was also flat.

"Son of a bitch," Jon mumbled under his breath.

"I can't believe it," one of the women exclaimed.

"Sorry about that. Who knew?"

"Thanks for trying." One woman got out her purse and tried to give Jon money for his trouble, but he waved it away.

Jon and Kolohe continued on to the jeep road where wild papaya grew. The jeep road was steep, dropping towards the ocean and connecting with Ulaino Road. Just before the jeep road was a papaya orchard, fenced off with barbed wire and hosting several big homemade KAPU, NO TRESPASSING signs. Jon kept out, although the forbidden fruit looked so much better than the wild ones, which often had bad spots.

Jon retrieved the picking pole he had stashed in the bush. It was a long, somewhat straight branch from a tree. He placed the end of the pole on the bottom of the papaya and raised the fruit until the stem snapped. He would attempt to catch the papaya before it smashed on the rocks and had become adept at catching them. The pole would sink into the soft flesh if they were overly ripe, and that could get messy. The papayas that were firm would go into his backpack to take home, with the greenest ones on the bottom.

On the way home they walked by the women with the flat tire, still waiting. It could be a while. Jon was sorry he couldn't have helped more. He gave a token wave as they passed.

As the two neared home they came upon a young man about Jon's age. He was haole, with a short beard, brown shoulder-length hair, and dressed in jeans with a faded tie-dye T-shirt.

"Hey."

"Were you . . . I think I saw you at Reed and Sunshine's wedding?"

"Up at the cross," Jon responded.

"Yeah, yeah. That's my brother. I'm Patrick"

"Oh wow." Jon didn't know if Patrick meant his *brother*, brother, or if he was just speaking figuratively. "That was a great ceremony. I enjoyed it."

"It was. It was. You live up at Rainbow's place? Up at the commune?"

"No, just down the street, past there. The old house on the right."

"Okay. Harry and Leanne's old place . . . and Faith. Do you know the two sisters?" Patrick asked. "Leanne is a beautiful blonde and her sister Faith, a beautiful brunette. Cool chicks. Do you have a girl?"

"No. It's just me and my little buddy for now."

They both looked over to Kolohe.

Patrick nodded. "You know the house you're living in, they used to have some outta-sight parties. At the last one there were cars parked all over the place. Both sides of the road, up and down. Two conga drum players and other musicians. Naked chicks dancing. I swear. It was great. A cloud of smoke from all the good pakalōlō being smoked, beer . . . the house was packed. There were so many people dancing, the kitchen was swaying. I thought it was going to break off and walk down the hill. Best party I've ever been to. It was tribal with those drums going off."

"Was Paulo one of the drummers?" Jon asked.

"Yep. He's good. Better than good. He lives out in Kīpahulu on Gene's property."

"Yeah, I know him and Dawn. They've invited me to visit but I haven't made it yet. He's an electrician too—multitalented guy."

"Hey Jon, do you play ball?"

"Ball?"

"Softball."

"No, not really."

"We have a team. Mostly the boys from Lower Nāhiku. It's fun. Slow pitch. We're the Nāhiku Gorillas."

"Nice."

"We play Saturdays at the Hāna ballfield. We're in a league so we get to play other teams from Hāna and around the island. Come check us out."

"I definitely will. I like watching softball. One of the hui, Blue, is on a team over on the other side."

"Blue? Don't think I know him," Patrick said. "Every now and then, I go down your trail, down below, to Stan and Susanne's."

"Hey stop by anytime."

"Right on man, I will." Patrick reached into the small macramé bag at his feet. "Check these out." He handed Jon one of several balls, crafted from soft leather, filled with sand, and made for juggling. "Do you juggle?"

"Actually, I do. Well, you know, not too often. I'm a bit rusty for sure."

Patrick started juggling. He began with the standard pattern for three balls.

"Here's another variation." It was one ball in the center and the two outside balls going up and down independently.

"I like that. I haven't seen that one before."

Patrick began to juggle the balls in a circle. "This one's actually hard. Got to be fast. I'm working on four. I'll get it. Okay, your turn."

Jon juggled three balls.

"Hey, you're good."

A car passed. Patrick stuck out his thumb. He was hitching towards Hāna. The car rolled by, and Patrick looked at his hand.

"My fingernails are pretty much gone. Ever since Vietnam they've been melting away." He showed Jon. "I don't bite them. Were you in-country?"

"I missed that one."

"You're lucky," Patrick said.

"It's true," Jon acknowledged. *I am lucky.*

8 | LINDBERGH'S GRAVE

"WELL, MY FURRY FRIEND, I THINK I'll get out and stretch my legs a bit. Hitch out to Seven Pools. You're going to have to stay home."

Kolohe was staring at Jon with a blank look on his face.

"Don't play dumb. You know what I'm talking about. It's a national park—no dogs."

Leaving him at home was easier said than done. Several times Jon tried to sneak out the front door, but Kolohe was onto him. Finally, he was able to get down the road a-ways, only to look back and see Ko lurking in the shadows.

"Go home now," Jon scolded. He skipped a small stone past him. Kolohe momentarily slipped behind some shrubs.

Jon caught a ride.

He turned in his seat and was happy to see they weren't being followed by the pup. Jon got out at Hasegawa Store. He didn't have much money but felt like having a treat. He bought a shiny red apple and a Barbara's Coconut Macaroon. The macaroons were individually wrapped, all natural, and made with honey. Carrying his treasures, he walked along the road, which was lined with tall Norfolk pines. He came to a building he liked and paused there; it had unique architecture, with wide steps, wooden columns, and an ornately carved fascia and curved roofline. Jon sat on the stone steps next to old, weathered sign that read "Hāna Soto Mission." He listened to the birds and to the wind rustling through the pines as he ate. He took a bite of macaroon followed with a bite of apple. It was a good combination. He continued to walk.

"Need a ride?"

Looking through the open passenger window of a small blue sedan, Jon saw a local man driving.

"Good morning. Thanks for stopping."

"No problem."

As Jon slid into the front seat, he noticed a young boy in the back seat holding something on his lap, under a blanket.

"I'm going out to Seven Pools," Jon said.

"We're not going that far but can take you a few miles. I'm Tevi and this is my grandson."

"I'm Jon." Jon turned and nodded to the boy.

"Show the man what you have under the blanket." Tevi motioned to Jon, "Try look."

Jon turned. The boy had a nervous smile as he peeled back the blanket. Jon couldn't have been more surprised as the hairy snout of a baby pig appeared, followed by the little pig's head.

"Now that is cool. Wow."

"Cute, yeah?

"Yeah."

"The mother was killed by hunters, so we saved the baby. We'll take him home to raise."

"Neat."

The little pig squirmed about in the boy's arms but relaxed once the boy covered him.

"Ever seen a wild baby boar?"

"No, can't say as I have." *Only at the House of Pancakes have I seen a pig-in-a-blanket.*

They drove by the pastures with huge bulls grazing, past the turn-off to Koki Beach, over concrete bridges with small streams, and through areas with scattered houses.

"Charles Lindbergh is here now," Tevi spoke. "Do you know who he is?"

"Oh, sure, the famous aviator."

"Yes. I work for him. I take care of their place. He's my friend, my good friend . . . my best friend. He's come home to die."

Jon didn't know what to say. He looked to the passing scenery.

"He's been all around the world, but Kīpahulu is his favorite place on Earth, his paradise. Mrs. Lindbergh is here too. They are good people. You know where the baby pig crossing sign is?"

"Yes, I've seen that. It's got the little cut-out pigs, on a big mango tree."

"That's the one. That's their driveway. Modest home. No electricity. He's got cancer. It's only days now. It won't be long."

Tevi looked Jon directly in the eye. His brown eyes were steady but sad. Sad to be losing his friend. He put his hand to his chin. "I'm going to miss him. We're preparing his grave. You should go see it. Do you know the Palapalo Ho'omau Church, out past the Seven Pools?"

"No. Is it that kind of funny looking building on the right?"

"No, no. Not that one," Tevi explained, "Farther up, past that one. You'll see some horses in a field on the makai side. Take the dirt road that goes alongside the field. If the cattle gate stay closed, it's okay. You can still go in."

"If the gate is closed, I can still go in?"

"Yes. Just close it after you. The church is not far. Go see the grave waiting for my friend," he said as he pulled the car over. "This is as far as we go today."

"Thanks for the ride." Momentarily, they locked eyes. All Jon could say was, "Sorry, man."

Tevi nodded.

Jon shut the car door. Through the open window he said to Tevi's grandson, "Hey, good luck with that little piggy."

The boy smiled.

Some tourists going to the Seven Sacred Pools gave Jon his third ride of the day. Along the way, he made sure to notice the "baby pigs crossing" sign. As they passed, a glance up the driveway revealed little. It was amazing the things you'd never know existed on this island, unless you met the right person.

Carved out of rugged terrain, the highway became very narrow. It was some of the world's most beautiful scenery, with spectacular roadside waterfalls amidst a lush tropical backdrop. This land haunted Jon, touched his soul, and called him back many times.

They stopped at Wailua Falls for pictures. Jon didn't mind. He enjoyed this lovely waterfall, even if for only a few moments. Farther on, they stopped alongside the Mother Mary statue standing peacefully in her roadside grotto. The Mother's hands were open in blessing, a serene expression on her face. Several flower leis adorned her neck.

At the Seven Sacred Pools Jon bid goodbye to the tourists and was once again on his own, and on foot. He stood on the bridge spanning 'Ohe'o Gulch, looking over the edge. It was a long way down to the stream below. The sides of the old concrete bridge weren't very high, and Jon always felt uncomfortable standing there for too long. His eyes followed the stream, over the waterfalls, into the large pools, and then flowing out to become lost in the ocean.

Jon was intrigued and curious to see the gravesite. He continued walking, past the Seven Sacred Pools, past the old sugar mill with its walls crumbling, the tall concrete smokestack rising above the encroaching jungle. Vines and tall vegetation were swallowing the past and reclaiming the area. Jon found the dirt road leading to the Palapalo Ho'omau Church, just as Tevi had described it, and was soon standing in front of the churchyard. A huge banyan tree grew just outside the rock wall surrounding the church compound. He ran his hand over the trunk and roots. As he walked to the front of the church, he noted the graveyard off to one side. The door of the church was unlocked. Closing the door behind him, he briefly placed his palms together and gave an almost imperceptible bow of his head. It was familiar . . . the old musty smell, the quiet, the subdued light filtering in from the side windows. Jon had been in many old churches in Hawai'i. They were always unlocked, kept clean, simple, and tidy. He sat on one of the wooden pews as his eyes wandered about the room. He liked the old churches. To him they represented a sanctuary from the world; a place to reflect, give thanks, and to share with others the mystery of life.

He thumbed through a songbook, then picked up a Bible. He purposely turned to the New Testament, randomly selected a page, and read to himself. "Except ye become like little children ye shall not enter the Kingdom of God." Jon chuckled to himself. *Am I childlike? That's easier said than done.* He put the Good Book down to continue exploring. To one side of the church was a glass bay window that went all the way to the floor. Perhaps a statue of Jesus or Mother Mary had once stood here. He came to a side door and emerged into the graveyard.

Jon was awestruck as he stood at the edge of the freshly dug open grave of Charles Lindbergh. Precisely cut from the hallowed Kīpahulu earth was a very large square. And, it was surprisingly deep. The sides and bottom were lined with large, rounded beach rocks. The corners of the grave were perfect, and the sides straight up and down. He had never seen anything like it. It was obviously made with great skill, but also with great care and love. A special grave for a special man, and someone's good friend. Beside the grave was a big pile of beach rock. Jon sat beside the grave in contemplation. *One day, we have to leave it all . . . our friends, family, and homes, our bodies. We all return to the earth. Who will be there for me when my time comes, to send me off with prayers of love?*

After some time, Jon headed back to the Seven Sacred Pools. He hiked up through the pastures, crossed the stream, and onto the trail leading deep into the bamboo forest. The bamboo here grew thick and tall. High above, the tops of the bamboo were swaying with the wind, making eerie creaking sounds as they rubbed each other. The trail was slippery from recent rain, and he had to skirt some areas to avoid the mud. Jon was hungry, so he returned to the pasture. These areas were interspersed with clumps of trees and brush where he hoped to find something to eat. He kept his distance from the cows and young bulls grazing, and eventually came across a tall papaya tree with a small ripe papaya on it. He threw sticks and even rocks to knock it down. The fruit was damaged from the abuse but tasted especially good after his long walk. Not far from the papaya tree was a chili pepper bush. The peppers were very small. He picked a bright red one, carefully sliced it open and touched it to his tongue. Big mistake. The burning sensation was instantaneous. His mouth was on fire and he had nothing to dull the sensations.

The burning gradually faded, yet Jon's memory of the day remained strong. Later that evening, in his Captain's Log, Jon wrote about his adventurous day. His journal entry ended with, *"It was a day to remember and one I will never forget."*

9 | NĀPILI

NĀPILI BAY WAS BEAUTIFUL. INSIDE THE cove, the tranquil ocean was a transparent blend of blues and greens. Beneath the shimmering surface you could see large and small rocks, coral formations, and tropical reef fish. The yellow tang were the easiest to spot. Across the Pailolo Channel, the peaks of Moloka'i were shrouded in cutout white and grey clouds, easing their way down the creases of the island. Jon stood under the only tree in Kathleen and Paco's yard, a large kiawe tree, gazing out on the peaceful setting. This was a refreshing change from the rain in Nāhiku.

Jon and Kolohe were watching Paco and Cha Cha on their morning swim. Cha Cha was a little chihuahua. The two swam across the small inlet of the bay and back. Paco swam slowly, using no particular stroke. Cha Cha kept up.

"Cool. Very cool," Jon murmured to himself.

Once out of the water, Paco jumped under the outdoor shower. Looking over to Jon, he asked, "Ready to do some airbrushing?"

"Sure."

Cha Cha gave herself a couple of good shakes and went to lie in the sun.

"First things first. You got any grass?"

"No."

"Okay. I'm about out. There's a guy up the street. He always has something. You can come with me if you want." Paco threw on one of his colorful air-brushed tank tops. They climbed into the Jeep and headed just across the Honoapi'ilani Highway, up the street to a non-descript duplex. Jon could smell a familiar aroma as they walked toward the front door. A couple of guys were just leaving.

"Hey Clark."

"Come on in."

Clark was sitting on the couch in the small living room. He was a tan, clean-cut haole guy with dark hair.

There were several grades to choose from. A decent Columbian at forty dollars an ounce, a lesser grade Mexican for twenty-five, and some local leaf for twenty.

"There'll be some good Maui bud coming in soon."

Paco bought the Mexican.

Kolohe had followed the Jeep up the road. He ran behind them on the way home. "I've clocked him at forty," Paco said.

"No way."

Paco cranked up the Jeep, and Kolohe also cranked it up. Jon turned in his seat to see Kolohe go. "That is one fast dog."

"Remember that time, in Hāna, when he fell out of the back of the Jeep?" Paco asked.

"Yep. He was leaning out too far and lost it. Lucky we weren't going very fast. I looked back in time to see him do a 360 and come up running, unfazed."

PACO'S STUDIO WAS A CONVERTED GARAGE. They smoked a joint while Paco explained the art of airbrushing. He started with the basics, instructing Jon how to mix the paint. A set of small plastic jars held paint colors and water. Paco diluted and strained an artist's acrylic paint through a nylon stocking.

"Very important," Paco looked up. "You don't want to be stopping to clean your airbrush. Nylon stockings are getting hard to find, though. Women don't wear them much anymore, especially in Hawai'i. I could buy new ones but I'm not going to do that. I get them from Debbie at the shop."

Paco had a talent for intricate stencil cutting. Many of his designs involved multiple stencils which he would use, one after another, to form a complex design. The stencils were meticulously cut out of manila file folders using a sharp precision knife.

"Ever seen one of these? A light table. I made it myself."

It was a shallow wooden box with two twelve-inch-long florescent tubes inside and a sheet of glass over the top.

"See, you can overlay two stencils and check how well the edges line up. Go ahead and make a design and cut some stencils, Jon. We'll paint later. Painting is the quick part. Here's the piece I'm working on. It's my own creation. I call it a mandala oblongata. Can you dig it? It's a mind fuck."

Paco tossed a drawing in front of Jon. It was a sphere of legs, arms, and other naked body parts, wrapped around each other in a tangled ball. Jon was at a loss for words.

He quietly watched Paco as he cut the final stencil for his new design, moving slowly and carefully.

"This takes a lot of patience," Jon finally said. Paco nodded and kept working. Jon began drawing his own design, a simple fantasy style sailboat.

"I used to play cards," Paco said after he'd finished cutting, holding his new stencil to the lightbox to admire its shape.

"Cards?" Jon didn't understand.

"You know, for money. I'm a sleight of hand artist."

"In poker? For real?"

"Yep. Things would heat up in Detroit, so I'd head out to LA. When it got hot in LA, I'd go back to Detroit. I'll show you some moves some time. Don't look so surprised!"

Jon couldn't help it. Paco was always surprising him.

"I've lived a lot of lives," Paco said. "I was also a second-story man."

"What's that?"

"Burglar. I'd enter a house through a second story window. One night I burglarized a judge's home. Went in the upper story bedroom window. The judge was sleeping."

"That's nuts. Did you ever get arrested?"

"Never arrested for burglary . . . or for gambling. I did a year in federal prison for a pound of Acapulco Gold. That was in LA, and the feds were bringing in bad drugs. Downers and speed. Trying to enslave the Chicanos. I was only selling grass and LSD—drugs that free the mind. I was doing my part to bring us all up, but they were trying to keep us down. It was war."

Paco had a distant look. "What was I going to tell you? Oh yeah, so in the joint there was this guy, Martin. Great artist. Every year the prison would have a big show of his work. Three months before the show, Martin would start painting. He would set up a bunch of canvases in his cell, all different sizes and shapes. He worked on all of them at once. Like ten at a time, going back and forth from one canvas to another. Same brush, same colors. A brush stroke here, a little color there," He gestured with his hands. "Here's the thing—every painting was totally different. It was all in his head. Nothing was drawn out. The guy was a genius. I would watch him for hours. He wouldn't let me talk while he painted."

Paco shook off the memory. He set his stencils onto the light table, gesturing for Jon to look. "I like my edges tight. But it's okay if they're not perfect. It gives you an extra little edge of color . . . or no color. That depends on if they overlap or, ah, underlap."

Jon began to cut his design.

"Save both pieces, inside and out. You need the cut-out piece as a cover to paint the background."

"Positive and negative."

"Right," Paco said, looking a bit irritated. He knew the effect but not the technical words for it and didn't appreciate his lack of a formal art education being pointed out, even if it was unintentional. Paco generally had a serious demeanor; it was hard to tell what was going on inside his head.

Paco gave the backside of his stencils a light coat of spray adhesive.

"You have any old T-shirts you can paint on?"

Paco slipped a white V-neck T-shirt on to a cardboard cutout to stretch it flat, then pinned it onto a 4' x 8' sheet which Jon realized was interior ceiling material, firm but easy to push a pin into. The backing was originally white, but now covered in a kaleidoscope of color.

Jon was happy to be in the studio learning. He watched closely as Paco's new design manifested on the shirt. Although he found the design strange, he appreciated the imagination and craftsmanship required to create it. Paco definitely marched to the beat of a different drummer.

Once he finished, Jon had a turn with the airbrush, grinning as his fantasy sailboat materialized.

When Kathleen came home in the evening, she fed the dogs. She mixed dry Friskies with warm water and set it out in a big tray for Ruffus and Kolohe to share with a few neighborhood dogs. Jon noted Ruffus was top dog; the other dogs waited for him to finish, then ate and growled at each other. Cha Cha, the only dog allowed in the house, dined indoors.

There were young women who stayed at the house and worked for the boutique, sewing. Zoe, an old friend of Jenn, was living there. She was moody and always seemed to be on the edge of depression. Elizabeth came and went, dropping by for hot showers and company; she mostly lived out of her car. She parked in the driveway which was unpaved red Nāpili dirt, usually pocked with puddles. Elizabeth was five years older than Jon, strait-laced and more reserved compared to many he encountered on the island.

Jon sat on the sofa leafing through one of Kathleen's books, *The Teachings of Ramana Maharshi*. One corner of the book cover had been chewed off, and the beginning pages were totally missing. It began mid-sentence on page fifteen: "the Self is not then perceived . . ."

Kathleen came into the living room, wrapped in a sarong. "Tonight, I'm making my shrimp curry and rice. How's that sound, Jon?"

"Great, thanks." Jon knew shrimp curry was one of Kat's specialties, and a real crowd pleaser.

"Blue and Judy are coming for dinner too, along with their kids. They're part of the hui; I can't recall, have you met them?"

"Briefly."

"Eventually you'll know everyone—we're all 'ohana. How about Georgia? Have you met her? She lives in Huelo, but I imagine she'll be coming out to Hāna soon."

"No, not yet."

"She and I discovered the Nāhiku property when it was for sale. You'll like her. She's a bit of a character."

Jon was never sure what "a bit of a character" meant. He had met a lot of characters along the way.

Blue and Judy, who lived around the corner, brought their two boys Cody and Seth, aged three and five. Blue was a potter who had his own wheel and small electric kiln. He had told Jon he didn't throw a lot of pots these days, as he was working full-time as a carpenter.

"So, what? Jerry's not here?" Blue said, holding up two six-packs of beer.

"He had to go to work." Jerry would be bummed to miss the meal *and the beer*. He was the head chef at the Tree House Restaurant in Lahaina, about ten miles down the road, and worked the night shift.

Blue was six feet tall, blonde, with broad shoulders. He was as athletic as he looked; on his days off he liked to surf and played on a softball team. Judy also had blonde hair which hung well below her shoulders but unlike Blue, she was petite. The kids explored the house.

Everyone enjoyed the meal. After dinner Paco retreated to his studio, Judy took the kids home, and Jon helped with the dishes. Kathleen retired to her bedroom to relax and read a little. Blue stuck around for a bit.

"Jon, do you play any ball? You have the body of a second baseman."

"Ah, no. Never got into it. Played tennis and surfed quite a few years, in San Diego. Wasn't into sports much."

"You want another beer man?"

"Nah, I'm good. Do you ever play any of the Hāna teams? There's a team, the Nāhiku Gorillas . . ."

"Yeah, I know some of those guys. They're actually pretty good. You know, for a bunch of stoners." Blue rolled his eyes, and Jon chuckled.

Jon slept on the living room floor that night, cozy in his sleeping bag. The house was full of activity early the next morning. Kathleen was washing yards of material to be sewn into clothing, while Paco threw his newly painted shirt into the dryer to heat-set. As usual, there wasn't much food in the refrigerator. Breakfast was honey wheatberry toast with peanut butter. On a good day, slices of banana were added. But as far as Jon was concerned, peanut butter on toast was a treat on any day. Perfect fuel for his hitchhiking journey back to the windward side, to Upper Nāhiku.

Kathleen was going to be deworming the dogs and figured Kolohe should be included. They would bring him out to Hāna in a couple of weeks. It was a strange feeling for Jon, now that he was accustomed to his little dog buddy following him everywhere he went—he was flying solo.

10 | LOCAL COLOR

J ON CAUGHT A RIDE TO THE outskirts of Lahaina. He stopped to see Mike, who worked at an autobody shop at the old cannery.

"Hey Jon. Getting out of the rain?"

Mike's friend Jimmy did most of the bodywork, while Mike was adept at painting the finished cars. He pointed to the car he was working on.

"Check this out. It's the layers of clear lacquer that give it depth."

"Looks like a little sparkle too."

"There's metal flake in the paint. A couple more layers of clear—that's the key. Not everyone understands that."

Mike showed Jon the gas tank of a Harley that he painted. Out of pitch black came deep blues and purples with stars, and on top of the tank, a sunrise bursting over a mountain peak.

"Wow. Good job, sir. Great depth." Jon was surprised. He had never seen this artistic side of Mike.

"Thanks. Layer upon layer, I'm telling ya. It took a while. You'd be good at this."

Jon shrugged off the compliment, then eyed a calendar hanging on the wall of the garage. *November already.* "So, I hear Thanksgiving is coming up."

"Me and the old lady are going to Mama's Fish House. That way she doesn't have to cook, and it's good grinds. What are you doing?"

"Not sure. Guess I'll see what comes up." Growing up, Jon had no extended family close by, so consequently Thanksgiving was a simple affair. Still, he hoped to have someone to share the special day with.

"We'll be home during the day. Stop by if you're around."

"Will do."

Jon walked the rest of the way into Lahaina Town. Stopping at Maui Ragtime, he saw that one of his puka shell necklaces had been sold. It was a fancy one with turquoise and silver. He was happy that someone appreciated his work and it would give him a bit of grocery money. Leaving the shop, he spotted Pancho. He was an old Filipino man, thin and wiry with a brown weathered face and a white wispy goatee. He wore a broad brimmed straw hat with a plastic flower lei wrapped around the brim, a long black trench coat, a T-shirt, and baggy trousers. He was barefoot. His coat was festooned with metal buttons displaying various slogans, and there were a good number of them. Jon watched Pancho haggle with some tourists who had just taken his picture. He was waving his hand with his index finger raised.

"Wan dala. Wan dala." With his thick pidgin accent, the tourists didn't understand; they smiled and laughed nervously while attempting to move away.

"You need to give him a dollar," Jon told the tourists as he passed them on the sidewalk. "If you take his picture you have to give him a dollar."

Pancho gave Jon a quick look, up and down. One of the tourists pulled a couple of bucks from a folded wallet and shot Jon an appreciative glance.

Jon continued down Front Street, stopping to talk to his friend Jamie who was managing his brother's jewelry store. The front and side walls of the shop rolled up, creating an open-air feeling. Waist-high jewelry showcases edged the sidewalk.

"My man," Jamie said with a big smile. "How you be?"

"Good, good. How about you? How's biz?"

"Wonderful. The snowbirds are starting to roll in."

"Snowbirds?"

"People escaping cold weather on the mainland. A lot of them come every winter."

As if on cue, Captain Kenny was lumbering towards them. With his big belly, white beard, double XL aloha shirt and dark sunglasses, Kenny looked like a Hawaiian Santa Claus. As usual, Kenny was pushing a shopping cart full of his artwork. He was talking to himself as he rambled down the sidewalk.

Kenny's fanciful creations were mostly stylized fish, in which sea creatures merged with everyday objects—fish with glasses, golfclub fish, guitar fish, an octopus bartender. The art was colorful, with well-balanced compositions. Colored felt pen on poster board was Captain Kenny's favorite medium, but he was known to paint on anything that wasn't nailed down. Jon once saw a plastic lid from a five-gallon bucket that Kenny had transformed into a seascape.

Kenny shot them a shy glance as he passed. "Eh, governor," he said softly.

"Hey Kenny."

The two watched Kenny roll past and on down the sidewalk. Everyone who spent much time in Lahaina knew Captain Kenny. When Jon had his bicycle shop, Kenny created a poster board piece for him that had a big bicycle tire in it, among the fish. Jon wished he had hung on to that poster; it was a gem.

Jamie was 6'2" with broad shoulders, a warm smile, and a clean shave. He had the smooth deep voice of a radio announcer—a natural charmer with a laid-back attitude. Jon imagined he could seduce a woman just by saying, "Well hellooo there." Jamie was forty-five, divorced, and presently single, which he seemed to enjoy.

"Jon, you ever need a place to crash, come on by. Here's my number," Jamie said. "I just rented a house up in Pukalani. It's in a neighborhood but has a huge back yard."

"Thanks Jamie. Hopefully I'll make it to Nāhiku before dark. Although all the tourists will be going the other way by the time I get out there."

"I'll be heading that direction later, pau hana. You got any dope?"

Jon shook his head no.

"You should get some growing out there."

"Yeah, I know."

A couple of tourist girls stopped to look at jewelry, and Jon watched Jamie shift into salesman mode.

"Right on Jamie. Catch ya later."

As Jon walked away, he heard Jamie greeting his female customers, "Well hellooo there." It made Jon chuckle.

A few doors down, he ducked into the Lahaina Book Store.

"Just the guy I wanted to see," Matthew said, extending his hand.

Matthew was the owner of the bookstore. He was a large man, tall and sturdy, with a few extra pounds on him. He had a dark scruffy beard and a slight New York accent.

"How's it going?" Jon asked.

"Good. Everything starts picking up about now. It was a slow summer."

"You probably sell a lot of books around Christmas, right?"

"Oh yeah." Matthew stepped closer to him. "Honestly, if I could sell girly mags, I'd be making a fortune any time of year," he said, raising his eyebrows. "Anything with any sex or nudity flies out of here."

Jon shrugged. He didn't see anything so wrong with that. Why not sell what the people wanted?

"We're in the Lahaina Historical District. Got to toe the line. Hey, I wanted to ask you to make me some new signs for out front. Maybe we can trade like last time?"

"Sounds good." Jon was thinking that the last signs he made for the bookstore still looked great but hey, he wouldn't refuse a trade.

"I just got some new books in I think you will like." Matthew handed Jon a book. *The Magic of Findhorn.* "Have you heard of that place? It's in Scotland. I know you're in to gardening. And here's another good one—"

Jon looked at the cover. "*Hey Beatnik! This is the Farm Book.* Steven Gaskin. Okay. I read *Monday Night Class.*"

"Here, check these two out." He pushed two more books into Jon's hands, both oversized paperbacks: *Tao Te Ching* by Lao Tzu and Chuang-Tzu, *Inner Chapters.* Jon leafed through and saw exquisite black and white photography overlayed with simple poetic ancient teachings. "These are great, thank you."

Matthew explained that he wanted the new signs to look like an old book.

"Too bad I don't have my leather tools. I could have actually made the signs out of leather." He enjoyed a creative challenge. "It would have looked really authentic."

"I trust you'll do a great job. You doing anything for Thanksgiving? You should come over. Linda cooks all day and makes a ton of food. She's vegetarian so there'll be plenty of options. Myself, I'm going to have to have some turkey."

"Ok, yeah maybe. Tell me again how to get there. In Ha'ikū, yeah? I'll come by if I can."

"Take the books, we can settle up later. You can always get a few more."

"Right on. Thanks Matt."

Jon turned up Prison Street, walked past the old whaler's prison to the highway, and stuck out his thumb. *What was I thinking taking these books*, he thought, feeling the extra weight in his pack.

A station wagon pulled over. Two young men were in the front.

"Thanks for the ride. It's hot out there."

Jon peered into the car. The front seats had been removed and replaced with two easy chairs, with their legs cut off. He had to smile.

"Now that's far out."

"Pretty cool, yeah? Don't worry—the chairs are bolted down."

Once he'd climbed in, Jon chatted with the driver. "Is it legal to have easy chairs for seats? What about safety inspections?"

"Once a year we have to put the real seats in. It's easy, just a few nuts and bolts."

"Too much, man."

They dropped Jon in Wailuku. He walked through town to find a good spot for hitching. Rides were sporadic and it was late afternoon by the time he reached the north shore. Walking up and down the hills approaching Huelo had worn him out. He sat on a guardrail, deciding he would stand only when a car was coming. The shadows were stretching long and he began to see hints of color highlighting the clouds. He was glad to have brought his sleeping bag and rain poncho; if he didn't get a ride soon, he would have to find a place to sleep in the bush. Occasionally, in moments like these, Jon missed the comforts of the mainland. *Living on the fringe of civilization has its drawbacks.*

11 | JERSEY TORNADO

An old four-door Ford station wagon pulled over. Jon climbed into the back seat and greeted three others in the car.

"Thanks. I was beginning to wonder. I'm Jon."

"Mark."

"Carla."

"I'm Mary Rose," said the young woman at the wheel. She patted the dashboard, smiling at Jon over her shoulder, and added, "This is Frank. Frank is a 1956 Ford. Mark and Carla are hitching too. We're headed for the Seven Sacred Pools, but stopping at Kaumahina State Park to stay overnight. I don't want to miss anything by driving at night."

Mary Rose had black hair tied into two braids. She wore thick coke bottle bottom glasses with wire rims.

"Jon, where are you going?"

"Headed home. I live out by Hāna."

"Sorry we're not going all the way to Hāna tonight."

"No worries."

At the park, Jon and Mary Rose walked to the viewpoint, naturally falling into step together. Mary Rose was short, her legs and arms were muscular, and she moved with confidence. The white Mexican peasant shirt she wore highlighted her deep olive-colored skin. Reminding himself not to stare, Jon turned to the horizon. Looking east towards Hāna, Ke'anae Peninsula was dreamlike in the twilight. Night was falling quickly.

As they returned to Frank, they passed a sign:

NO OVERNIGHT CAMPING

"Will that be a problem?" Mary Rose asked.

"Nah."

"You can sleep with me in Frank if you want."

"That would be great. Most likely it will rain during the night."

Mark and Carla were going to sleep on a picnic table, up off the ground and away from the bugs. They said they didn't mind a little rain.

"I borrowed Frank from a girlfriend in Wailuku. She works at the hospital and couldn't get off, so here I am."

Jon and Mary Rose put down the rear seats, spread out their sleeping bags, and sat leaning against the back of the front seat. It was a bench style seat and spanned the width of the car.

"Where do you live?" Jon asked.

"San Francisco. I have a little apartment. A cozy little nest. I'm a Cancer. What sign are you? Where are you from, originally?"

"Taurus. From San Diego."

"A Californian bull. Interesting." Mary Rose had a mischievous smile on her face. "I'm originally from New Jersey. Italian girl from Jersey, but I love San Francisco. Love, love, love it. Love the city. Love my funky little place. Love my job."

"Where do you work?

"I'm a head nurse at a hospital. On my vacation time I like to travel, and to hike and camp in nature. There are so many beautiful and inspiring places in the United States. Have you been hiking in Haleakalā Crater, the National Park? I want to camp up there."

"Oh yeah. It's amazing. Definitely a great experience." Jon found himself distracted by Mary Rose and how close she sat.

"I'm going to save my battery," she said, turning off her flashlight.

The two sat in the dark.

"Not much of a moon out," Jon said.

Mary Rose reached over and put her hand on the inside of Jon's leg. He turned and touched her face. Their eager lips found each other.

"Umm, that's nice," she whispered. Their hands explored each other's bodies as they kissed. This sensual moment was heightened by the darkness. Jon was quickly becoming swept up in their shared passion.

She pulled back. "Jon, I want to make love to you. But I think we should get to know each other better first." She took his hand and squeezed it. "Let's get some rest for now. I'm looking forward to tomorrow."

"Me too."

A LIGHT RAIN FELL DURING THE NIGHT. Jon and Mary Rose slept cuddled up for warmth, and Mark and Carla took shelter under the picnic table with the rain fly from their tent draped over it. By morning the rain had stopped, and the four travelers sat at that very picnic table eating trail mix and bananas.

"Jon, will you drive so I can enjoy the scenery?" Mary Rose asked.

He didn't mind. He was getting to know the road well. There was little traffic with the exception of a few Hāna locals making an early morning run to the other side.

He drove slowly as the beauty of Maui unfolded before them. It was refreshing to be with someone who was seeing it for the first time. He offered his house for everyone to stay the night, but Mary Rose was intent on sleeping under the stars.

"I didn't come to Hawai'i to sleep under a roof! Jon, are you coming to the Seven Sacred Pools with us?"

How can I say no? New friends, intriguing woman, the call of adventure.

He stopped at home to drop off his books and grab his tent. The house was strangely quiet; Kolohe was still in Nāpili at Kathleen's. In Hāna, Jon drove by Hāna Bay, past the ballpark, and then pulled into Hasegawa Store for supplies. They all piled back inside Frank and continued to the Seven Sacred Pools in the National Park. They dropped down to the camping area which was adjacent to the 'Ohe'o Gulch and the pools. No permit was necessary, with a three-night maximum. It was a spot with stands of trees and open grassy areas that stretched to seaside cliffs.

Jon and Mary Rose stood on the bluff overlooking the ocean.

"That's the Big Island. Looks like snow on the peaks," he said, pointing. Mauna Kea and Mauna Loa could be seen in the distance, across the channel, rising above the clouds.

"Snow in Hawai'i. That's so cool. I visited the Big Island before coming to Maui."

Mark and Carla had gone to explore the area on their own. Jon and Mary Rose grabbed a beach towel and walked to the pools for a swim.

The large pools were fed by a stream that wove its way from high in the mountains. The water moved all the way down to the last pool, close to the ocean. They jumped from the ledges into the cool water. They climbed rocks and stood under small waterfalls together, laughing and grinning at each other. When they'd had enough of swimming, they sat in the sun, talking.

As night came, there was little more than a sliver of a waning moon. Mary Rose grabbed her flashlight and Jon carried a sleeping bag as they slipped out of camp. Carefully, they crossed the stream near the ocean where they could step or jump from rock to rock. On the other side of the stream, they climbed a grassy knoll. There they spread their sleeping bag. The trade winds softened. The waves provided a soothing percussion in the background. Hala trees were dimly silhouetted against the sky.

She peeled off her clothes and lay on her back. All the nearness and kissing the night before had left Jon with an aching desire. Naked, he fell into her arms. The lovers enjoyed each other, their bodies writhing in pleasure until they collapsed onto their backs, looking upwards into the night sky.

"Umm."

"Umm hmm."

"Is that the Big Dipper?"

"I think so."

"Were you holding back that second time?" she asked.

"No." He suppressed a smirk; he didn't realize he *could* hold back, even if he wanted to. But her eyes were serious, curious. She was unlike any woman he'd met before.

THE NEXT MORNING ARRIVED WITH MUTED reds, yellows, and oranges, the sun rising from the ocean as the Earth turned to another day.

"I want to find some mushrooms. Are there really psychedelic mushrooms that grow out of the cow pies?" Mary Rose asked.

"Yep. They're not *super* psychedelic, but they can certainly get you high. Psilocybin."

"Do you know what they look like? Think we can find some?"

Jon led her to the trailhead above the highway. From there the trail wound through the pastures and skirted the stream. They checked the dried cow pies but didn't find any mushrooms. They paused where the trail crossed the stream.

"Jon, do you know what a coven is?"

"No," he answered honestly.

"I belong to a coven. It's a group of witches. A group of women that I get together with. We're good witches. We don't cast spells on anyone or anything like that. We play music together, with bells. We sit in a circle with just candlelight, lots of candles. Everyone has a different sounding bell, and we make music. It's amazing."

He had never heard of someone calling herself a witch before. Not in real life.

"Also, we do spontaneous writing . . . automatic writing." She saw by the look on his face that he had no idea what she was talking about. "It's a spiritual way of writing—you don't think. You just write. Whatever comes. No mental editing. It doesn't even have to make sense. We have a time limit. Five minutes or something like that. Then we read them aloud. Someone else reads yours."

"Right on," said Jon. Who was this woman? She was even more fascinating than he'd thought.

"I'm really close to my coven sisters. You know, I'm bisexual. I like women as much as I like men." After a moment of thought, she added, "Maybe more."

He wasn't sure how to respond. After a moment of awkward silence, he blurted, "Can't blame you. I like women too."

They both laughed a little, then continued up the trail winding their way into a dense bamboo forest.

"This is incredible," she said.

Emerging from the bamboo forest they ventured up a riverbed, walking on large rocks and boulders. They came to a large pool and waterfall.

Jon had been here once before, by himself. He was happy to be able to share it with someone. Unlike the pools they swam in the previous day, the water here was murky. To Jon it looked like a place where, in the movies, a dragon or other mystical creature would rise out of. Normally he wouldn't have gone in, but Mary Rose wanted to take a dip, so he followed. They left their clothes at the edge of the water. He surfaced next to her and kissed her. She dove underwater and swam away. Later, on their way back through the bamboo, she said, "I know you wanted to get together back there, at the pool. It just didn't feel right."

"That's okay."

"That area felt like a very sacred spot. While I was floating on my back," she continued, "I looked up, and the shape of the sky looked like a uterus, a womb. Did you notice?"

"No. Can't say as I did."

They hiked in comfortable silence, until Mary Rose turned and asked, "Do you want me to eat you?"

"Uh . . . sure." Jon felt his cheeks heating.

"Here this looks good." She placed the folded towel on a stump that had been cut along the trail. "Make yourself comfortable."

He sat on the stump and leaned back against some bamboo. She unzipped his pants and pulled them down. They were still on the trail, although they hadn't seen any other hikers all day. He relaxed, looking around at his surroundings and Mary Rose. He ran his fingers through her thick black hair then rested his arms to his side and closed his eyes, the center of his body alive with feeling. Afterwards she looked up at him, smiling. Wordlessly they got up and continued down the hill.

The group of four stayed one more night at the Seven Sacred Pools then headed to Wai'ānapanapa State Park, on the outskirts of Hāna town. Jon was enjoying the feeling of moving with a pack, and sleeping next to Mary Rose each night. It was a different rhythm than being on his own. He wondered what mischief Kolohe was getting into back in Nāpili.

Wai'ānapanapa State Park had restrooms, outdoor showers (cold), and a mowed lawn for camping. It was a picturesque and historic area. The entrance and parking area were shaded by stately kamani trees. Their large rounded multicolored leaves littered the road. Looking up towards the sun, Jon saw an illuminated, layered canopy of colors and shades. Oranges, reds, greens, browns, and yellows.

Mary Rose and Jon hiked the ancient Hawaiian coastal trail, a rugged path that passed over barren lava. Hala trees and low shrubs grew out of the rocks. The trail rewarded them with spectacular views of the Hāna coastline, small offshore islets, and the slopes of Haleakalā. Wai'ānapanapa means "glistening waters" in Hawaiian. True to its name, the ocean here sparkled with a million tiny points of light. After lunch, they took a dip at a small black sand beach, framed on either side by lava cliffs. They stayed in the shallow water as the currents here were not to be trusted.

Not far from the beach, they stopped at the freshwater caves. Jon told Mary Rose the legend he'd learned about the caves: *A young Hawaiian Princess named Popo'alaea once fled here to escape her cruel husband, Chief Kakae. Popo'alaea brought a trusted female companion along with her. The women hid on a ledge just inside the underwater entrance to the caves during the day, and came out at night in search of food. One day while Chief Kakae was at these freshwater caves, he saw their reflection in the water. They were discovered and killed. Blood darkened the rocks and water. Even now, in the spring, the time the tragedy occurred, the water turns red in remembrance.*

"A sad story," she said. "Poor Princess Popo'alaea. And her friend."

He nodded. "The legend coincides with the gathering of the red 'ōpae 'ula every spring, a tiny red shrimp that colors the water."

That evening the four travelers came together. They sat exchanging stories of their adventures. Mark and Carla had hitched into town to go swimming at Hāna Bay. Jon had asked them to pick up brown rice and lentils at Hasegawas, which he was now cooking compliments of Mark's camping pot and sterno.

"Umm, that smells good," Carla said, referring to the small pot of rice mixed with lentils.

"I know," Jon replied. "Something about it, yeah?"

"I'm surprised Hasegawas has brown rice," Mark said.

"Hasegawas has everything. If you don't see it in the front, it's in the back. They even have art supplies."

After dark, Jon and Mary Rose took a walk. They sat in a grassy area not far from the campsite.

"I think there are gravesites right here," Jon said pointing to the area just above them.

"That's okay," she said, with confidence. "If there are spirits here, they know we come with good intentions."

The two kissed.

She whispered in his ear. "Do you want to make love? Or do you want me to eat you?"

"Decisions, decisions," he whispered back. They giggled. Then he remembered their encounter in the bamboo forest and chose the latter.

She made her magic, then said, "Your turn."

He agreed, shyly.

"Have you done this before?" she asked.

"No." He felt comfortable enough with this woman to admit that.

"Okay. I'll help you. Lick it like a lollypop. That's it. Keep licking. Good. Right there. Right there."

Afterwards, they lay watching the stars dancing between the clouds. She touched his face. "Your beard is soft. I think of beards as being rough and scratchy. Yours is soft." Jon felt strangely proud that his beard was soft for Mary Rose. He wanted to make her happy.

THE PLAN FOR THE NEXT DAY was to head for Haleakalā Crater. They all rose early and got back on the road with Frank. Mark and Carla sat in the back. Jon drove, and Mary Rose slid over to sit right next to him. This affectionate gesture made him grin. He felt loved. In Nāhiku Jon grabbed extra clothes for the crater, as it would be cold at night. He would have to layer as his warmest coat was a denim jacket.

Reaching Pā'ia, they turned up Baldwin Avenue then stopped in Hāli'imaile where Mike and Shay rented a small plantation-style house. The house sat at the end of the street, next to sugar cane fields, and had an excellent view of the West Maui Mountains. When Jon came to this side of the island he often stayed with them. They were one of only two haole families in the Hāli'imaile area.

"Mike," Jon called out.

"In here. Hey Jon. What you up to?"

"Heading to the crater to camp for a couple of nights."

"It's going to be cold."

"I know. These are some friends of mine. Mary Rose, Mark, and Carla.

"Nice to meet you. Smoke a joint?"

"I think we have time for that."

While the group passed a joint around, Mike unfolded a cloth and held it up to Jon. Inside was a piece of ivory. "Check this out."

"Scrimshaw?"

"Yep. You know Jimmy, the guy I work with at the cannery, in Lahaina? Surfer dude. Does the auto body work, yeah? He's a really good artist and is doing scrimshaw now too. He gave me some small fossilized ivory chips to practice on, along with some samples. It's piecework. Once I get fast, I can make good money."

"Far out."

Mike was tall, with a wiry build. He was bald on top and had a beard which he kept neatly trimmed. He was an ex-biker and once rode with a motorcycle gang similar to the Hells Angels in California. His tattoos told stories: *U.S. Marine Corp* in small letters, *Satan's Slaves* in cursive, and a skull with a dagger through it. He didn't talk about the old days often, but every now and then after a couple of beers and a good joint, Jon heard some interesting tales.

"The old lady went for a job interview. It's for manager of the shopping mall," Mike said.

"The big shopping mall?"

"Yep. She'll probably get it too."

Jon tried to imagine Shay as a corporate type. Shay was thin and lanky, with very short blonde hair—boyish. She was strong-willed and determined. Jon knew that whatever job she took, she'd do it her way, that was for sure. As the room fell silent, Mary Rose caught his eye and gave him a small wink. The troop, sitting in the small living room, had just finished the joint. Each used the restroom, waved their thanks to Mike, and continued up the mountain.

12 | MILAGROS

"I COULD GET USED TO THIS," RAOUL said. They were having lunch at the Pā'ia streetside café, Milagros.

Jon raised his glass. "Cheers."

"That Mary Rose was a trip. She sounds very SF."

"We kept in touch for a long time. She came to visit me in Half Moon Bay some years later. I was just passing through visiting my mom." *Memorable day.* "Saw her again in Nāhiku once or twice, and even in Volcano on the Big Island. She hiked to the top of Mauna Loa by herself."

"That's a strong woman. Hey, these nachos are good."

"So good," Jon said, helping himself to more. "She eventually got married."

"To a woman?" Raoul asked, half in jest.

"Yep . . . to another woman. She was ahead of her time."

"I may have crossed paths with her in The City. There were always a lot of interesting folks in and out of the library."

"I'll bet."

"You know I'm from New Jersey too."

"Oh yeah, that's right. Another time when Mary Rose was back in Nāhiku, she had a new tattoo—a rainbow above her pubic hair. She said it was a rainbow over her pot of gold."

"Wild child."

"We were at the hui house. Judy was there, and Mary Rose asked me if she should show Judy her tattoo. I just raised my eyebrows. Then she asked Judy if she wanted to see her tattoo. Judy looked at me and asked, "Jonnnn, do I want to see her tattoo?" I said, *Sure, why not.* So, there in the kitchen, Mary Rose pulls her pants down. She was very comfortable with her sexuality."

"Oh yes, sounds like San Francisco, alright. When I first moved there, I thought it might be hard to get a date. But actually, being a straight guy in San Francisco had its advantages."

"Supply and demand."

"Right! Although in that town, when a guy is really staring at me, I never know if he wants to fight or ask me out to dinner."

They sat and watched the colorful parade of people passing by.

"I could do this all day," Raoul said. "I already said that didn't I?"

"Something like that. But, you know Raoul, just like anything, even doing nothing—it takes practice to get really good at it."

"I'm willing to put the time in."

"Right."

"You saw a lot of action in your day, yeah Jon?"

"Once upon a time," Jon murmured.

"Well, I'm still having fun. I brought my little blue bombers."

"Your little blue what?"

Raoul whispered quietly, "Viagra. If we hook up with some hot chicks you can borrow some. They're great. Get things pointed in the right direction, if you know what I mean."

"I don't know. I'm such an old hippy. I don't trust the pharmaceutical companies. I'm trying to age gracefully," Jon said.

An attractive young woman strolled by.

"How's that going?" Raoul jabbed.

Jon smiled.

"Ready for another Maui IPA?"

"Okay, since nobody's driving," Jon said. "But I don't know about the pills, man. I can see the headlines now: 'Old Man with an Enormous Four-Hour Erection—Emergency Air-Lifted from Haleakalā Crater'."

"Oh, it's enormous now is it?"

The two friends laughed.

"How many times have you been in the crater?"

"I was asking myself that very question the other day. Seven times. Out Kaupō Gap three times."

Two fresh beers arrived at the table.

"In 1972 I was living in Makawao. My friend Jeff was working at Haleakalā Dairy as a cowboy, rounding up the cows in the morning on horseback, for milking. The dairy provided living quarters for the workers—an old plantation-style house. It was the bachelor quarters where my friend lived, along with another guy, his girlfriend, and her little girl. I stayed in a small shack behind the house. Jeff knew all about the crater, obscure trails and interesting spots. Once we hiked the ridgeline above Palikū Cabin. That's at the far end. He had read about a small lake up there, so we went looking for it. We were on a section of trail that very few people go on. The clouds enveloped us in thick mist. Hiking parallel to us, along the edge of the ridge, was a herd of goats. They were headed in our same direction, disappearing and reappearing in the mist. The head honcho, leader goat or whatever you call him, had a long white beard and big horns that curled around."

"So cool."

"It was. They kept alongside us for a ways."

"Did you ever find the lake?"

"No. Never did. Gave up. Set up our tent in the clouds." Jon paused and sipped his beer. "After being in the tent for quite a while we noticed it wasn't getting any darker. Neither of us had a watch. We were bored out of our minds, just hanging out in the tent, so we packed up camp and hiked back the way we came. We stopped at the trail junction on the ridge above Palikū Cabin. From there a switchback trail dropped down to the cabin area below. We camped on the ridge and built a nice fire behind a huge boulder. Of course, open fires are not allowed in the crater. Anyway, to make a short story even longer . . . sorry man, I'm rambling."

"No, no."

"Okay. Well, the next day, we split up. Jeff hiked back up Halema'uma'u trail, to his Jeep, and I hiked out Kaupō Gap by myself."

"What did you take to eat?"

"We had these papaya bars—papaya rolls. There was a place here in Pā'ia called Papaya Hill. They made these concentrated papaya rolls. They were fat like a big sausage and one quarter inch slice was a serving. We had a breakfast, lunch, and dinner roll, and an energy bar. We traveled light. Maybe an apple and an orange if we wanted to go gourmet."

"You probably had trail mix too."

"Guaranteed. Hippy food. At Papaya Hill they also had frozen treats. Like ice cream but made with stuff that's good for you. Whey powder, figs, I forget, but it was tasty. Always a treat when passing through Pā'ia. I stopped at Papaya Hill one time after returning to Maui from the mainland. The salesgirl asked me if I'd had the products before so I told her yes, but not for a while as I had just gotten back. She said, 'Welcome back home, brother.' That's just how it was," Jon smiled.

"If they're still around we could get some bars for our crater trip."

"I'm not sure—there was a fire, and Papaya Hill closed, at least for a time. I heard later that the old guy who developed the process died. It's too bad, because those bars really did give a person energy. Once, hiking the Gap Trail by myself, I paused to look back up the mountain and could just barely make out a tiny figure. This dude caught up to me. He was tired and hungry. I had just finished the last chunk of my energy bar and told him I was sorry I couldn't share it with him. He took off down the trail, but it wasn't long before I passed him by. He was a healthy guy, but he had to move slowly to conserve his strength. Meanwhile, I hiked all the way to the ocean and lay my wet gear and myself on the rocks in the sun. Fueled by papaya and Mother Nature. Of course, you prayed that the Kaupō Store would be open. A cold soda and an ice cream always hit the spot."

Jon looked to Raoul to see if he was storied out. He still seemed to be paying attention, so Jon went on.

"Something interesting happened on my way back to Makawao, that trip. I stayed one night at the Seven Sacred Pools then started hitching home. Coming out of Hāna I got picked up by this hippy guy. Long hair and full beard, driving a VW van. He made a stop at a house on the highway in Upper Nāhiku. He said that he wouldn't be long and left me sitting in the van. I was hoping he would invite me in but, no. So, I'm sitting there, checking out this place, and thinking, wouldn't that be a great place to live.”

"Nooo way. This was the hui house?"

"Yep. Before the hui bought it. Crazy yeah? A couple years later I was living there. Destiny is a trip."

"That's nuts. You going to finish your beer?"

"Nah, I'm full. Go for it."

The men walked back to the inn. Raoul smoked a bowl and joined Jon on the rooftop patio.

"What? I'm on vacation."

Jon didn't comment.

Raoul brought out his recorder, some sheet music, and a foldable music stand. "Would you like to hear me play something?"

"I would like that. I can't believe you haul that music stand around. I'm glad you brought your recorder. I was hoping you would."

"It's an alto," Raoul said as he slipped the sections of the recorder together.

Raoul played well. Jon closed his eyes and savored the moment.

"That was nice."

Raoul bowed. "Thank you."

They sat for a minute before Raoul said, "It might be fun to bring my recorder to Haleakalā. You talked about someone trailing us through the crater carrying our supplies or something?"

"Yeah. They're young, we'll probably be trailing them. Good kids. They work on our land in South Kona. You'll like them, especially Annet."

"Is she cute?"

"Stay in your lane, dinosaur. Her husband is a hunter and has a lot of guns. He's an excellent shot, by the way. We don't need any old goats going down on this trip. But yeah, she's cute. She'll have you wrapped around her little finger in no time. She's kinda like the heroine from the latest Tomb Raider movie. Anyway, they're going to carry food, drinks, and a tent. Actually, two tents, one for them and one for us."

"Don't we have the cabins rented?"

"Yeah, but I thought we'd stop halfway down the gap and camp a night. All that downhill gets to your legs. We're not young and invincible anymore, Raoul. I've even got a helicopter lined up to be on standby while we're up there. Just in case you fall and break something."

"Oh, thanks. Isn't the helicopter a bit extravagant?"

"Not bad just to have them on standby. If they have to rescue us, then, yeah . . . could get pricey. So be careful."

"Damn. And why are we carrying your manuscript with us?"

"Symbolic. I don't know. Just an idea I had," Jon said.

"Because you could?"

"Something like that. Isn't that what Bill Clinton said about his affair with Monica? Because I could . . ."

"That's right."

"Funny we both know that. I thought it was such an honest answer. Typical man."

"True, true. But really—and don't give me the Clinton answer again—why did you write this novel Jon? What is all this effort for?"

"It's my futile attempt at immortality."

"Okay, I'll buy that," Raoul said. "You're the judge, jury, and executioner."

"Huh?"

"If it makes the book, you're the one responsible. Do you promise to tell the truth, the whole truth, and nothing but the truth?"

"Oh hell no. It's a novel."

"And the part that is true?"

"I'll take the fifth."

"Wise choice."

"I can blame you for the questionable material."

"Perhaps you could *credit* me for the questionable material," Raoul countered.

"That's the thing, I want it to ring true to the experience and the era. Sex, drugs, and rock -n-roll. No apologies."

"I like it. Though you need a strong ending." Raoul suggested, "Maybe something unexpected. Some drama."

"Still working on that. But this isn't a murder mystery. Unless . . ."

"Jon! No! Put down that knife!" Raoul screamed. "You see, I'm good at this."

Jon smiled. "And it's not a tragedy."

"Although if I run out of weed, that would be bad."

"It's more of a journey," Jon continued, "A young man who's trying to understand what life's all about . . . looking for love and hoping to find where he truly belongs in the world. It's an adventure. I was lucky. Fate landed me on Maui before it was overrun with yuppies and the rich and famous. Back when even Lahaina was mellow with mom-and-pop stores on Front Street. Yamamoto Store was a classic," Jon paused. "Stop me if you've heard this one. One side of the store was fishing supplies and the other half was an old-school soda fountain. Hamburgers and shakes whipped up by Mrs. Yamamoto. She would have her apron on and her grey hair up in a bun. Super sweet. They both were. In the center of the store was the shaved ice machine. Mr. Yamamoto manned the shaved ice machine. To us pineapple pickers, that shaved ice machine was the Holy Grail."

"God likes you."

"I've been set up. God set me up. I owe Him, big time."

"So, let me get this straight. To pay Him back, Him, Her, the Great Spirit, Whatever, for payback, you're writing a trashy novel?"

Jon's eyes darted around the surrounding area. He bit his lower lip, shrugged his shoulders, and sheepishly replied, "Guess so."

"You're going to hell!"

The two friends began to laugh, heartfelt, pit of the stomach, whole body laughter. Wiping tears from their faces they struggled to regain their composure.

"Gonna be one of those . . ."

"Yep. Hey—tell me more about Mary Rose."

13 | HOUSE OF THE SUN

"I'M SO EXCITED," MARY ROSE SAID. "Are you excited Jon?"

"Haleakalā is always a treat. It's been a couple of years since I've hiked in the crater."

Jon was a bit nervous, wanting the trip to go well for Mary Rose, who was practically vibrating with enthusiasm, her eyes wide and strands of dark hair freeing themselves from her braids.

After a stop at the ranger station for a camping permit, Jon drove Frank to the Halema'uma'u trailhead. The foursome took their usual positions: Mary Rose rode shotgun, and Mark and Carla were snuggled in the back seat. As much as everyone wanted to see the view from the summit, they were anxious to get hiking while there was plenty of light. The trailhead began at eight thousand feet, which was two thousand feet below Haleakalā's Summit. From here it would be a four mile hike into the crater, to the Hōlua Cabin and camping area.

On the trail, Jon's anticipation melted away. Haleakalā was an old friend.

"Feels good to be out of the car," he called out to Mary Rose. She vigorously nodded her agreement, cheeks flushed and arms swinging at her sides. Even with the sun out, the wind was chilly. Jon took a moment to fold and tie a red bandana to create a headband. It would keep his hair out of his face.

They came to one of Jon's favorite spots. Both sides of the trail dropped away, leaving them standing on a narrow ridge. On the right was their first glimpse into the crater. A few clouds lingered on the upper slopes of the chiseled ridges that dramatically plunged to the crater floor. In the opposite direction, Jon knew, was the north coast of Maui and the road to Hāna, although a thick layer of clouds obscured any hint of it.

The group paused upon reaching the top of the switchbacks. They took a minute to contemplate the trail below, snaking its way down the nearly vertical wall of the crater. On the descent they spread out a bit, each hiking at their own pace. The air was clear, sharp, fresh. The sun felt warm and welcoming, but distant. Jon's hands and nose were cold to the touch. The only sound was the wind against his ears and his breathing. It had been a long day already, but he was invigorated, glad to be once again dropping into Haleakalā. The trail provided a good vantage point of the entire crater. To the north, clouds were licking through Ko'olau Gap, advancing and retreating. At the far end was Kaupō Gap, with a trail leading to sea level. The floor of the crater, some six miles across, was a surreal moonscape of lava fields, colorful cinder cones, and home to a rare plant, the silversword. The volcano felt alive, and it was—Haleakalā was dormant, but not extinct.

Jon noticed that Mary Rose was falling behind. He stopped to let her catch up. She stopped where she was, so Jon made use of the break, easing his pack off and sipping some water. He turned to stand facing away from the wind, the sun at his back, and was struck by the rich textures and colors on the cliff face beside him. It was a microcosm of high-altitude tundra—a mixture of mosses, lichens, and ferns. The colors were fluorescent. Chartreuse green, neon oranges, yellow, rust, deep reds, and shocks of purple. Even the ferns were orange and red, their new growth curled into tight spirals. *It's all a myriad of worlds upon worlds.* He was reminded of Paco's intricate stencil designs and Captain Kenny's brilliantly colored fish.

He looked back up the trail to see Mary Rose still standing in the same spot. He waved his arms, and she waved back. Jon started hiking again. After a few minutes he looked back. She had resumed hiking too. The trail was rough here, and he had to watch every step. It was wide enough for horses and there was evidence of their recent passage. He stopped again to be sure Mary Rose was alright, and she stopped too, stretching. Mark and Carla had caught up to Jon.

"She looks okay," Carla said, looking up the trail to Mary Rose. "Sometimes a woman wants to be alone."

At the point where the trail met the crater floor, Jon took off his pack and sat in the grass. Soon Mary Rose joined him there, while Mark and Carla continued hiking.

"I wanted to take it all in," she explained. "I wanted to see everything, hear everything, experience it myself."

Jon nodded. That made sense. Sometimes he liked to be alone, too. But he sure was enjoying her company. They set out again, together this time.

Along the trail, Mary Rose found three mushrooms growing out of a dried horse pie.

"What do you think?"

"Well, that's what they look like—almost. Usually the dome is flatter, not so humped up. That one is a big one."

"Maybe the elevation makes them a little different. Plus, it's horse poop, not cow. Would you eat them?"

"Nah, I don't think so. A lot of mushrooms are poisonous."

"I'll hang on to them and think about it," she said, closing her hand around them.

When they reached the cabin Jon saw that Mary Rose no longer had the mushrooms in her hand.

"Did you toss them?"

"I ate them."

THEY WALKED UP THE PATH TO the camping area. Mary Rose wanted to sleep under the stars, so they didn't put up the tent. They put their sleeping bag down next to a corrugated metal shelter—a small stable for horses, open on one side, the floor covered with straw. The National Park rangers traversed the area on horseback; Jon had previously seen a ranger cabin at the far end of the crater at Palikū.

"We can retreat into the shelter if it rains," Jon said.

Mark and Carla found their own spot and set up their tent.

Jon and Mary Rose zipped their sleeping bags together to form one large cocoon.

"I didn't know you could do that," Jon admitted. On Mary Rose's suggestion, they slept naked to share body heat.

"Did you feel anything from those mushrooms?"

"A little something."

The night was clear and cold. The stars above them appeared to be thrown from a saltshaker. The Milky Way was distinctly evident. They were tired; they held each other close and slept well.

In the dim early morning light, Mary Rose quietly asked, "Do you want to cum?"

After a pause, Jon teased, "Is that a trick question?"

Mary Rose turned over on top of Jon. She eased herself onto him and began to slowly move. Jon could hear other campers walking by. The two were still under the sleeping bag but he imagined it was obvious what was going on. He closed his eyes and shut out the world—everything but Mary Rose, his body, and the warmth between them.

As the sun rose, the four hikers sat watching Hawaiian Nēnē Geese loitering on the grass in front of the cabin. This was one of their usual hangouts, as evidenced by a small sign that read:

"PLEASE DO NOT FEED NĒNĒ GEESE."

A man, unshaven and short-haired, hiked in from the direction of the switchback trail, stopping in front of the cabin. He nodded in greeting and took off his small backpack.

"This is incredible." He gestured towards the crater, then turned back to the group. "I'm Robert. I'm here in Haleakalā doing research for a book."

"Hi Robert. What's your book about?" Mary Rose asked.

"Sacred places. Power points on Earth that expand your consciousness. Effortless nirvana through physical presence, so to speak. My job is to travel to these spots to experience the energy there."

"That's a good job," Carla said. "Are you getting paid?"

"Ah, no. That's just it. I'm on my own. It takes time and money. So far, I've been to Machu Picchu, Sedona, Mount Shasta, and now Haleakalā. It's so quiet here."

"What about Stonehenge?"

"That's on my list." He noticed a large horse fly hovering three feet in front of him, at eye level. "Am I going to have to listen to this fly all the way across the crater?" He frowned.

"Yep. One fly per hiker," Jon said.

Another fly joined the first one.

"I guess you get two. They must have heard you were coming."

"You're kidding?"

Jon smiled. *Maybe this guy will reach nirvana by accepting the unfortunate reality of horse flies in paradise.* Hadn't he read something about that in one of those books at Kathleen's house?

"I'm going to keep moving. Nice meeting you all."

They watched as he disappeared down the trail, then had a little laugh. Eventually, they too packed up and headed out.

Hiking across the crater floor, silence was accentuated by the sound of footsteps crunching along the cinder trail. They took the Silversword Loop trail to view the magnificent plants it was named for. The trail passed through an area of large, rounded cinder cones; the earth here was an amazing array of reds, oranges, and yellows. They rested at the "bottomless pit," and then the two couples parted ways. Mark and Carla continued to the Palikū Cabin, planning to hike out Kaupō Gap. Jon and Mary Rose followed the trail to Kapalaoa Cabin.

They were the only ones at Kapalaoa. The cabin was locked, so they set up their tent, leaving the flap open so that they could still see the stars. In the morning they sat in the sun, letting the day uncurl before them.

"Do you know what today is?" she asked.

Jon drew a blank. "Ah . . . I give up."

"Thanksgiving."

"That's right! I knew it was close. I had forgotten. Thank you, God."

"Thank you, Goddess."

"Some friends of mine in Ha'ikū invited me for Thanksgiving. We can go there."

"You have a lot of friends on this island. That's wonderful. But Jon, have you had many lovers? Before me, I mean?'

"Just one." He never did care much for the word *lovers*.

"Was she your girlfriend?"

"No. Just a friend. And it was just the one time. I mean, I did have girlfriends but . . ."

"Just one time? Once? How long ago was it?" She was smiling, but she didn't seem to be teasing. Just interested. She leaned forward, waiting for his answer.

"It was a while ago." He was feeling uncomfortable. "Maybe two or three years. I was about twenty."

Mary Rose kissed his cheek. "I think that's sweet. Late bloomer."

"Yeah. Guess so."

The two crawled back in the tent and into each other's arms, spending a bit of time there before it was time to pack up and retrace their footsteps back towards Hōlua Cabin.

Something felt off. Mary Rose had been unusually withdrawn for the past mile or so.

"Is something wrong?" Jon asked.

"You know, in the tent this morning, what I did for you?" With her hand, she made an up and down motion in the air.

"It would have been nice for you to return the favor."

He was embarrassed that he hadn't thought about it.

"It made me feel bad. I got my feelings hurt."

"I'm sorry."

She stopped hiking and turned to face Jon. She held his gaze with a focused look, as if trying to read his mind. Finally, she said, "Okay. I forgive you. I'm good now."

As they continued on the trail, Jon had time to reflect. He regretted upsetting her but was grateful for her frankness and willingness to express her feelings. He realized how important communication was to a relationship. It was something he needed to practice more of.

They hiked past Hōlua Cabin, slowly climbed the switchback trail, and made their way back to the car. Frank started right up, and they drove to the summit. There were a few small patches of snow on the ground.

"No wonder it was so cold," Jon noted.

In the distance Mauna Kea and Mauna Loa of the Big Island rose above the clouds, capped with snow. They browsed through the visitor building then climbed into Frank and began to descend the mountain.

They drove through a blanket of clouds, then dropped below the cloud-line into a clear sky. As they passed a large pasture above Makawao, Mary Rose asked, "Can we stop and check for mushrooms?"

He pulled over. They carefully climbed through the barbed wire fence. The pasture was littered with cow pies; almost every cow pie hosted many psilocybin mushrooms. He smiled as he looked over to her. She was beaming. She thrust both arms into the air, shouting, "Thank you Divine Goddess."

She turned to Jon. "I'll be right back." She navigated the barbed wire fence again. It was harder without his help. Determined, she deftly dropped to the ground and crawled beneath the lowest strand of wire. She returned from the car with two jars of honey.

Under his breath, Jon mumbled, "You have got to be kidding." And then, louder, "You've been carrying that with you?"

"I have."

"You're crazy."

"I heard that it's a good way to preserve them. I promised my coven sisters I would try to bring some home."

"Wow. Now that's a good friend."

To make room for the mushrooms, they poured some of the honey into a plastic bag that they'd emptied of trail mix.

"Let the picking commence," Jon said in his best announcer's voice.

"And on Thanksgiving. It's truly a special day. Thank you for this bountiful harvest."

That afternoon, they pulled up to bookstore Matthew's A-frame in Ha'ikū.

"Jon, you made it." Matthew gave Jon a hug. "Who's your friend?"

"Mary Rose."

"I'm Matthew," he said, holding his arms out to greet her.

"Hey Jon," said Linda, poking her head out of the kitchen door. "Welcome."

"It sure smells good."

Linda refused any help in the kitchen. She was a great cook and had prepared many dishes, but she shooed them out of the kitchen and told them to relax.

Mary Rose handed Matthew a plastic bag. He was excited to see the mushrooms in honey. "That could make for an interesting Thanksgiving," he said with a mischievous look on his face.

Linda didn't eat meat, but had cooked a small turkey for Matthew. Mary Rose also enjoyed the turkey.

"Coming out of the crater to a feast. It's amazing. Thank you, it's delicious."

"We are blessed," Linda said.

"And thank you for bringing the extra dessert," Matthew said with a twinkle in his eye.

It took Jon a few seconds to realize what he was referring to. He smiled. *Ah, the mushrooms.*

After dinner, Matthew, Jon, and Mary Rose stood on the lanai looking out towards the ocean.

"I was surprised to see fields of pineapple on the way up," Jon said.

"Yep, there's a bunch," Matthew said. "Hey, see that gulch over there?"

"Uh huh."

"Pretty nice stream at the bottom of it, with some good pools."

"How did you ever figure that out?"

"Some neighbors told us about it. There's a trail that goes down. Lots of surprises on this land."

"Nice."

"Speaking of surprises, I am now the sole owner of the bookstore," Matthew announced proudly. I bought my partner out." His expression turned to exasperation. "The sorry son-of-a-bitch. I was the one doing all the work, everything. He was still in New York. Even so, he didn't want to sell. I grabbed him by his scrawny neck. I was so pissed. I told him, *listen motherfucker, you're going to sell me your half or I'm going to kill you.*" Matthew cleared his throat. "He came around to seeing my point of view."

Whoa. Down boy. You'll scare the guests. Jon was somewhat amused by Matthew's intensity. He knew he was passionate but had always assumed that his bark was worse than his bite.

There was pumpkin pie, followed by magic mushrooms. They unanimously decided it would be fun to get out of the house and go to a movie, and *2001: A Space Odyssey* was playing in Kahului. Jon drove himself and Mary Rose in Frank as they were planning to stay overnight among the kiawe trees in Olowalu, where Mike and Shay would be car camping. Everyone was feeling good during the movie; the mushroom high was mellow. Few words were spoken, only smiles and knowing looks exchanged. Jon was struck by the artistic camera work and the symmetry of the images on the screen.

After the show Jon and Mary Rose bid their friends farewell and drove to the beach at Olowalu. Jon spotted Mike's truck backed into the trees, and parked nearby. Mike and Shay appeared to already be sleeping, so they sat on the sand talking quietly for a while, then climbed into the back of Frank. She would be flying out the next day.

Morning came soon. They hung out with Mike and Shay, enjoying the morning under the kiawe trees, observing their twisted trunks and vast branches. Small waves broke haphazardly on the outside reefs that sheltered the area. The ocean along the shore was soft and soothing as it caressed the golden sand. Mike cooked bacon, eggs, and some homestyle potatoes on a little hibachi. Mike and Shay left not long after breakfast.

Jon and Mary Rose reflected on their time together; her Hawaiian vacation had come to an end. He had come to love her energy. She was real. He moved closer to her and put an arm around her waist, tugging gently.

"It was wonderful Jon. I really needed this. I really needed you."

"It was great for me, too."

"Something happened to me on the Big Island." Mary Rose closed her eyes and pinched her eyebrows together. He waited, unsure if she'd share more. She inhaled sharply. "I was raped."

"Oh no. I'm sorry, Mary Rose . . . what happened?"

"I was hitchhiking. It was in Kona. Down south, in the middle of nowhere. I was trying to get to where I could camp. It was after dark. I got a ride with this guy in an old pickup truck. A big local man. Suddenly, he pulls over, grabs me by my hair then pulls a big knife from under the seat."

"Holy shit."

"Yeah, tell me about it. I asked him what he wanted. This was a big guy and we're in the middle of nowhere. It's all lava fields. I was really scared and shaking but I forced myself to be calm. He made it clear he wanted sex, and he's still holding this knife. I told him, if we're going to do this, let's find a spot. I asked him if he had a blanket or something we could put down." She sighed. "There wasn't much I could do. Very little traffic, like none, and nothing but lava fields. Afterwards he told me that his wife didn't want to have sex with him anymore because he was so fat."

Jon felt his heart beginning to race as his facial muscles tightened. If only he could go back in time to protect Mary Rose from being hurt by this man. He took a deep breath, "Did you report it? Call the cops?"

"No," Mary Rose answered. "I was too shaken up afterwards. But meeting you, Jon, was just what I needed for my heart and soul—emotionally and physically, for my healing. I prayed for something good, something positive, and you're it." She looked into Jon's eyes. He put both arms around her and gave her a good squeeze.

"You're a sweet man, Jon. Kind and gentle."

Jon just shrugged his shoulders. He wasn't always great with words in moments like this. But Mary Rose had been what he needed, too. A companion. A mirror to help him see himself.

She dropped Jon off at the beginning of the narrow winding road. They exchanged addresses and hugs. Jon waved goodbye as Frank disappeared into the distance.

Alone again. As a car approached, Jon stuck out his thumb.

14 | BROWN EYED GIRL

A LARGE MONKEYPOD TREE CAME INTO VIEW.

That must be it. Jon and Kolohe were on foot. Jon saw Paulo's truck, along with another car, parked off to the side of the road. A young man came up the trail next to the huge tree.

"Hello."

"Hey."

"I'm Elliot. Going to Paulo and Dawn's?" He reached down to pet Kolohe. "Hey dog."

"Yeah. Never been there before. I'm Jon."

"Just follow the path through the tall grass, Jon. Paulo is up on the hill but Dawn's home. Aren't you the guy living in Faith and Leanne's old house?"

"Yup."

"I heard that you're from the Bronx. Paulo and I are both from the Bronx."

"Oh, no. I'm from San Diego."

"Huh. Okay. Someone told me you were from the Bronx." Elliot sounded disappointed.

Elliot had dark hair, eyes, and beard. His hair was tied back in a short ponytail.

"What sign are you?" he asked.

"Taurus."

"Meet the local astrologer," Elliot said extending his hand. "I'm a Gemini. Do you know your moon and rising sign?"

"No not really. I think my moon is in Venus or something like that."

Elliot chuckled. "Those are both planets. Ever had your chart done?"

"In college one of my art teachers drew everyone's chart. It was his hobby."

"Who knows how accurate that was? I can draw and interpret your chart sometime. I just need your place and time of birth. Do you know Charley Butterfly?" Elliot asked. "He's on the mainland, sailing or something. I'm staying in Charley's tent, on his property. It's the tent in the pasture—not far from where you live."

"I've seen it."

"If my car is there, then I'm home. Stop by. See you, man."

Jon wove his way down the hill through the tall grass. Paulo and Dawn's shack was perched on a cliff above the ocean. As he neared the building Jon gave a couple of hoots. It was protocol. Dawn came out of the open doorway. She was naked.

"Hey Jon. Come on in."

She gave him a hug.

"You're nice and warm," Jon said.

Dawn smiled. "Good to see you."

She was thin. Her skin was brown as was her long straight hair. Her large brown eyes sparkled with kindness.

Kolohe was content to sniff about the yard.

"Location, location, location," Jon said looking out at the ocean. "How far are you from the Seven Sacred Pools?"

"About a mile. Is your dog okay? Does he need water?"

"No. He's fine."

Dawn had the radio playing.

"You actually get radio reception out here?"

"Big Island. It's a Hilo station."

The shack was built with recycled materials. There was one small room that served as a living room and kitchen, and a narrow side room which had built-in bunk beds. Jon noticed how ridiculously uneven the floor was.

The wall facing the ocean was mostly glass, made of old salvaged windows with multiple panes. On the wall were pictures of Paramahansa Yogananda and his lineage of gurus alongside Krishna and Jesus.

Paulo and Dawn's four-year-old girl, Anna, was sitting on the bedroom floor in a faded floral print dress. Her light brown hair was cropped to her shoulders, and held to one side by a barrette.

"Hey Anna."

"Say hi to Jon, honey."

"Hi." She gave a small wave, then went back to playing with her stuffed animals.

"Would you like some tea? I made lemongrass and peppermint sun tea."

"Sounds good. How do you make that?"

"Cut up peppermint and lemongrass, put it in a gallon glass jar with water, and let it steep in the sun. You need a jar with a lid to keep the bugs out. It makes a nice mellow tea."

"It's good."

"I can give you a cutting from my peppermint plant if you want. It's been a while since I've seen you, Jon. What have you been up to?"

"Hmm. Well, around Thanksgiving I spent a couple of nights in the crater with an amazing woman from San Francisco. It was damn cold, but beautiful as always. Other than that, not too much. With all of the rain, I've had plenty of time for art and reading. Just hanging out . . . ."

"This year is flying by. I can't believe that the first day of spring is in two weeks. You know, the sun comes up right out there." She pointed to the horizon.

"What a spot."

"Paulo will be coming down soon. He's working on the mountain. You know, doing some gardening." Jon knew she was referring to a "cash" crop of marijuana.

The song "Brown Eyed Girl" came on the radio.

"You know this song? I was living with Van Morrison when he wrote it."

"Oh, wow . . . brown eyed girl."

Dawn gave a little wink and turned the radio up. Jon noticed Paulo's conga drums standing in the corner. He gently tapped them.

"You can play them. Paulo doesn't mind, really."

Jon tried his hand at drumming along to the music.

"Hey man."

Jon turned to see Paulo. "You always make it look easy, Paulo."

"I've had a lot of practice." He flashed a smile. "I knew someone was here. It sounds different when Dawn plays. I think I spooked your pup. It looked like he was copping a nap." He looked at Dawn. "You should put something on."

She stepped into the bedroom, emerging moments later in a pair of cut-off shorts and a tank top.

"So, how's this place?" Paulo asked.

"I like it. Did you build it yourself? What's up with this floor?"

"What? I'm an electrician, not a carpenter." Paulo sounded insulted. "I didn't have a level, so I just eyeballed the posts. Here I am, an electrician living in a place that doesn't have any electricity. Funny, yeah?"

"Can you do electrical work here in Hawai'i?"

"I can, but not legally. I'm not licensed in the state of Hawai'i. I keep busy with projects around here plus I'm playing more gigs now too."

Paulo took off his headband. It was soaked. Then he put on a dry T-shirt. He had a strong upper body.

"Paulo dug us an outhouse," Dawn said.

"I saw the toilet over there. Is that it?"

"Lucky that hillside is all dirt. I dug down six feet and stuck a sheet of plywood over the hole. A friend gave us an old toilet."

"Not much privacy." The toilet was in the open, on a grassy slope and not far from the house.

"I was going to close it in, but we've gotten used to it. Kind of nice sitting there looking out at the world."

Jon laughed. "Puts everything into perspective I suppose."

"Before I dug the outhouse, we damn near got our butts kicked out of here," Paulo said.

"Literally," Dawn added.

Paulo motioned Jon over to the side window, next to the homemade kitchen counter. It was low to the floor and wide open.

"Look out this window, straight down." He instructed.

Jon was shocked to see what looked like a pile of dried excrement mixed with toilet paper. There was a brown stain running down the outside of the building.

Paulo began to explain. "One day Anna really had to go so I told her to just hang her butt out the window. Then we all started using it as a toilet. It dried out quickly with the sun. It was easier than going out and digging a hole every time, which is what we had been doing. Anyway, Gene's family from Honolulu were here visiting—you know Gene? He's the cowboy who lives on the top part of the property, across the road—and they own the property. They're of Hawaiian ancestry, connected to the Royal Family. Gene is the black sheep of the family. So they came down to check us out. You know, come see who their brother had allowed to build a shack on their property." He paused. "Everything was going fine until they saw Anna take a dump out the window. They lost it—totally freaked out. Major drama."

"It was horrible," Dawn agreed.

"They wanted us out, like right now. I had to get down on my hands and knees and beg. Dawn and Anna were crying. Finally, they agreed to let us stay. We were so close to being out of here."

"And now you have an outhouse," Jon said.

"We're happy to still have a place to live. Just getting by can be hard. Jon, do you get food stamps?" Dawn asked.

"No."

"Do you have any money?"

"No, not really. A little, not much."

"And no job?"

"No."

"You definitely qualify. It's like $60.00 worth of food a month. You should get them. The government is spending all our money on bombs. We should get something back. Think about it. I'm going to go take a dip. Want to come with me to the stream?"

"Sure."

Kolohe trotted in front of them only stopping at the highway to see which way they'd be going. He made himself look busy.

Dawn and Jon walked up the path, through the grass, to the road. Across the street, on the upper section of the property, were some corrals for rounding-up and loading cattle.

"Gene's cabin is a little farther up the hill."

They walked fifty feet along the Hāna Highway. The roadway wasn't much wider than a car's width. Just before a small concrete bridge, a narrow path dropped through yellow ginger plants to the stream. The stream was flowing nicely, filling the bathing pool waist-deep. They took off their clothes and slipped into the water. The water was brisk.

"This isn't bad," Dawn said. "I can always tell when there's snow on Haleakalā. The stream water gets colder. I know, hard to believe, but I can tell." She pointed to Kolohe who had stationed himself on the bank.

"He doesn't like the water?"

"Nah, not so much."

Dawn had brought some liquid peppermint castile soap. She washed her hair. Jon also used the soap. Any cars passing could easily see them, through the foliage, if they turned their head, but Jon knew the drivers were focused on the challenging road in front of them.

After their bath they walked towards the shack, refreshed.

"Jon, can you babysit sometime?" she asked over her shoulder, as they walked single-file down the path. "Anna is easy. She's pretty much self-sufficient, you just have to feed her. Paulo has some gigs coming up on the other side. It's hard when we have Anna with us. We're up late. It's a bummer for everyone."

"I get it."

"Do you like kids?"

Jon did like kids. He appreciated their spontaneity and unfettered creativity. It was not beneath him to get down on the floor to partici-pate in imaginary scenarios. Although he didn't have a lot of experience babysitting, he assured her he'd be happy to help.

"Did you see the papaya tree out front?" Paulo asked proudly, once they'd made it to the shack.

"I did. Looks like it's on steroids."

"I figured out that if you treat them like pot plants, with lots of good fertilizer and tender loving care, they thrive."

"You've got a green thumb." Jon had learned a lot about plants care-taking the land. The papaya tree was a male and would produce no fruit. He didn't mention it, not wanting to be the bearer of bad news.

"I've got to go in to Hasegawa's and can give you and your dog a ride."

"Absolutely. That would be great."

Paulo dropped Jon and Ko at Hasegawa's. From there they began to hoof it out of town and hadn't gone far when a VW van pulled over. It was Skip, Jon's neighbor.

"Hey man. Thanks."

"Howzit Jon," Skip smiled. "Looks like your rascal smells 'opihi. I've been diving, picking 'opihi. Got some big ones. They're fresh. Jon, help yourself."

"Ah, no thanks."

"I went in the water down by Wai'ānapanapa. It's a stretch of coast not too many people go. Hard to get to. Jon . . . eat."

"Nah, I'm good."

"The current was strong. When it came time to go back, I couldn't swim against the current. I tried. Couldn't do it. Luckily, I have a lot of experience in the water. Swimming against the current tires you out pretty quick, so I relaxed and went with the flow, drifting with the current down the coastline. Had to go quite a ways before I found a spot where I could get out of the water. Plenty cliffs. I had to walk back to my car. But hey, that's why there's big 'opihi there. Have you had 'opihi before?"

"No."

"No way. It's a delicacy. You got to try it."

"Uhh . . ."

"Do you eat fish?"

"Sometimes."

"It's seafood. Not much different from fish."

"I don't know. You eat them raw?

"Yep. These are fresh. You're not going to get any fresher. Try it. It's not going to kill you."

"Okay, I'll try one."

"Here's a good one. Use this shell to scoop it out, then pop it in your mouth."

Kolohe was watching intently.

The look on Jon's face, as he ate it, made Skip laugh.

"Doesn't look like you like it. Hey, at least you tried it. That's one Hawaiian food that." Skip shook his head. "You tried it," he chuckled.

After a moment, Skip said, "They just launched the Hōkūle'a."

"What's that?"

"The Hawaiian sailing canoe. It's a big deal. Someday they're going to sail to the South Pacific, to Tahiti, and who knows, probably all around the world."

"Nice."

"Yep, it's good to have some good news, right? To balance out the sad parts of life. You know why they have those barriers, the barricades, on the pier in Hāna?"

"No."

"That's because of my friends and me. They never used to have them. One day my friends were driving my VW van—not this one, my old van. They drove off the pier." Skip paused. "I'm not sure what happened that day but . . . they all died. They all drowned. Usually, I would have been with them. It was my van. You know, we all drove each other's cars. Nobody got out. Those were my friends. My good friends."

Jon was silent.

"That's the day I stopped drinking."

At home, Jon sat beside Ko and petted him a long time.

Life is uncertain. Every minute is precious.

15 | FLASH FROM THE PAST

"Knock, knock. Hello. Anybody home?"

Jon walked towards the front door to see who was there. It was early morning.

"Eddie. No way man. Long time. What a surprise."

The two hugged. Eddied reeked of weed.

"Is that your dog out there? White with spots."

"Yeah."

"I heard you were living here. Can't remember who told me."

"Maybe Joseph."

"Could have been."

Jon knew Eddie from high school in San Diego. Eddie and his older brother, Jim, surfed Scripps, La Jolla, north of the pier. It was where Jon and his close friends surfed. Jon had also dated Eddie's younger sister. She was Jon's first lover, although Eddie didn't know that. Nobody did. Linda didn't even know she was Jon's first.

"It's been years, yeah?" Jon said.

"Been a while. Where's your furniture?" Eddie asked.

"Yeah, no. No furniture."

"What's this?"

"Piano backboard."

Eddie strummed the strings. "Hey, I have a roach. Not much left, if you want to finish it. Home grown. Good stuff. It's from last year's stash. Pretty oily."

He handed Jon a wooden matchbox. Jon retrieved the roach.

"Jim and I are living on the other side of Hāna."

Eddie was wearing work boots, camouflage shorts, and a black T-shirt with a few small holes in it. He carried a small military green canvas pack. With his Spanish heritage, he could easily pass for local. His skin was dark, along with his eyes and hair. He wore an Aussie-style bush hat, his shortish hair sticking out from underneath.

"We're living on a property with a local family. Aunties, uncles, tutus . . . we're one of the family. 'Ohana brah." He paused. "You know, I walked all the way here from the Hāna airport road."

"That's a long way, bro, and uphill too."

"I got a ride with a tourist dude, you know, about our age. I asked him if he wanted to smoke a joint. He said no, he didn't smoke much. I asked him if he minded if I smoked one and he said okay. I lit it and took a big hit. I started coughing my head off. He told me he was going down to the airport and that he'd drop me off and pick me up on his way back up. It seemed a little weird, but I thought, okay, whatever."

Eddie hadn't shaved in a couple of days. His eyes were blood-shot, glassy, and wild looking. He was speaking with a strong pidgin accent, which he'd picked up from having lived in the islands for many years.

"So, he comes back up and drives right by me. Didn't even look. I should have seen that coming. Guess I scared him."

"He probably had the doors locked too."

"I hoofed it up the hill and here I am. Good weed yeah?"

"Umm hmm." Jon had taken some LSD earlier that morning and was feeling the effects. It was coming on strong but he didn't mention anything to his friend.

"Jim and I are growing some great pakalōlō. The folks who own the property have no clue what we're up to. We have it growing everywhere. Flower beds, hedges, even up in a big mango tree on a platform. We keep the place looking good and the folks love us. We're like their sons."

Jon was appalled at the deception. He frowned.

"You have some weed growing Jon?"

"No."

"I've got a few seeds I can give you." He pulled a ziplock from his pocket. "There's a few crumbs here too, enough for a small bowl maybe." He picked the seeds out and held them in the palm of his hand.

"They're huge."

Jon had never seen such large seeds before. They had dark irregular stripes running lengthwise like little watermelons. He could literally see energy radiating from the seeds—jumping off them.

"You gotta take good care of them. Do you know how to get them started?"

"Stick them in the ground?"

"No, no. This is what you do. Get a wet paper towel but not too wet, more like damp. Put the seeds in the paper towel folded over several times. Don't let it dry out. In a few days, the seeds will begin to germinate and start cracking open with a little sprout coming out. That's the root. Here's the deal, you plant them when the root is just barely coming out, about a 1/16 of an inch. But, you plant it with the root up." He looked Jon in the eye. "You getting this?"

"Up?"

"Up. The root comes out, curls over the seed, and goes down." Eddie demonstrated the curling action with his index finger. "That springs the little plant out of the ground and you're on your way. You should get some peat pellets or potting soil. You'd think the root would point down, but no. Won't grow like that. Mother Nature, man."

"Yep. That's interesting. Thanks."

"Hey, I need to go see about catching a ride. One time my brother picks up this chick hitchhiking, you know, backpack and all. She was going to the airport. He asks her if she wants to smoke a joint so they stop at our place, Paukūkalo. They're in the bedroom smoking a joint and the woman starts taking off her clothes. Jim takes off his clothes, and, well, she gives *him* a ride. How's that?" Jon gave a faint smile but didn't say anything. Eddie paused, looking around the room then looking back to Jon. "I better keep moving. Good seeing you." With that, he was out the door and gone.

Jon took this opportunity to slip out the back steps. He stopped below the house. The intensity of the moment struck him as he turned. He stood in one place and moved his head. Jon could feel the weight of his head—the physical weight. Everything centered on this moment, and then that too was gone.

Kolohe had heard the back door close and was now alongside. They started on the trail that led down the property and hadn't gone far when Jon heard a humming. He stopped and looked up, trying to locate the source of the sound. The large kukui nut tree beside him was full of blossoms and there were hundreds of bees working the flowers. He looked to the top of the tree, then his eyes wove their way down, jumping from blossom to blossom until coming to rest directly in front of him on a cluster of flowers. The individual flowers were tiny white five-petal stars with delicate creamy yellow centers. The little flowers grouped together to form clusters. He watched the honeybees climb about as he listened to their collective hum.

Farther down the trail, a branch of ripe strawberry guavas hung invitingly at eye level. He took a moment to appreciate the deep red color and smooth outer surface of the fruit. As his teeth pierced the thin skin, a tangy sweetness filled his senses.

"Umm. Thank you."

A swarm of mosquitoes were following him but weren't biting, just along for the hike. Jon and Kolohe headed to Ulaino Road and found Blue Pond was dry. Usually, from there they would go left to Emerald Pond to enjoy the waterfall on the ocean, but today Jon decided to go exploring. He turned right. Like a big swell on the open ocean, the dirt road rose and fell as it cut through the forest. The surrounding trees were tall; their branches intertwined to form a thick canopy. The sound of the birds was constant.

They came to a cattle grate across the road—the kind that cows are afraid to walk over, with barbed wire fencing connected to either side of the grate. Up against and growing through the barbed wire was a huge coleus plant. It was six feet tall and even wider. The vibrantly colored leaves were electric. Deep purple centers blended into brilliant pink that sat upon shocking green fringed in yellow. Jon was impressed. He used to see small compact coleus plants at nurseries in California. He breathed in the wonderful colors through his eyes. *Amazing.*

The forest gave way to large swaths of pasture. Encroaching into these cleared areas were guava, kukui, and African tulip trees.

Looking up the mountain Jon could see where the Hāna Highway dropped from Upper Nāhiku, winding its way toward Hāna town. Many large old mango trees stood near the highway. Kolohe was nosing around some brush on the side of the road. Behind him, Jon noticed an intriguing spot where the vegetation grew tall and thick. There was a big mango tree and an old avocado tree. Jon waded through grass and weeds and was soon peering over a barbed wire fence. He slipped through the fence and Kolohe followed, crawling under. Inside was a plumeria tree and impatien flowers. Jon saw some low rock mounds that appeared to be gravesites. He didn't see any markers or headstones. It had been many years since the burial site had been cared for.

"Forgive us our trespasses as we forgive those who trespass against us," he said aloud.

He scanned the trees. The avocado tree had small fruits on its branches, but none were to be found on the ground.

They continued hiking, turning away from the dirt road. Jon knew the ocean wasn't far. He had seen the tops of some tall coconut palms rising above the trees. He couldn't see them now, but headed in that general direction. The jungle was thick. Kolohe stuck close. They hiked around large 'ulu trees and treaded carefully beneath hala trees with piles of dried leaves; the long dry hala leaves were slippery to walk on. Jon marveled at the scarlet blossoms filling the mountain apple trees, along with clusters of small light green mountain apples.

He climbed a rocky slope that leveled at the top and stopped abruptly. He began to turn and look around in all directions. He realized the plateau wasn't natural. It was man-made. The flat area had been created and it was big, very, very big. Although overgrown, the vegetation here was much less dense than the surrounding area. Jon wandered, just observing. Kolohe too seemed curious. It was a wonderous site, with rock walls of various heights, enclosures, pits, raised flat areas with small smooth ocean stones along with large ocean rock embedded in the pathways. The stonework of the rock walls was skillfully set and superbly fitted. Jon had never seen anything like it. It appeared that the ancient ones had filled in a gulch with an enormous—a mind-boggling amount—of lava rock. Much of the visible "filler" rock was of uniform size. The sheer volume of rock was staggering to imagine.

He came to the stand of coconut palms he had glimpsed from afar. He had totally forgotten about them. Coconuts littered the ground. He picked out a big one and shook it. It held a lot of coconut water. He smashed the ends of the coconut on a rock over and over until he could grab a piece of the fibrous outer husk and strip it off. A slow process. Once the husk had been removed, he used his pocketknife to bore through two of the three eyes at the top of the hard shell. He enjoyed the delicate flavor of the coconut water. Thirst quenched, he cracked the shell in half on a rock, and cut pieces of the hard white coconut meat from the shell. Fresh coconut was a treat that Kolohe liked too. Jon had heard that traditionally the native Hawaiians would plant a coconut palm when a baby was born as it would provide food and shelter for their lifetime. The fronds were used for thatched houses, and the coconuts for food and drink.

Jon moved closer to the ocean and stood on the foremost edge of the plateau, looking over. The stone structure dropped dramatically, and was terraced. Jon marveled at the vision, engineering, and the vast amount of work it took to create. Unknowingly, this stoned-out haole boy had stumbled upon an archeological site of great historic and cultural importance. It was Pi'ilanihale, a sacred Hawaiian temple. Years later, Pi'ilanihale Heiau would be restored and recognized as the largest heiau in the Hawaiian islands and perhaps the largest ancient temple complex in all of Polynesia.

Jon sat with his back against a large smooth stone. Kolohe lay nearby, resting with one ear up, just in case. Through the trees Jon watched the clouds dance. The forest birds caught his attention, then his eyes fell back to the sky and clouds which the tree branches broke into a thousand pieces of a mosaic puzzle. He sat, watched, and listened. His thoughts, and the day, drifted. Time fell away. In the wind, blowing through the trees, Jon could hear chanting, strong and mesmerizing. His mind melted into the moment. He was aware of the rock beneath him, the cool stone pressing against his back, the breeze upon his cheeks. The sun was playing a game of light and shadow about him. Jon's breathing was slow, deep, and easy. The air of this sacred place filled him.

This trance was broken by a sharp cry, a calling, coming from the sky. Jon and Kolohe looked up. High above, two 'ios—Hawaiian hawks— were effortlessly riding the air currents. Together they drew large circles in the deep blue.

16 | HOT DOG ANNIE

JON LINGERED ON THE ROAD ABOVE his house, hitchhiking to the other side of the island to do laundry. Kolohe would be tagging along. It was still early morning and there was little traffic. As he waited, he took cuttings from impatien plants that lined his walkway and stuck them in the ground along the roadside. He used a stick to make holes, and would jab several spots before the stick would sink in far enough to plant each cutting. Kolohe sat on the front step watching. Jon had his small duffel bag filled with dirty clothes at the top of the walkway.

He noticed a man walking up the road towards him. He was older, had a slight limp, and was using a cane.

"I'm out getting some exercise. What's your name son?"

"Jon."

"I'm Earl. Most people call me Colonel. Retired military. Were you in the service?"

"No."

"That's okay." Earl was wearing a baseball cap that said John Deere on it. He appeared to have a buzz cut, judging from the tight, clean sides visible below his hat. "I'm your neighbor. I live around the corner, past the Medeiros. My place is the house overlooking the stream. So you live here now?"

"Yeah."

"Where you from, Jon?"

"Originally San Diego."

"That's a good town. Military town. I've been there."

"Big Navy town."

"Did you see there was a platoon of men here, doing some R&R at Wai'ānapanapa? I took some cases of beer and pūpūs to them. The men appreciated it. It was bending the rules, but the lieutenant let it slide. It felt good to do something for the boys."

"Good for you, sir."

Kolohe came out to say hi.

"Hey, pooch. He doesn't chase cows, does he?" the colonel asked.

"No. Never seen him chase anything 'cept a mongoose."

"I raise cows. Once a dog starts chasing cows it gets in their blood. They'll run the cows right through the barbed wire fences. You have to shoot the dogs. I've had to shoot some wild dogs." The colonel was staring down the road. "You gotta do it. They'll ruin a cow."

Jon had a concerned look. *Is the colonel threatening to shoot my dog?*

"Hey, if you want to grow some pot, put it down below . . . down on the land."

Jon was surprised by this change in topic. He nodded.

"Nobody is going to find it down there. My wife is from Vietnam. She knows how to grow it. Okay, Jon, nice to meet you. I gotta keep walking." With that, he turned and walked back in the direction he had come.

You never know who you're going to meet out here. The colonel did not seem like the type of guy to give me tips on how to grow marijuana, but that's Maui for you.

EVENTUALLY JON AND KOLOHE GOT A ride; a young local woman, about Jon's age, was driving with an older haole woman riding shotgun. The older woman turned in her seat. She was wearing a lauhala hat and had on large horn-rimmed glasses. She was a petite woman.

"I'm Hot Dog Annie and this is my friend and associate, Honey Girl. We're over from O'ahu playing tourists."

"I'm Jon."

"How the hell are you, Jon?"

He grinned, "Great."

"And your friend?"

"This is Kolohe."

"A rascal, eh? Honey Girl is a bit of a rascal."

"Hey, watch it, Grandma."

"I'm not your damn Grandma, sweetie. But I still love you," she said, looking at Honey Girl. "So, Jon. How long do we have to drive on this fucking bumpy road?"

"Oh, it's a ways. Thirty, forty miles."

"It's the same road we came in on yesterday," said Honey Girl.

"I know. I know. Don't remind me."

"We work together in Honolulu," explained Honey Girl. "This woman is a *big* celebrity."

"Are you entertainers?"

"Yep. We sing, dance, and play ukulele."

"And tell dirty jokes," Hot Dog Annie added. "All while selling hot dogs."

"Jon, do you know where the Banana Patch hippy commune is? I read about it. We want to go see some naked hippies."

"Yeah, kind of. I've been past there. Pretty sure I could get you there. It's up near Ha'ikū. But I think it was closed down by the health department because of hepatitis."

"Son of a bitch," Hot Dog Annie said. "Just our fucking luck. If I wanted to catch a damn contagious disease, I would have fucking stayed home. Still, I'd like to see it. Can we drive by?"

Jon managed to navigate to the Banana Patch. The country road skirted the commune. It was in a small, steep valley, with unpermitted shacks lining the sides and floor of the gulch. The property was thickly planted with banana trees. There were signs posted by the health department that read:

QUARANTINE. HEPATITIS OUTBREAK.
NO TRESPASSING.

It looked deserted, but the women were happy to see the spot they had read about. Honey Girl took pictures out the window.

"Where are you going Jon?"

"To Hāli'imaile . . . to my friend's house. Probably stay one or two nights, do laundry, then hitch home. They usually let me use their car."

"You're coming from Hāna to do laundry? There's no laundromat there?"

"No."

"You've got to be fucking kidding me. Could you get a washer?"

"I don't even have electricity where I live."

"That's the shits. Give Honey Girl directions. We'll drop you at your friend's house."

"That would be great. Thank you."

"I had a husband that looked like your dog. Same black lips and beady eyes."

"Kolohe doesn't have beady eyes," Honey Girl protested.

"No, not him—my husband. Big patch over one eye . . ."

"Now you're exaggerating. Next, you'll say he had a wooden leg."

"Don't be ridiculous, the dog doesn't have a wooden leg."

Everyone laughed.

Before Jon and Kolohe climbed out of the car at Mike and Shay's, Hot Dog Annie grasped Jon's hand in hers.

"It was nice meeting you, Jon. Aloha."

MIKE AND SHAY WERE IN THEIR living room watching tennis. It was Sunday and the Wimbledon Tennis Championship was on.

"I *thought* it was Sunday," Jon said. "Today is Sunday, right?"

Shay laughed and continued to watch the game. Mike smiled while shaking his head.

"Yes Jon, it's Sunday. Grab a cold one from the fridge."

Jon helped himself to a Lowenbrau. He was looking for an opener when he heard Mike call from the living room, "It's a twist off, Jon. You don't need a church key."

Jon put Kolohe into the fenced yard with Mike and Shay's dog, Max. Max was a Scottish Terrier and an outside dog. The two got along well. Jon sat on the leather couch next to Mike.

"Do you know who these guys are?" Shay asked.

"I'm a little out of the loop," Jon admitted.

"Arthur Ashe and Jimmy Connors."

"Who you going for?"

"Ashe is going to win," she announced.

Mike looked at Jon, raised his eyebrows and then went back to rolling a joint.

Arthur Ashe did win.

"First Black male tennis player to win a major championship. It's history," Shay told Jon. "Miguel, we're going to be needing some more beer."

Jon rode with Mike in his vintage pickup truck to the Hāli'imaile Store. The owners at the store knew Mike and gave them a free bag of shrimp chips to go along with the beer.

Back home, Mike and Jon sat on the porch. It was only big enough for one chair, so Jon sat on the steps. They had a great view of the West Maui Mountains where the sun was setting. Kolohe and Max were lying at the bottom of the steps.

The mango tree in the front yard was full of blossoms.

"Looks like a good year for mangos."

"Yep." Mike said. "Though I can't eat mangos. I get mangoitis—it's like poison ivy to me. I break out in a mean rash. Itches like hell. They are good mangos, or so I hear. It's a Haden variety."

"That sucks that you can't eat them."

"I can't even look at the tree without getting a rash."

Shay poked her head out the door. "You boys hungry?" She had cooked red snapper with mushrooms and onions, white rice, and a salad.

The three sat down to eat at a small table in the kitchen.

"Sorry, Jon. I know you would prefer brown rice."

"No problem. It's all good. Thank you. So, Shay, you're managing the big shopping center now?"

"Yeah. It's too much work. I can do it, but . . . geeze Louise." Shay took a swig on her beer. "I just started studying for my broadcasting license. I'm going to be a DJ."

Mike gave Jon a knowing look.

"That would be cool." It was much easier to imagine Shay thriving as a DJ than suiting up to run the mall. As Jon observed Mike and Shay that evening, he realized that although they were two very unique individuals, they had figured out how to make life work together. He admired and even envied their close relationship.

After dinner, they all sat in the living room drinking and talking.

"Smoke a joint?"

"Sure."

"Did you hear about the tourists driving off the road on the way to Hāna?"

It sounded like the beginning of a joke, but it wasn't. Jon shook his head no.

"Jon doesn't read the paper, honey," Shay said.

"Down a big cliff." Mike made a downward motion with his hand. "Ka-boom. All dead. The tourists think they're at Disneyland and the rental cars are on tracks."

"Miguel, don't be like that," Shay said sternly.

"It's true," Mike added quietly. "Makes you think about the big picture, though. We just saw a program on space. You know, the universe and all that. Amazing. You would have liked it."

He took his eyes off Jon to light the joint.

"Do you think there's intelligent life on other planets?" Shay asked Jon.

"I'm still trying to figure out if there's any intelligent life here on Earth," Jon smiled.

"Touché. The jury's still out on that one."

"No, yeah," Jon said. "There's got to be life on other planets. I mean, we're in space. It's not out there somewhere. We're in it. Floating through space on this spinning ball. It's crazy."

Mike and Jon passed the joint between them. Shay didn't smoke.

"With all of the gazillion stars, planets, universes, and galaxies," Shay said, "it would be a miracle if there wasn't life on other planets."

"I agree. It's nuts that any of it exists in the first place. Scientists say there are galaxies as far as their instruments can see, or sense, in every direction."

"Seems unreal, but scientists give us a sense of reality. What they've observed and discovered. Where we live."

"The distances involved are mind boggling. Between stars, and planets, and galaxies. We can't even comprehend, right?"

"How do you wrap your mind around infinity? It goes forever?"

"And if it stops or has an end—what's on the other side?"

"God or no God," Jon said, "it's totally nuts. Makes absolutely no sense."

"If God created the world and man, then who created God?" Shay asked.

"As my dad would probably say, man created God to help him sleep better at night," Jon said.

"What was it Karl Marx said?"

"Religion is the opiate of the masses."

"I think it's been replaced by Budweiser."

"Keeps the natives from getting restless."

"The wild thing is," Mike said, "nobody even thinks about this stuff. Not as much as we should, anyway."

"I know." Jon nodded. "We're all in our own little worlds. All mental. In a sense all made up and determined by time and place."

Shay excused herself. "Thanks for the deep thoughts, boys. I'm going to bed. I've got to get up early."

"Night, Shay."

Mike fell quiet for a few moments, then spoke in a soft, wistful tone. "When I met the old lady, my life changed. I was headed for a dead end. I was still riding in the club. I got into some trouble and had to go to court. The judge, who I'd been in front of before, looks at me and says, 'If I see you in my court again—that's it. I'm going to put you away,'" Mike sighed. "I realized there was something bigger and badder than me. I did a 180° flip. Totally turned my life around. Shay was there for me. We hit it off from the start. You know, most of the guys I rode with are either dead or in jail. Some of the guys would ride the line."

"Ride the line?"

"The centerline. Literally ride down the center line on the road. They thought they were invincible. That's just who they were. They paid the price. Ended up in the morgue. After I got out of the Marines, I wasn't sure where I fit into society. I didn't know what to do with myself. Joined the motorcycle gang. I swear, Jon, I didn't eat a vegetable for fifteen years. Well, French fries. Guess that's a vegetable. Burgers, shakes, and fries. Crazy yeah?"

"Yeah."

"We had a house in Mission Valley, right next to the freeway. Highway 80. I had gotten my hands on an electric guitar. I kept playing the same chord, over and over, for hours. You know, higher than a kite. Drove the guys up the wall. They were ready to kill me . . . screaming at me to stop and threatening to shoot me."

Mike had Jon's full attention.

"I had this chick over. We were in the bedroom." Mike glanced over his shoulder. "These guys would shoot into the air, through the ceiling and even through the walls. There were bullet holes all over the place. A couple of bullets came whizzing through the wall. Luckily, we were sitting on the mattress on the floor, and the shots went over our heads. After that I spray painted a line on the living room wall, about waist high, and wrote NO SHOOTING BELOW THIS LINE. Hey, it worked."

Jon shook his head and laughed.

"I was reckless. One time this dude and I were driving down Sunset Boulevard in Los Angeles, stoned out of our minds on downers. Got pulled over. My friend, I don't know how he was even driving. He couldn't even talk. His words came out all garbled. You couldn't understand a thing he said. The cop pulled me to the side and asked, 'What's wrong with your friend?' Now I was just as out of it as my friend, and to this day I don't know how I did it, but I pulled it together, mustered all my concentration, and spoke perfectly clearly. I told him, 'Man, if he knows you're making fun of his speech impediment, he'll kill you.' The cop let us go."

"Miguel," Shay called from the bedroom. "Jon doesn't want to hear your old stories. Time for bed."

17 | ANOTHER ROADSIDE ATTRACTION

THE TIRES NEEDED AIR. JON CHECKED the brakes. He adjusted the rear brake. Lifting the back of the bike, he turned the pedal. The crank wheel had a slight wobble, but everything was working. He ran through the gears. It was a ten-speed. While living in Lahaina, Jon had painted the bike frame with a night sky, clouds, and mountains—blues and greens. It was a good bike, made in Mexico.

He hadn't been on his bicycle since riding to Hāna from Kīhei and crashing along the way. Jon recalled the accident . . . . Before moving from Lahaina, he had stashed his bike at a friend's house in Kīhei. Once settled into Nāhiku, it was time to retrieve it. It would be an ambitious ride of over fifty miles, which would be split into two days. He was excited for this up close and personal adventure along the road to Hāna.

At his friend's rental home, he was surprised (and impressed) to see several large, beautiful, pakalōlō plants growing in the inner courtyard. The plants were protected from public view and got plenty of sun.

Jon rode his bike out of town, past the sugar cane fields and through Pā'ia. By the time he got to the winding Hāna Road, his legs were toast. He began to walk up the steep hills and ride the downhill sections. As he approached Kaumahina state park where he planned to stay overnight, there was a light rain, enough rain to wet the road.

He was riding down a hill, coming around a hairpin turn, when he came face to face with an oncoming car. The road was narrow to begin with, so he had to cut it tight to avoid a collision. Both tires slipped out from under him. He did a 180° flip, still holding onto the handlebars. He jumped up quickly in case another car might come around the corner and run him over. He was bleeding from a gash on his head, by his temple. He walked the rest of the way to the state park, where some tourists driving a VW camper van checked out his wound and insisted on giving Jon and his bike a ride to the medical clinic in Hāna which was still a good ways off. It was dark by the time they got there. The clinic was closed. The pay phone was out of order, so they drove to Dr. Howell's house, just down the street. The doctor opened the clinic and stitched Jon up. Seven stitches. He still had a trace of a scar. His ribs were sore for a while after that, but for the most part the whole ordeal made him appreciate being alive and grateful for the generosity of strangers.

Today's plan was to ride to Hāna, which was five miles, one way. He walked the bicycle up the driveway, Kolohe alongside. He figured Kolohe would tire quickly and turn around, but *that* never happened.

They stopped near the airport turnoff, at the bottom of a long downhill run. The return would be the hardest with lots of uphill. Jon was feeling alright himself—taking it easy, being careful—but wishing he had some water for Ko. They continued to town. Jon rode slowly, amazed at Kolohe's stamina. Upon reaching Hasegawa Store, he sought out a hose bib on the side of the building. He turned the water on, cupping his hands underneath. Kolohe lapped the water greedily. Jon smiled.

"I'm next."

Startled, Jon looked up to see Paulo.

"That's one thirsty pup."

"He just ran all the way from Nāhiku. I was on my bike."

"That's crazy."

Dawn walked up with Anna in tow.

"Hi Jon." Dawn gave Jon a hug. "I have a favor to ask you. Paulo is playing on the other side on Friday. We want to stay the weekend. Can you babysit?" Before he could respond, Dawn kept talking. "She's low maintenance. Dresses herself. Uses the bathroom by herself. She has books, crayons, and paper. We just got some new colored pencils. I can give you some food stamps and getting rides is easy, hitching with Anna."

"I guess so. Okay." Jon thought it strange that Dawn was talking about Anna as if she wasn't standing right there. He looked at the child, who appeared to be in her own world, staring at something on the sidewalk that was captivating her.

"You'll do it?"

"Yeah." He was apprehensive, but always had a hard time saying no.

"You're a sweetheart. We appreciate it. We'll drop her off tomorrow. I'll pack her a bag with extra clothes, a toothbrush and stuff." Paulo had already slipped into the store. Dawn kissed Jon's cheek to thank him.

After picking up a few things at the store, Jon and Kolohe started back to Nāhiku. They stopped at Hāna Bay. Sitting in the shade, Jon drank a small bottle of apple juice and gave Ko water from the faucet on the outdoor shower.

On the way home Kolohe and Jon were both moving slower, climbing hills, enjoying the views. Deep green pastures flanked both sides of the road. There was a car up ahead, pulled over to the side. It was pointed in the same direction Jon was traveling but parked on the opposite side of the road. As he got closer, he saw Patrick, the juggler, along with two other young men. They were talking to a blonde girl who was standing in the pasture alongside the barbed wire fence.

Jon stopped.

"I'm drawing a blank," Patrick said, pointing at Jon.

"Jon."

"That's right. Hey Jon. Do you know Paul Fingers?" he asked, introducing the fellow standing closest.

Jon shook his head no.

"Incredible flute player. Bamboo flute."

"Nice to meet you."

"And this is Wolf. He's giving us a ride to the other side. And this is . . ." Patrick turned toward the girl.

"I'm Laura," she said. "Just checking this pasture for mushrooms. Found a few."

"Did you eat them?" Patrick asked.

"Yeah, duh . . ."

Laura had long blonde hair. She was wearing dirty blue jeans, a loose fitting T-shirt, and a braided leather headband. She looked somewhat disheveled.

"Jon lives in Leanne and Faith's old place in Upper Nāhiku," Patrick said to Paul.

"Is that piano backboard still there?" Paul Fingers asked.

"Yep. Harry is threatening to come get it but it's still there for now."

"Praise the Lord. Maybe I can stop by sometime?"

"Sure."

"I'm living in Kanaio . . . out past Kaupō. Quiet and peaceful," Paul reflected. "Just me and the wind. I'm staying in the old church. Taking care of the place. Keeping it clean."

Paul Fingers was slight and wiry with short dark hair and a short beard. He was soft spoken but animated as he talked, revealing a wildness that sparkled in his eyes. It was a wildness tempered by a sweet demeanor.

"Your dog looks thirsty," Laura said.

"We're almost home," Jon nodded. "He'll get more water soon."

"The cows must think we're crazy," Laura said. "They have all this pasture and acres of green rolling hills and we humans are confined to this narrow strip of pavement." She waved her arms in the air as she talked and then placed them on her hips. "We're the ones fenced in."

"I never thought of it like that. That's so true," Patrick said. "It's all a matter of perspective."

"Hey, we better keep on truckin'. I'm supposed to fix up a van this afternoon," Wolf said.

"Wolf is a good mechanic," Patrick told Jon. "He can fix anything."

Wolf had a thick beard and short dark hair. He was the stockiest of the lot. His oil-stained overalls made him look the part.

"I'm a bit of a grease monkey, it's true."

In a deep voice Laura said, "How far do you go? I'm going all the way." She grimaced, and in her regular voice added, "I've heard that one a million times. Har, har. So funny I forgot to laugh. So, which way are you guys going?"

"You need a ride? We're going in the direction our car is pointing, obviously. Towards Kahului," Wolf teased.

"Okay, smart ass," Laura paused. "Ah . . . do you know which way *I* was going? I can't seem to remember."

"No. You were in the pasture when we pulled over."

"I've been eating mushrooms for the last three days. I'm getting a little spacy. Which way should I go? I'm trying to remember. I think I'll go towards Hāna. Yeah, I'm going towards Hāna."

"Alright then, we're going to hele on. Have a nice day. Take care, Laura."

"Bye guys."

Wolf and the boys hooted and hollered as they passed Jon on his bike. Paul Fingers had his arm out the window giving a shaka sign.

I WONDER WHO'S HERE, JON THOUGHT AS he neared his house. There was a beater of a car parked across from the walkway to the front door. He rode down the driveway to the underneath of the house, and called out as he walked up the interior stairs.

"Hello." It was a woman's voice that answered. Jon popped up into the dining room.

"Hey, Cheryl."

"Hi, Jon. Hope you don't mind me making myself at home. It was open."

"No, not at all. I'm going to take a quick shower, I'm really sweaty–just rode my bicycle to Hāna and back."

"You have a hot shower?"

"No. It's cold water. That's why it's quick."

Jon grabbed some clean clothes and ducked downstairs. Kolohe was happy to have his water bowl filled.

"Ah. That's better," Jon said as he walked back up, drying his hair with a towel.

"Your hair is getting long. Did you wash it?"

"Yep. I don't often get special company."

"I'm honored. So, I'm special?"

"Did I say that?"

"Think so."

"Well, you are," he smiled across the table.

The two knew each other from Lahaina. Jon, Cheryl, and their friend, Butch, used to hang out together. Butch and Cheryl seemed like boyfriend/girlfriend, but Jon was never quite sure. Together they would all ride bikes to swim at the beach park on the outskirts of town. Eventually Jon moved to Hāna, Butch moved to Moloka'i, and Cheryl remained in Lahaina.

Cheryl had a pretty face and long brown hair. She was sweet.

"How's life in Lahaina?"

"I got a new job. I'm driving taxi."

"Driving taxi?"

"It's okay. Working mostly at night. The tips are better at night. Most of the people you meet are nice. There are some assholes though."

"Guess that comes with the territory."

"It's a job. I don't take any shit," Cheryl said. She pulled a plastic bag out of her backpack. "I brought you some cookies. Enjoy. Oatmeal with walnuts. Help yourself."

"Thank you. Don't mind if I do. Want one?"

"Sure. Jon, you said that there are waterfalls nearby. Can we go see them?"

He looked out the window, observing the clouds. "Ah, looks like it might rain, but we can chance um."

"Do we have to drive?"

"Nope, it's a short hike."

"Tomorrow I have to head back to Lahaina. I work tomorrow night, so today is all I have. You up for it?"

"My dog Kolohe is going to be dragging. He ran behind me all the way to Hāna and back."

"He could stay here."

Jon smiled. "Nah, he won't stay."

They hiked to the ocean and to Emerald Pond. Kolohe, not to be left out, tagged along and soon was leading the way. The sky was dark and ominous, but Jon and Cheryl sat enjoying the waterfall.

On the way home, on Ulaino Road, the clouds opened into a sudden downpour. They were soaked. With water dripping down their faces, they looked at each other. Laughing, they wrapped their arms around each other in a warm embrace. They took shelter under a large mango tree, and Kolohe stuck close by.

"Welcome to Nāhiku," Jon said. "And I already had a shower today!"

The rain let up as they sloshed up the hill to the house.

Dry clothes felt good. Jon cooked brown rice for dinner.

"It was either this or oatmeal. On the bright side, there is soy sauce."

"I'm sure it will be good. And cookies for dessert."

"That's right. Yum."

Night was falling. Jon lit a candle inside a gallon glass jar and the kerosene lamp.

"You must go to bed early, with so little light here."

"I do."

"I checked out your drawings. I like them." Jon's drawing tablet was on the table. "Pen and ink?"

"It's just a regular pen. I like to draw. Gives me something to do at night."

"Do you know who Maharaji is?" Cheryl asked.

"Isn't that the kid guru?"

"Some people call him that."

"He's like thirteen years old or something?"

"Maharaji is seventeen now. He's my guru."

"Oh. He's the one who asks followers to bring him stuff, yeah? Jewelry, cars, boats, TVs . . . ."

"That's part of his teachings; not to be attached to your possessions. You know how materialistic Americans are. The offerings are sold, and the money is used to do good."

"I saw a program on TV. Some guy threw a pie in Maharaji's face," Jon said. He'd watched the show with Mike and Shay. "His disciples attacked the guy and came close to killing him. Literally stomped him and crushed his skull. He barely survived."

"Maharaji can't be responsible for everything his disciples do. Free will—they're responsible for their own actions. That's not Maharaji."

"I don't know."

"His teachings are good."

Jon could see Cheryl didn't want to be pushed on this. "As long as you're happy and comfortable with him, that's all that matters."

"I'm happy."

"Have you seen Butch lately?" Jon asked.

"He was in Lahaina a couple months ago. We hung out a bit. He's making jewelry and pipes out of the Moloka'i deer antler. Even doing some carving and scrimshaw on some."

"That's cool."

"I'm thinking about moving. I like living in Hawai'i but I'm ready for something new. It's hard to get ahead here. Not sure where I'll go. Maybe San Diego."

Jon yawned.

"Bedtime?"

"It's been a long day."

They slept in separate rooms, and in the morning Jon made oatmeal.

"Jon, I appreciate that there's no pressure from you to have sex. That's nice. It feels good to enjoy our friendship and to let it unfold. We'll see what happens."

"Absolutely." Jon too valued their relationship and was willing to see how it played out.

"I'm hiking through the crater in two weeks," she said. "I'll come and see you. In the meantime, I'll bake you more cookies."

"Thank you. I love cookies."

"I know. Me too. Do you get mail at your mailbox here?

"Yes. I just got that set up. It's great."

"Be expecting some homemade cookies in the mail. Aloha, Jon."

Jon stood in the road as Cheryl drove off. His eyes scanned the sky. *Looks like a good day to paint the mailbox.*

The aluminum mailbox was mounted on a fat guava post that Jon had cut with his bow saw. The mailbox had to be a certain distance off the ground and from the road so that the postal carrier could pull up to it in their car to deliver and pick up mail. Paco had asked Jon to paint it— just not too wild. Not like Rainbow's mailbox, around the corner at the commune, which had—no surprise—a rainbow on it. Jon had bought a small can of cobalt blue enamel paint. It didn't take long to coat the mailbox. Once finished, he stood back to admire it. *Perfect.* The cobalt blue color was bright, cheerful, and not overly flashy.

He was cleaning his paintbrush when Paulo and Dawn pulled up. They were dropping off Anna. Jon hadn't forgotten.

Jon and Anna spent their time at the house. She was too little to hike to the ocean; the trail was dangerous in spots, and it was too far. It was true what Dawn had said; Anna was used to playing by herself. She played, drew, and colored, and was happy to have a real bedroom all to herself to spread out in. She left books and toys all over the bed and floor while her favorite doll sat neatly against the pillow. In the evening Jon read aloud from Anna's books. Jon enjoyed the children's stories, the way they were musical like poems, and delivered positive messages. Unlike the Grimm's fairy tales Jon had read, which could be quite dark. He checked in on Anna a couple of times after she fell asleep, happy to see her "snug as a bug in a rug." He wondered what it would be like to be a father, to see a little face resembling his own, to take on the responsibility of caring for another human being.

One day they hitchhiked into Hāna town. Jon spent the food stamps that Dawn had given him. Having never used food stamps before, he was apprehensive, but it was fine. No questions asked. Dawn had told him not to tear the coupons out of the booklet ahead of time. "They don't like that."

It *was* easier hitchhiking with a child—people felt sorry for Anna, he guessed, seeing her on the side of the road—but Jon took his responsibility seriously and kept a close eye on her. *Precious cargo,* he thought.

After several days of babysitting, he was happy to see Paulo and Dawn coming down his walkway to retrieve their little girl. Anna was also happy to see them and to be going home, though she flung her arms around Jon's leg to say goodbye.

Jon and Kolohe stood on the front step watching as they walked to their truck. Anna turned and waved, "Bye doggie."

After they left, Jon looked to Kolohe. "Shall we?"

You didn't have to ask Ko twice. They walked along the highway, and hadn't gone far when Jon spotted something along the edge of the road. It appeared someone had tossed two pumpkins out their car window. They were green on the outside, orange on the inside, and broken into large and small pieces that were scattered about.

"Come on."

Jon motioned to Kolohe as he turned back toward the house. He fetched his small nylon pack and returned to salvage what he could. Back home Jon rinsed the pumpkin, skinned it, and boiled it in water. It cooked quickly and was delicious. Jon thoroughly enjoyed it. He wrote of it in his journal that night.

What a week! A great bike ride to Hāna town along with the pooch. Felt good. I love riding . . . especially the downhill runs—silently zipping along with the wind in my face, hair flying. Also enjoyed spending time with my Lahaina friend, Cheryl (not to mention the oatmeal cookies). On our hike, we got caught in a downpour. Good fun. Survived several days of babysitting. And, now, in a nice turn of events, and a great way to end the day—vegetarian roadkill.

18 | PĀʻIA BAY

"**D**O YOU HAVE REGRETS?"

Jon and Raoul were sitting on the sand in the dappled shade of an ironwood tree. Jon's eyes wandered from the small waves breaking on the shore to the clouds gathered on the horizon. Pieces of clouds drifted overhead. Down the beach, a guy was jogging with his dog. A young couple lay sunbathing. Jon was rolling one of the roughly textured cones from the ironwood between his palms.

"Yeah." He glanced briefly to Raoul. "Sure, I have regrets. I have a boatload of regrets. I've done a lot of stupid things in my life."

"Even though your decisions have got you to where you are now?"

"If I had a chance to do it over, I would do it differently and have faith in the outcome. I know what you're saying, but I would make some different choices. We're basically who we are. I don't know. Anyway, it's not so simple. You only get to do it over in the movies."

"At our age, we're closer to the end than the beginning," Raoul said.

"All we have is this moment."

"This is a good one."

"This is a great one. We tend to miss the moment. The here-and-now."

"It's hard to hang in the here-and-now."

"True," Jon agreed. "Although there are situations that are more conducive to being aware than others. Life and death. Anything that requires your whole undivided attention. Like when you're pulling in a 200 pound ahi."

"Or having sex with someone for the first time."

"Or the 20th time. Certain activities: sex, cooking, eating . . . walking a tightrope."

"Or when a baby croc latches on to your nuts," Raoul jested.

"I hate when that happens." Jon tried to maintain a serious expression but couldn't. "That would do it. The whole world would disappear."

"It would be a situation that would require one's full attention."

"I went to a *playshop* in Hilo with Paul Reps. It was a playshop as opposed to a workshop. He was a Zen guy. Widely known for the book *Zen Flesh, Zen Bones,* which is a collection of Zen koans and texts that he compiled. As a painter and a poet, Paul Reps created his own form of "Haiku" picture poetry. When I saw him, he was an old man, in his mid-eighties, but he had a sparkle in his eyes and a deep presence. I feel fortunate to have spent an evening with him. The charge for the playshop was an oddball amount, $7.53 or something. He made this theoretical offer. He said if a person was truly interested in living in the moment, he could shadow that person for two or three weeks, twenty-four seven, constantly bringing their attention back to the present. After which, the mind would surrender, and they would be grounded in the here-and-now. I may have it all mixed up, but it was something like that. He said if you want to awaken, you have to shake life up. Do things as you wouldn't usually do them. If you normally sit at the table, then sit on top of the table or underneath the table."

"He sounds like a stoner."

"You know, that was an interesting thing about LSD—not that I'm recommending it, at this point—but acid brought you into the present. You would see things that were always there, around you, but might go unnoticed. Colors, shapes, sounds. And you might be experiencing it all at once—taste, sight, hearing, all the senses. Which is what we're always doing anyway. But we're focused elsewhere. In our heads. In our dreams. We learned to navigate different levels of consciousness. There was no choice, once you jumped off that cliff. It's a powerful drug and unfortunately, not everyone lands on their feet."

"I don't know who's more stoned," Raoul said. "Me or you."

Jon nodded. "I think it's pretty interesting that some of our past presidents admitted to smoking weed."

"Is that true?"

"Yep. Bush, Clinton, and Obama. Clinton said he smoked but didn't inhale. Totally bogus. Obama, on the other hand, said, 'Hey, inhaling was the whole point.' Gotta love that."

"The times really are changing. Jon, if the goal is to experience the present moment, how is it that you are writing a novel about the past?"

"Go figure," Jon mused. "I had some great reference material I had saved. *Lahaina Sun* newspapers and miscellaneous info from the seventies. Then in the mid-eighties we were hanging out with a young yogi from the Himalayas. Cool guy. Long hair, full beard. He wore traditional garb, a robe. He was saying, *Live in the present. Forget the past. Let it go.* I tossed my material. I regret that." Jon laughed. "It would have made for a fuller, richer narrative. Because in the end, I couldn't let it go. Writing the book, it's something I wanted to do for reasons I don't fully understand. So, I persevered. Believe me, writing is a ton of work. Not always easy. I would just as soon be working in the garden and watching the carrots grow."

"You know your spelling is atrocious," Raoul said.

"I know. Would you mind using smaller words? Because I'm probably going to write this down later. Maybe say something like, *Your spelling is bad.*"

"I will endeavor," Raoul grinned, "to effectuate a concerted and bona fide effort."

"Just shoot me now."

"You know your story, Brown Eyed Girl?"

"Umm hum."

"That story gives a whole new meaning to brown eyed girl."

"What?" Jon didn't get it.

Raoul repeated slowly, "brown eyed girl."

"You're sick. Brilliant, but sick."

"I'll take brilliant but sick. Could be worse, right?"

"It can always be worse. Shall we keep walking?"

The men continued down the beach along the waterline.

"The colors are amazing," Jon said, looking at the ocean's brilliant blues.

"Is that still Maui we're seeing across the water?"

"That's the backside of West Maui. Out past Wailuku and around to the Lahaina side. It's a gnarly dirt road. I hiked it with a couple of friends. Took us three days. Camped for two nights along the way."

The long stretches of sandy beach they walked were broken by areas of lava rock and boulders that reached out into the water. Here there were trails that ran parallel to the beach and skirted the rocky outcroppings. At the edge of Baldwin Beach Park, they stopped to admire a tangled root mass that had been weathered by the wind and waves. It was one of many, each with their own character.

"I say we dig it out and ship it to San Francisco to a high-end gallery," Raoul said.

"Big bucks. Going to need a backhoe. Check out the shadow. I had a metal sculpture class in college. The teacher always brought the finished pieces outside so we could check out their shadows."

There were many people there, enjoying the day; walking, swimming, having fun with family and friends. There were lots of kids. One young mother, in her bikini, did yoga in foot-deep water while keeping one eye on her toddler who was playing next to her.

"How far does the beach keep going?"

"Maybe another mile. I camped here for a month. In the ironwoods."

"No way."

"It was a tent city. Haoles, locals, families. Some people had cars. They would drive in and park next to their camps. It was pretty sweet, with Baldwin Park right here. We had bathrooms, outdoor showers, a big pavilion, and barbecues. All of this, and not far from Pā'ia. I had oil paints and was painting on driftwood in those days. The camp area was on private property, so they eventually closed it down. By that time I'd met Steve, Jackie, and their dog Bear. They were driving a Jeep Scout and living in a big canvas tent. Steve informed me they were relocating to Windmills Beach in West Maui to pick puka shells. He offered me a bag of weed to come with them and paint a mural on the inside of their tent."

"That was probably a no-brainer."

"Got that right. Picked a good amount of puka shells too. Puka shells had value for necklaces and jewelry making. One night we played puka poker using the puka shells for chips. The shells were assigned value according to size. The small pukas were the most valuable. Good fun."

"Puka poker."

"Hey, I brought a poem for you to read." Jon pulled a folded paper out of his pocket.

"Is this something from back in the day?"

"Kind of. It's more recent, but basically a vintage sentiment, whatever that means. Inspired by this area."

I was walking
along the shoreline,
a hippy chick
walking towards me,
our eyes crossed
well I should say
her eyes crossed
she had crossed eyes,
a lovely smile
floated upon her face
as she gazed at me,
at least
I think she was
looking at me,
her hair was dark,
curly and thick
and that was just
the hair under her arms,
a scent of ripe mango
followed her every step
I was aroused.

"I like it."

Jon laughed. "You would be my target audience. It is, of course, a commentary on perception."

"Of course. Shall we head back? Must be about lunchtime. I'm making a point not to be checking my phone every ten minutes."

"Yeah, we haven't eaten in a couple of hours."

"And my blood alcohol level is dropping dangerously."

"Roger that."

The two began to walk.

"I liked your vegetarian roadkill story. Hardcore."

"That pumpkin was so good. I was hungry. It was a treat. I have another vegetarian roadkill story."

"Let's hear it."

"I'm walking to Emerald Pond, along Ulaino Road. Do you remember how people used to grow their own alfalfa sprouts from seeds in glass jars?"

"Yeah, yeah."

"You'd put screen over the end. Rinse them every day."

"Um hum."

"So, I'm walking along the dirt road, in the middle of the jungle, and I come across some alfalfa sprouts growing alongside the road in a bed of broken glass. It turned out Stan or Susanne, I forget which, were carrying sprouts to the freshwater pipe down at the ocean to rinse them when they dropped the jar. I found that out later. At the time I had no clue how the sprouts got there. Nāhiku is so wet, the sprouts continued to grow where they were. I carefully plucked them from the roadside, avoiding the larger pieces of glass. I took them home and rinsed them many times before eating them."

"You're crazy."

"That's a possibility."

"I may be getting ahead of myself—haven't read the whole book yet—but did you ever hookup with Cheryl?" Raoul asked.

Jon looked down the long stretch of beach then back to the sand in front of him. He cleared his throat. "I was expecting her to drop by after her hike through Haleakalā, but she never showed. I had received a box of homemade cookies in the mail along with a note that said, *See you soon.* It was unusual for her to not follow through with plans. I figured something had come up. A couple weeks later I was in Lahaina, so I went by her house in town. The front door was open with the screen door closed. I called her name. I knew Cheryl had a roommate, but no one was around. Didn't think much about it. Not long after that I was in San Diego visiting my dad. I went to dinner with my sister and brother-in-law to a place called The Prophet. It was a vegetarian restaurant where you sat on the floor. Our waitress was someone I knew from high school, who also happened to be a good friend of Cheryl's. I asked her how Cheryl was doing. She was taken aback.

"You don't know? You don't know what happened? Don't you read the newspaper? I'll tell you after dinner. I don't want to spoil your night."

"Throughout the dinner, I'm wondering what the hell happened."

"What did happen?"

"Well . . ." Jon took a deep breath, and let it out heavily. "Ah, she was murdered. Shot to death."

"What?"

"While she was working, driving taxi. They didn't know if it was a rape attempt or a robbery, or what. Someone even insinuated that she was involved in drugs. Highly unlikely."

"Did they ever catch the person responsible?"

"I'm not sure. Never really found out any of the details."

"Sorry, man."

"Yeah."

Big fluffy clouds were passing overhead. Although the sun was out, a soft mist began to fall. Jon noticed a faint rainbow forming above them and silently pointed to it.

19 | SAN PEDRO

Without a phone, Jon never knew when someone would be stopping by for a night or two. Whether it was one of his friends from the other side, or the hui and their 'ohana. Ready or not, he was called upon to be a host and occasionally a tour guide. For the most part he welcomed the intrusions.

On this day Jon sat in the dining room writing in his journal. The sound of car doors shutting brought him back to this world. He heard women's voices, and stood up to see Georgia, one of the hui, coming in the front door. Trailing her was a young woman around Jon's age.

"Hey Georgia."

Georgia was sixty years old. She was thin with dark hair and olive brown skin. Georgia had wrinkles upon wrinkles. The skin on her arms hung loosely. Jon had met her several months earlier. At first, all he could see were the wrinkles. Very quickly, as he got to know her, the wrinkles disappeared. She was a fun-loving rascal with an impish grin. Not a toothy grin but more along the lines of Dopey of the Seven Dwarfs.

"Jon, this is Jenn. She just got back from South America. She's Kathleen's partner in the Maui Ragtime, and part of our hui.

"Nice to meet you Jenn. How was South America?"

"Absolutely wonderful," she said. "I've heard a lot about you."

"All lies no doubt. That was my evil twin brother. I didn't do it."

"No. It was good things."

"Well, yeah. That was me."

"You're funny."

Jenn had brown eyes, long light brown hair, and girl-next-door good looks.

"We're just here for the night," Georgia said. "Jenn brought something special from Peru." Georgia had a mischievous look.

"Star of the Andes," Jenn said. "San Pedro cactus."

"It's a psychedelic cactus," Georgia added.

"Oh?" Jon said.

"It contains mescaline," Jenn said. "This is dried and powdered. It isn't as strong as when it's prepared fresh. Are you game?"

"Sure."

"It tastes terrible. Very bitter. We brought some orange juice to mix it into. That's the only way we'll get it down."

"Brunch."

"I like the sound of that."

"I have some papaya I can cut. Let me put this stuff away."

Jenn put a spoonful of the powder into each of the three waiting glasses of OJ. "This is probably all we'll be able to get down. You'd have to take quite a bit to actually hallucinate. In Peru, San Pedro is for healing and spiritual practices. It's said to be a bridge between the visible and invisible worlds."

They gagged down their exotic brew followed by some slices of papaya.

"Is that your white dog in the yard?" Jenn asked.

"Yep."

"He looks like one of the dogs in Nāpili."

"That's him. He *is* one of the dogs from Nāpili."

"I thought he looked familiar. Is he good company?"

"Oh yeah. Very attentive. Doesn't talk back."

"Watch it now," Georgia said.

Jon smiled.

"He can be our spirit guide," Jenn said. "What's that buzzing? Is that bees?"

"There's a beehive above the kitchen in the attic space. Bees coming and going all day long."

"If you open the attic crawl hole in the bedroom, are they in there?" Georgia asked.

"No. Since the kitchen was an add-on, the bees are confined in the one area. It's blocked from the rest of the attic."

"Maybe we can drill a hole in the ceiling and get honey," Georgia said.

"Yeah, we'll just put a cork in it," Jenn added.

"Better yet, a spigot."

"Honey on tap," Jon said. "Could be handy. Shall we take a walk?"

"Where to?"

"The ocean and the waterfalls."

There was a resounding, "Yes."

Kolohe lead the travelers down the hill.

"Is it going to rain?" Jenn asked.

"It might. There are some really dark clouds up the mountain. Definitely raining up there."

The San Pedro was not disorienting; in fact, it imparted a sense of well-being and an expanded physical awareness.

"I feel all electric," Georgia said, holding out her arms.

Jenn and Jon smiled.

They paused on the bluff next to the broken-down shack.

"I heard there used to be a jeep road that went past here all the way to Ulaino Road," Jon said.

"This would be a good place to build a house," Jenn said.

"You'd have a great view."

They crossed the lava bridge. Kolohe went up and around. Coming down the final steep slope to the Blue Pond, the strap on one of Jon's slippers broke. He was forced to go barefoot over some rough rocks. The San Pedro had numbed his body. Some weeks later he tried walking the area without shoes again, and couldn't do it.

True to its name, Blue Pond was a magnificent blue color. The small waterfall was gently flowing into and projecting over the ledge and the pool.

"It's so beautiful."

"It is. It truly is."

Jon and Georgia stripped and waded into the pool for a dip. Jenn was on her period and didn't go in the water, for which she apologized. Kolohe sat next to Jenn as Jon and Georgia enjoyed the cool water. Then they all walked to the ocean, and finally to Emerald Pond. They sat entranced by the waterfall; engulfed in the moment. Jenn put her hand on Jon's arm and softly said, "Listen. It's the voice of the angels."

They all sat quietly, listening.

Kolohe was close by. Jenn had helped him over some of the large boulders near the pool. He was restless and sniffing the air.

"He smells danger. I think we should head back," Jenn said.

As they got back to Blue Pond, they saw that the water was rising quickly. The road crossing which had been completely dry a short while before was now covered with flowing water. They crossed quickly. It was still shallow enough for Kolohe to cross. They stood watching as the water continued to rise. What had been a tranquil setting was becoming a rushing torrent of muddy water. In a matter of minutes, the stream was uncrossable.

Wow."

"And it's not even raining here."

"It's a flash flood from all that rain up the mountain."

"Amazing. I've never seen that."

Blue Pond had become unrecognizable. The tall waterfall upstream from the pond was rushing hard and roaring.

As they hiked back, a misty rain began to fall.

Back home, Jenn made some hot chamomile tea. They sat at the dining room table.

"I got busted," Georgia announced.

"Busted? For what?" Jon asked.

"Growing."

His eyebrows raised, "Growing?"

"Cultivation of mary-j-wanna. We had some plants at our place in Huelo, in a thicket of hau trees. You know how hau grows?"

"All tangled together." Jon weaved his arms around each other.

"Yep. We had a pathway through the branches. It was perfect. They got full sun and were protected from the wind."

Jenn listened quietly. She had heard the story.

"Solomon Lee had it out for me."

"Solomon Lee?"

"Vice Squad. I had previously lodged a complaint against him. He didn't like that. He wanted to get me. They sat in a car up on the road, about a mile away, with high-powered binoculars—watching our place. Targeted me. They saw us going in and out of the hau patch. For the bust they showed up with a helicopter and all. Hauled me away in handcuffs in the back of a cop car."

"Dang. That name sounds familiar. Solomon Lee," Jon said.

"He told me that my complaint was permanently on his record, and he'd been wanting to bust me."

"Payback's a bitch. You know," Jon said, "he's the guy who busted me and my friend Butch in Lahaina a couple of years ago. We were smoking a joint in front of the library, next to the ocean. This local guy walks up to us. Plain clothes. He says, 'Can I have a puff?' I'm thinking, now that's a little strange. My friend hands him the joint. He flashes his badge and tells us we're under arrest. He takes us to the Lahaina Police Station. Twenty-five dollar bail. Neither of us had twenty-five bucks on us. They let Butch go get the money to bail us out. We were never in a cell or any-thing. But I had to go to court, upstairs at the harbor. It was a twenty-five dollar fine. They just kept our bail money. The thing was, Lee was leaning on Butch because he was living at Kobetakes. Up by the sugar mill. They knew someone up there was dealing but didn't know who. Butch knew who it was but played dumb."

Georgia shuddered. "Enough talk about the cops. Let's change the energy in here. Does anyone want to do some chanting?" Georgia had recently returned from a retreat for Swami Muktananda, in California. "On the retreat we sang a chant, *Om Namah Shivaya*." She sang the words slowly, with the vowels drawn out.

"Let's move to the bedroom. We can sit on the bed. That will be more comfortable."

They relocated to the bedroom that faced the ocean. It was the nicest of the rooms. Someone had previously added windows down low, just above the floor where the mattress sat.

Georgia demonstrated. Jon and Jenn joined in, *Ommm Naaaamaaaah Shiiivayaaaa*, over and over. They all worked on their harmonies.

"Jon, you're good at holding those notes," Jenn said.

"I've done breathing exercises for a number of years. Part of Yogananda's teachings. You're to do breathing exercises before meditation, although I'm not really meditating regularly these days."

"I love Yogananda," Georgia said. "He *is* amazing."

"He keeps an eye on me," Jon said. "Any guru with a surf spot named after him, Swami's in Encinitas, is my kind of guy."

"Is he still alive?" Jenn asked.

"He passed in 1952."

"Now that we're centered, how about massages? We can give each other massages," Georgia said.

Jon and Jenn looked at each other.

"Okay."

They took turns getting massaged, leaving their clothes on.

Afterwards they voted to eat. Georgia pulled something out of her large canvas shoulder bag.

"Jon, do you like ramen?"

"Ramen? What is that?"

"Noodle soup."

In a miraculously short five minutes, the ramen was ready, and the trio was back in the dining room drinking soup out of coffee cups.

"It's salty but tastes good. I like it," Jon said. "Is slurping allowed?"

"Absolutely."

Jon had an idea. "Scott, one of our neighbors around the corner, has often said that we are all welcome to come up and use their sauna. I've never checked it out."

"That sounds *goood*," Georgia said. She drew out the word *good* so long, it almost sounded like she was chanting again.

"Where is it?" asked Jenn.

"Up at the commune. The property where Rainbow and Patchouli live. It's walking distance."

"Perfect day to check it out."

It had been raining off and on. Georgia grabbed her umbrella from the car, and they walked to the commune. The dirt road leading into the property was steep. Just out of sight of the highway there was a flat area, some parked cars, and a garden. Kolohe came along even though Jon tried to discourage him. Jon knew that Scott had a couple of big dogs.

Farther up the hill they came to Rainbow and Patchouli's homemade house. It was small, funky, and as one might imagine, colorful. Patchouli directed them to continue up to Scott's place and the sauna.

"It's a good day for it. We were in the sauna earlier. Scott should be home."

As they approached the sauna, Scott's dogs appeared, and rushed to surround Kolohe. A dog fight broke out. Scott came quickly, charging towards the dogs, shouting sharply. The dogs stopped. He told his dogs to go home. They went most of the way but turned around outside of the house, lay down, and watched.

"It's all in the tone," Scott said. "That's what they understand. I just yelled gibberish."

Kolohe sat next to the sauna, keeping an eye on the big dogs. Life as a spirit guide wasn't all fun and games. Scott showed his visitors the sauna.

"It's still hot, but I'll throw a couple of logs on the fire," he said. "If you want more steam, there's water in the wooden bucket. Use the cup and throw water on the hot rocks. When you get good and hot and sweating there's buckets of cold rainwater here. Just pour one of those over your head. I know. Believe me, it feels great. There's more rainwater in the plastic trashcans. It collects off the roof." He smiled. "Enjoy."

A misty rain enveloped the area. The sauna was small and had windows up high for light. Jon and Georgia stripped naked. Jenn stripped but left her panties on. Jon couldn't help but notice what beautiful breasts and body Jenn had, but he tried to avert his eyes, to be respectful.

Everyone was quiet. After a long day it felt good to just sit in the warmth. At first, they looked at each other with shared satisfaction, but then they settled into their own private worlds.

Twenty minutes passed. Georgia was the first to speak. "It's hot in here."

They all joined in a good laugh.

"Umm hmm. Ready for a rinse?" Jon said.

As they left the sauna and poured cold water over each other's heads, they squealed and giggled, then pulled it together. They solemnly reentered the sauna. After several times in and out of the sauna they decided to head down the hill and home. The rain was light. They used Georgia's umbrella but couldn't fit the three of them underneath at the same time. They laughed as they bumped hips, jockeying for a spot.

For dinner Georgia and Jenn had brought a can of vegetarian chili and a bag of Dr. Bronner's Corn and Sesame Chips. Jon pulled two beets from the garden. It made for a wonderful dinner.

"What's our spirit guide dining on tonight?"

"Oh, Kolohe? Friskies. Dry crunchies but I mix it with warm water. It makes a gravy. I learned that trick from Kathleen."

As Jon came back upstairs, Georgia said, "Jon, you were saying you like to write. Do you have something we can read?"

"Ah, I guess I could dig up something. I don't really have much that's good." Jon took the kerosene lamp from the table and went to his room. "Let me see."

Blue had brought Jon an old desk. Jon loved having a desk. During the day he would sit at his desk looking out the window, drawing and writing. Jon began to paw through one of the drawers. Jenn used Georgia's umbrella and went to the car. She returned with a long cloth bag.

"What's that?" Jon asked as he returned to the table.

Jenn eased an unusually shaped musical instrument out of the bag. "Show and tell night," she said. "It's a dulcimer. Have you seen one before?"

"No. I don't think so. It's cool looking. And the cloth on this bag is amazing."

"Handmade fabric from Peru. I sewed it for my baby."

"Jenn plays really well," Georgia said.

"I'm a little rusty. This weather messes with the tuning." Jenn laid the instrument across her lap, strumming and plucking, and stopping to tune.

"Very cool."

"Let's see your writing, Jon. I'll get back to this in a bit."

"Okay. This one is a short story. I don't know if you want to take the time to read it. It's like eight or nine pages."

"I'll read it to myself," Georgia said, "while you check out the other stuff."

"Some of these are just random thoughts," Jon said.

Be unattached to words
and thoughts
which you call your own.

He rifled through scraps of papers, pulling another from the pile. "One time I bought a concrete statue at the flea market—a mythical creature playing a hand-held flute type thing. Very cool. He was around two feet tall. I gave it to my sister and wrote this to go with it."

> *I hear say, in days of old,*
> *trolls and fairy folk*
> *did these hills rove,*
> *and I do believe*
> *in yonder garden,*
> *one does sleep,*
> *as dawn's first light*
> *did catch him,*
> *and he,*
> *in stone did freeze.*

Jenn clapped her hands a little. Jon grinned and shuffled his papers some more.

"This is kind of a funny story. I wrote this while I was camping for three weeks in Waipi'o Valley, on the Big Island."

Coming on to midday, of the second day, in a six day fast. Hiking to the store for to mail some letters, get some popcorn (for later) and some matches. Hippies along the trail.

Raisins?

Oh, ah, no thank you.

Hey wild tomatoes alongside the road. What do you know? Nah, I'm fasting. Hmm, four more days, awreet. Fasting all the way to the store. Let's see now, popcorn, yep here. What else? Hippy:

Hey lady this bag of Bronner Chips is open.

Boy those sure would be good. Hmm, hey look, ice cream. Fuck it, I'm getting some. OK, strawberry sundae, ice cream sandwich. Guess I don't really need popcorn, put it back. Ah, Bronner Chips. This ought to do it. Outside store, not fasting, munch munch. Hmm. Think I'll cruise down to the Natural Foods store. Um boy, I'll have an avocado and cheese sandwich with a large carrot juice.

Ok, is that all now?

Well, all except one of the oatmeal cookies. Thank you. Welp, might as well stick out my thumb, can't walk far in this condition. Hey a ride. All the way. Okay thanks. Would you like a beer?

Well, hey, Millers, my favorite, I sure would, thanks. Up the trail very slowly. Well I guess tomorrow's another day.

Moral: Why be attached to food?

Why be attached to fasting?

"Kind of silly, I know," Jon said.

"No. I like it. It's funny."

"Here's another . . ."

> *She was cloaked*
> *in mystery*
> *beneath layers*
> *of illusion,*
> *secrets untold,*
> *a timeless pyramid,*
> *coyly glimpsed*
> *through the early morning mist*
> *that blankets the Nile.*
> *Into the dawn,*
> *she came riding*
> *on a white Arabian,*
> *past ghost-like images*
> *of windblown tents*
> *that cover*
> *the shifting sands*
> *of time.*

"Here's one I wrote for a friend of mine—my surfing buddy, Mark. We were pretty crazy. The reference to holding hands and skating on the ice—we used to go to this ice-skating rink, in seventh grade. When it was couples only on the ice, we didn't want to hang out waiting, so we would skate together. It's called 'How We Loved to Ride the Waves.'"

friends of the long years
we've grown as brothers
and though now we live
with many miles between us
how I love to share
this world with you.

I remember skating on the ice
holding hands and laughing
and how we drank
and rambled about the night.

many a sunrise morning
along the blue pacific
we walked across the sand
and rode the waves to shore.

when so high and alone
our thoughts we did share
many times, laughing
and in wonder
of this life so strange.

seasons come to go
the moons change
life I see in the living trees
is the life that moves through you
and all things.

the clouds they dance
a ballet so rare and beautiful
seeing these things
I feel much joy.

"Ah, that's sweet. Friendship is important," Jenn said.

"Here's one more," Jon said. "I was living in the Bay Area and reading a lot of fairy tales at the time."

Clouds of white,
rain washed night,
fade away with
dawns first light.

elfin queens upon
river roads,
fruits, nuts,
heavy loads
of silver stars
and precious stones.

dancing waters
deep, twilight clear,
fairy children singing,
voices golden
drifting near.

On, on, on
the river long,
as leaves gently spin
a melody soft
of whispered wind.

"Nice Jon. Very nice. I like what you do with rhyme."

"I've always liked that one."

"Have you heard that song on the radio—*Poetry Man?*" Jenn asked.

"No."

"Jon, you are the poetry man. You make it all rhyme. You're the poetry man, brother."

Jon smiled.

"I like your Joshua the woodcarver story," Georgia said handing it back to Jon. "Jenn, play us something on your dulcimer."

Jenn began to play. It sounded like a cross between a guitar, banjo, and mandolin. After two songs, Georgia went to the living room and began to play on the piano backboard.

"Jon, come on," she urged. Jon joined Georgia. The piano backboard was big enough to easily accommodate them both even if they had no clue as to what they were doing. The "music" merged with the increasing tempo of the rain. Georgia and Jon soon grew tired and rejoined Jenn, who was still playing the dulcimer. They listened as she transported them across time and space. When she stopped, they sat listening to the rain.

"It was such a lovely day," Georgia said.

"It really was an amazing day," Jenn added.

Jon looked at the girls. "Amen."

They all retired to their own bedrooms. As Jon lay on his bed, he just barely heard a voice from the other room.

"Good night, poetry man."

20 | DOG GONE

Sitting on the step, facing the house, Jon was painting. The door was screen on top and wood on the bottom. Jon had begun by tracing a circle using a plastic dinner plate on the wooden panel; he was now painting inside the circle. It was a simple scene of sky, clouds, and mountains. No rainbows, no waterfalls, no unicorns. Jon mixed his oil paints on a piece of cardboard that lay beside him. He turned when he heard a car stop. A man around Jon's age came down the walk.

"Are you Jon?" he asked, extending his hand. "I'm Sean. I'm one of the hui."

"Yep. Sure, I've heard of you."

Kolohe came up behind Sean to give him a sniff.

"Well hello there."

"That's Kolohe."

Sean turned back to Jon. "I haven't been back here since we bought the place. I love Hāna. I want to come more often. I've been on the *mad-land* selling puka shell necklaces and other things," Sean said, his voice trailing off.

His tone made Jon curious as to what the *other things* were.

"That's looking good. Is that acrylics?"

"Thanks, its oils. Hey, come on in."

Jon sat in the dining room. Sean was examining the books on the bookshelf. He was clean shaven, square jawed, with short blonde hair combed straight back. He looked like a jock.

"Have you read all of these?"

"Uh-huh. Lots of reading time out here."

"What's the Findhorn Garden? I'd like to read about it. Can I borrow this one?"

"Sure. It's a place in Scotland. They communicate with devas; nature spirits. They grow these amazing gardens with forty-pound cabbages and what-not. Pretty interesting."

"There must be a lot of nature spirits out here, the way everything grows."

"No doubt. You can cut branches off a tree, throw them in a pile, and they keep growing. Plants have strong wills to live. If there's any way to survive, they will. And then there's all that rain."

"So, you like to grow things?"

Jon nodded. "I'm a gardener."

"I'll be straight up with you. Every year we have a balloon payment on the property here. It's hard to put the cash together. You know how it is." Sean paused, "I know we just met and all, but I have a proposition for you."

"Shoot."

"How about we grow some pakalōlō? Just me and you. None of the other hui have to know. It's better if no one else knows."

"Hmm, maybe. I don't have any money for fertilizer or anything."

"I can cover our startup cost. Grow bags, fertilizer, whatever we need. I've got seeds too. I've been told that this is the start of long season so the plants will get big. I can sell it on Oʻahu. I know a lot of people. Maui Wowie is in demand. I can help us get set up, and then I'll be going back and forth between here and there. You'll keep an eye on the plants. What do you think? Sound good?"

"It could work."

"We'll split everything we make, half-half. Fifty-fifty."

"Let's do it." The two men shook on it.

Sean stayed the night, leaving the next morning and promising to be back in a week. As he was taking off, he hung his head out of the car window, shouting, "Talk to those pot devas."

Jon took the promise with a grain of salt. *People say a lot of things.* He was surprised, a week later, to see Sean pulling into the driveway in a rented van.

Sean opened the side door of the van. Jon was amused. *Damn. This guy is serious.* The van was packed. Most of the space was taken up by large commercial-sized bags of vermiculite. The bags were five feet tall and two feet wide. Vermiculite is a lightweight granule that can be mixed with soil to improve aeration and drainage.

"Wow," Jon said, grinning and shaking his head.

"You like?"

"Yes, I like. Looks good, man."

"Let's get this unloaded and go find a spot."

As they unloaded Jon discovered more treasure including several bags of time-release triple sixteen fertilizer, rock phosphate, dolomite, and bone meal. Also, a new shovel, some clear plastic, a camouflage tarp, peat pellets for the seedlings, and slug bait.

Once the supplies were stashed under the house and covered with the tarp, the two headed down the property trail. They carried Jon's machete and bow saw. Kolohe followed. Not far down, they left the trail. The foliage was thick.

"Careful," Jon said, "we don't want to leave any signs that we've been through here."

They picked a spot just thirty feet off the trail. The area was populated with ferns and inkberry trees. They began clearing, placing the cut trees this way and that and along the edges of the patch. The small side branches of the inkberry trees were easily cut off with the machete. Kolohe lay in the shade. At first, he was concerned at all of the chopping and activity, but after a short while he relaxed and took a nap. Both men were soon covered in sweat and had clouds of mosquitoes following them as they moved about. They cleared an irregular area approximately twenty-by-thirty feet.

The weather was holding, with the sun ducking in and out of the clouds. After lunch they began to shuttle supplies to the site. Kolohe shadowed the men on their many trips back and forth. In a stroke of good fortune, their spot contained a bank of black cinders. Jon dug into it, creating a pit which they used to mix the cinders and vermiculite. They began to fill the grow bags. The plastic grow bags were a six-gallon size. Jon added the fertilizer and other ingredients, layering them throughout. The filled bags were placed throughout the cleared area.

"This triple sixteen is a chemical fertilizer. It's strong. It will be interesting to see how the plants do. Good thing it's time release," Jon said.

The next day they were back at it. Some of the bags of vermiculite had gotten wet from the night's rain even though they were covered with the tarp. The bags were paper, and tore easily when wet. They used those first.

"That's about it for this patch," Jon said.

"How many we got?"

Jon started counting.

"Forty-five, forty-six, forty-seven. Three more and we have fifty."

"Let's do three more."

They built a small three feet high lean-to using thin inkberry trees and clear plastic. This would be the nursery. Sean had bought some plastic trays to set the peat pellets in, and some Miracle Gro to give the seedlings a kickstart.

"Let's get this one going," Sean said, "and then we can find another spot or two."

Sean left Jon with seeds. Jon picked out the larger ones and sprouted them, as his friend Eddie had instructed him, in a damp paper towel. He had never used peat pellets before. They started as a quarter inch compressed disk, and when soaked in water they expanded to two inches tall, their shape contained by a thin nylon webbing. They were made from peat moss and were perfect, once hydrated, for young seedlings. He watched them carefully. Once the plants were two- or three-inches tall, he began using the Miracle Gro. The plants became strong, green, and healthy. Soon, small white roots were poking out from the sides and bottom of the peat pellets, and Jon began placing them in their permanent homes. Dead slugs littered the ground where Jon had spread the slug bait.

It was three weeks before Sean returned. He brought a battery powered radio for Jon.

"Not sure what kind of reception you'll get out here. Hopefully something."

As it turned out, there was a radio station broadcasting from Hilo on the Big Island that Jon could pick up at night. The DJ was named Thor and he played acid rock music. Not Jon's favorite.

Sean was pleased to see how well the plants were growing. Jon had also started working on another patch. It was much harder than the first one. Jon had to scrape what soil he could find beneath nearby mango and kukui nut trees. There were no cinders here to mix with the vermiculite. The patch held twenty plants.

Sean was outgoing and social. Through him, Jon began to get to know some of the "local" boys better. When Sean was in town, they would stop by for a beer.

"Jon, this is Sandy, he lives in Lower Nāhiku."

"Hey man."

Sandy was a barrel-chested blonde haired surfer dude. He was born and raised in Hawai'i. His mother lived in Ha'ikū.

"I like that truck," Sean said.

"She go," Sandy replied. He was driving a full-sized four-wheel drive pickup truck. It had two surfboards strapped on the lumber rack.

"I want to get a beater to use when I'm here," Sean said.

"Honomanū Bay was cranking this morning, out on the point," Sandy said. "It was four to six and pretty smooth. I was stoked. Caught it early. Jon, do you surf?"

"I used to, in San Diego, but it's been a while."

"You're welcome to come along sometime. That place can be a little spooky out there by yourself, if you know what I mean. The men in the black suits. You're no longer at the top of the food chain." Sandy finished his beer. "Alright gentlemen, mahalo. I'm gonna hele."

Soon after Sandy left, Sean suggested they visit Skip, down the road. Kolohe came along but stopped near the entrance to Skip's driveway.

"Skip," Sean called out.

"Up here in the kitchen."

The kitchen was up some outside stairs.

"What's up?" Skip said. "This is my good friend, Nainoa."

"Hey."

"Nice to meet you."

"These guys bought the place next door. It's a hui," Skip explained.

"Nainoa and I went to school together on O'ahu."

Nainoa nodded.

Skip's wife, Kim, came up the stairs. "Hey guys. Hi Jon. Do you want some homemade guava juice?" she asked. "We have a new blender. I throw the whole guava in, seeds and all."

"She grind 'um," Skip added.

"It's good, 'ono," Nainoa attested.

After serving Jon and Sean fresh juice, Kim went downstairs.

"Nainoa is training as part of the crew for Hōkūle'a, the Hawaiian sailing canoe," Skip said. "He's a great waterman."

Looking at Skip, Nainoa smiled and said, "The Hōkūle'a is going to sail from Hawai'i to Tahiti and back again. That's about two thousand six hundred miles, one way. We'll be using old-school navigation. The stars, currents, and wind."

"That's so cool," Jon said.

"Are you the navigator?" Sean asked.

"No. That will be Mau Piailug. He's from Micronesia. Mau is one of only a handful of traditional navigators in the world."

"When do you leave?"

"The Hōkūle'a leaves Honolua Bay next month. I've been assigned to the return trip, so I'll be sailing from Tahiti to Hawai'i."

"What an honor," Sean said.

"It is. It truly is."

"Honolua Bay," Jon mumbled to himself. "I've heard," Jon said, "that *Nāhiku* is Hawaiian for Venus, the evening star or morning star, or whatever it is. Is that true?"

"*Nāhiku* actually refers to the Big Dipper. It's important in navigation because the Big Dipper rotates around the North Star, and one of the sides of the Dipper points to the North Star. The North Star is stationary and sits directly over the North Pole. Even though the Big Dipper moves, it always maintains its relationship to the North Star. So, it makes for an easy way to find the North Star. Of course, you can't see the North Star once you sail south of the equator." Nainoa laughed. "That's your lesson for today, boys. As far as *Nāhiku* as the name of a place, I'm not sure. It's quite possible the word has other meanings. Cleared that up, yeah?"

Everyone laughed. Jon liked Nainoa. He had a calm and deliberate manner about him.

When Jon and Sean headed home, Kolohe appeared out of nowhere and joined them. Sean stayed in Nāhiku a few more days.

After he left, Jon fell into a routine. He'd slip down the trail in the early morning to check on the plants, unless it was raining. The pakalōlō was thriving. He set up a third patch. This one was the smallest, with only twelve plants. It was closer to the house. Jon, on hands and knees, burrowed through thick ferns to create a secret access.

One afternoon, having just gotten home from hitchhiking into Hāna, Jon called for his four-legged friend. "Kolohe." Jon walked downstairs. "Ko." Kolohe was nowhere to be found. It was unusual that he wasn't right there. "Ko?"

Jon walked up and down the road, in both directions, calling his name. No luck. He made *LOST DOG* signs and posted them along the road. Without a phone, the only contact information he had was the number on his mailbox and his post office box in Hāna.

Kolohe wasn't lost. Jon knew that something had happened, he just didn't know what. It was a helpless feeling. That night, it rained. He had a restless sleep. The morning came and still nothing.

Kolohe loves to go for rides. He would jump in with anyone for a ride. Jon sighed. *Maybe his old owners from Nāpili drove by, saw him, and picked him up.* Jon knew that Kathleen had adopted Ko from the neighborhood dog pack, or more accurately, he had adopted her. *He still might show up.*

Jon pushed darker thoughts to the back of his mind.

He posted notices on the bulletin boards at Hasegawa Store and the Hāna Ranch Store. The rain from the night before had ruined the signs he had placed on the road. When he got home, he made new ones.

The days passed. One week, two, then three. Still no sign of Kolohe.

Below the house, the top of a large banyan tree could be seen. Jon had thought someday he would climb it. Today was the day. It was a perfect climbing tree, with a multitude of branches. He slowly made his way up, higher and higher. He held on tight while looking for his next foothold. He stopped near the top, seventy-five feet above the ground. The tops of the forest trees were moving gently with the wind. Standing on a branch, his eyes scanned the ocean and clouds in the distance.

He heard voices. Someone was at the house. He eased his way down the tree.

As he neared the house, Blue and Judy's boxer, Molly, came running up to him.

"Hey Molly."

Blue and Judy had stopped by. They had their two boys with them and Judy's older sister, Rebecca.

"Howzit Jon," Blue called out. He was in the yard having a beer and smoking a cigarette. "Where's your pooch?"

Jon explained the situation. "It's been around three weeks."

"Bummer. I swear I saw him in Lahaina the other day."

Judy came downstairs followed by her sister. Judy was wearing bell-bottom jeans and a crocheted bikini top.

"Maybe he'll show up," she said.

"I sure hope so."

"How's that desk I brought you working out?"

"I love it, Blue. Having a desk is great. Thank you."

"Jon," Judy said, "this is my sister Rebecca."

"Hi. Where do you live?"

"San Rafael, in the Bay Area. On the other side of the Golden Gate Bridge from the city.

Rebecca was thin and had shoulder-length dark brown hair. She was an ex-airline stewardess, now a teacher. Rebecca was Judy's older sister, just a bit older than Jon.

"Jon is there somewhere, nearby, where we can hike to the top of a waterfall?" Rebecca asked. "That's a view I want to experience."

"I know one we could get to," he replied. "Although the stream may not be running. It's been drier this week."

"That's okay. Can we go see?"

Jon led the way down the property. He veered off the trail and they made their way through the brush until they reached the streambed. It was dry except for some pockets of standing water. They walked on the water worn rock to the edge of the top of the waterfall, which didn't currently exist. It was a long way down. Jon stayed away from the edge.

"It must really be something when it's running. Shall we sit for a bit?" she said. "There's a grassy area on the bank."

They sat and talked. Jon noticed she was extra-friendly, but it wasn't until a year and a half later she revealed to him that she had ulterior motives at that first meeting. Those intentions went right over his head. After a while, she assumed he just wasn't interested, and they hiked back to the house.

"Jon, how about a beer?" Blue asked.

"Sure. Thanks."

If Blue wasn't working or surfing Nāpili Point or Shark Pit, he was drinking beer.

"Did you hear Kat-guys have to move out of the Nāpili house?" Judy asked. "The property sold to a developer who is going to tear down the house and build a big hotel. They have a month to find a new place.

"Oh, no. That's such a great spot. Things are changing."

They talked about the tight housing market on the island, development and big bucks, then turned to more cheerful things—the weather, the beach, their kids, and their plans for the day.

"We're going all the way back to Nāpili today if you want to catch a ride," Blue offered.

"I am about ready for a break. It's been a while since I was Lahaina side," Jon said.

"Blue," Judy protested, "we don't have a lot of room in the car."

"Ah, yeah . . . that's right. What was I thinking? Sorry man." Blue held up his hands.

"Hey, no problem."

"Nothing personal Jon," Judy said, "we have the kids and Molly, and my sister."

"The dog and my sister," Rebecca said dryly. "That sounds pretty personal."

AFTER HIS COMPANY LEFT, JON WENT to check on his gardens. He made it back to the house at dusk and lit the kerosene lamp and a candle in the gallon glass jar. He walked to his room and from his desk retrieved a drawing tablet, pencil, ruler, and a clear plastic drafting triangle. He returned to the dining room and huddled over the table in the dim light.

For a long time, Jon had held on to an idea. His idea was to create a coloring book. A Maui coloring book. It would have a colorful cover and simple, easy to color line drawings inside. Special places like Haleakalā Crater, Seven Sacred Pools, ʻĪao Needle, plus waterfalls, tropical flowers, and underwater scenes.

Jon could hardly think of Kolohe. It made him so sad to wonder where his sweet friend had gone, and what might have happened to him. And now—even though the dog had always slept outside at night—Jon felt extra alone. *At least I have this,* he thought, looking at the art in front of him. He had several of the drawings finished. This work he kept tucked away in his desk and only brought it out when no one was around.

21 | LAHAINA SIDE

"That sucks when your dog goes missing, Jon. That was a big deal. You must have been heartbroken," Raoul said.

"I was sad. Kolohe was my good friend and companion, you know, out there together, living in the jungle. He was cool. Loved that rascal."

"I like this section of road. Any closer to sea level and you'd be driving in the ocean. What is this area called?"

"Olowalu."

"Is that island Lāna'i?"

"Yep. Lāna'i is the pineapple island. Although I'm not sure there's many pineapples left. Some billionaire dude bought the island."

"Oh yeah. Larry Ellison? Co-founder of Oracle."

"Sounds right."

"You picked pineapples here on Maui back in the day?"

"Maui Pineapple Company. 1969."

"We're old, aren't we?"

"Roger that." Jon reflected. "I guess it beats the alternative."

"Abso-freaking-lutely." Raoul pulled a pouch from his pocket and retrieved a small pipe. "For traveling. You mind?"

"Go ahead."

Raoul had a couple of tokes. "Jon, you want?"

"No. I'm good."

A few miles down the road Jon spoke. "I'm realizing that I have a problem . . . with the writing. This here, the *present*." Jon waved his hands around. "You and me. As soon as I write it, it becomes the past. In the book, it may only be a couple of weeks of time passing. But if it takes me months to write it, it all changes. The present changes. I'm not sure if that's all clear."

"Clear as mud."

"One solution is to pick a time period for the present and stick to it. Or to keep the present time nebulous with no definite historical references."

"Are you saying that this *present* doesn't really exist? I mean, this here, this now." Raoul had a concerned look on his face. "And furthermore, are you insinuating that I'm a fictional character? Someone you've created . . . ? A figment of your imagination?"

"Possibly."

"Can a figure of your imagination do this?" Raoul held up both hands with the middle fingers raised high.

"I don't know. Maybe."

Raoul kept waving his hands in the air, flipping the bird, and looking to see if the cars passing in the other direction were noticing.

"That's not nice."

"You're the writer. Make me stop."

Jon looked out toward the ocean then back to the road. Raoul put his hands down. They rode in silence.

"You know," Raoul said, "you should let me write some of your book. I could spice things up. I'm not getting enough action."

"Action? Even if it is just on paper?"

"Jon, you're creating a world. In a sense it has its own reality."

"I like that—creating a world."

"You should let me contribute. Let me write some."

"We'll see."

"We'll see. Isn't that what you tell a kid instead of just outright telling them *no?*"

Jon shrugged his shoulders.

"I could accidentally knock you out," Raoul teased. "while I'm waving my arms around."

"Accidentally knock me out?"

"Yeah. So, then I'll have to drive from the passenger side of the car and will inadvertently pull off onto an abandoned sugar cane road, only to get lost and drive smack dab into the middle of a high-grade marijuana patch," Raoul took a deep breath, "with tall plants towering over the car—dripping with buds. I'll throw you into the back seat and tear on out of there. There will be buds stuck all over the outside of the car and a band of locals, driving monster trucks, on our tail. I'll give them the shake, losing them in a maze of cane roads. We'll make our way back to the highway where we pick up two hot surfer chicks hitchhiking home from the beach. You'll wake up to a smiling surfer girl. What do you think?"

"I like that last part," Jon smiled. "I can see the disclaimer now . . . *Not suitable for mature audiences.* As I may have said before, you do have a vivid imagination, my friend. I mean, you know, for a fictional character."

"Bastard."

"Here's our turn. It always sneaks up on me." Jon turned onto Front Street.

"So, chief. What's on the agenda?"

"Thought we'd cruise. Take a little break. Not that you've been doing much."

"Brahh. Just correcting your spelling is a full-time job."

"Okay, sorry. I know. I know," he admitted. "I thought later we could have lunch at the Maui Brewing Company."

"Now you're talking."

"Thank you, baby Jesus," Jon said as he found parking next to the Pioneer Inn.

"Have you stayed at the Pioneer Inn?"

"Oh yeah." Jon said. "Location, location, location."

"Samantha."

"What?"

"Oh, ah . . . Samantha. I met a girl named Samantha when I was here in the seventies. Sweet girl. We spent a lot of time in her room here."

"I'll bet you did," Jon said, with a courtesy smile.

"Shall we take a stroll down Front Street?"

"Strolling down memory lane perhaps?"

"Something like that."

"That's one big banyan tree," Raoul said. "Mucho grande."

"It's a big one."

"That's what she said."

"Right."

Just past the Pioneer Inn, they stopped in the open area behind the library. The land here jutted out into the ocean and offered an interesting perspective. A handful of surfers were out riding the reef break adjacent to the harbor entrance. Looking toward Front Street across the water as one would from a boat, Lahaina appeared to be a sleepy seaside village. Picturesque and charming, a slice of paradise. It was a view that had remained unaltered by time. Jon had taken many photos here. He couldn't help himself.

"Great view." Raoul was watching a female surfer stretching next to her surfboard before going in the water. Jon rolled his eyes.

The old storefronts were built shoulder-to-shoulder, and most of the buildings were two stories tall with railed balconies. Along the shoreline were shops and restaurants sitting at the water's edge, their post and pier footings literally in the water. In the distance a rocky point, covered with coconut palms, reached into the ocean. Lahaina town was anchored in a sea of blue against the backdrop of the West Maui Mountains, whose ridges and valleys rose into clouds that crowned the peaks.

"Technicolor," Jon said.

"What?"

"Technicolor. In Kona we get so much *vog* from the volcano that often the sky is brownish. You can't even see the horizon some days. Even the hills can be hidden in the haze. It looks like Los Angeles. Maui is still technicolor."

"Okay. I get it. Is this where the Hari Krishnas served their free meals?"

Jon looked surprised at the question.

"I already read some of the next chapter," Raoul explained.

"Oh, okay. Yeah, it is. They used to set up right over there. And behind us, that grassy area, was a hangout spot at night. Guys would sit around drinking and talking story. It was an interesting mix of characters. That's where we met Clark Carmel, the Major. He was a pilot who flew bombing missions over Vietnam, became disillusioned, and dropped out. He was just sleeping on the beach, not ready to go back to where he was from and face reality. The war was still ongoing. There was a Hawaiian guy, also a vet, who was one of the regulars, always wore a floppy hat. One night I was there with my friend and fellow pinepicker, Jim. There was a good crowd. They took up a collection to buy wine along with some acid. The idea was to put the acid into the wine. We would then pass the jug and everyone would be happy campers. We threw in the few dollars and change we had in our pockets, not really knowing what to expect. After a while they came back with a gallon of Gallo Vin Rose and some LSD. Everyone got some. We never felt any effects from the acid so we didn't know if they even put it in or if whoever had the last gulps spent the night tripping."

"Wild times."

"Indeed."

They walked along Front Street.

A young woman sitting on a low rock wall was playing ukulele and singing. They stopped to listen. She played passionately with her eyes closed. Between songs they chatted. Her name was Grace, and she was from Australia. Grace currently lived in Colorado and worked as a nanny. She was visiting Maui with the family she worked for. On her day off, Grace decided to stretch her wings and do some street performing. Jon threw a couple dollars into her open ukulele case, then he and Raoul continued down the street. They sat on a bench facing the ocean.

"You've lived in the islands a long time. Over forty years, right?" Raoul asked. "Do you consider yourself a local?"

"Not really. I'll always be a haole from the mainland and I'm okay with that. It's different for my kids who were born and raised here. They're not from somewhere else. They're from here. They walk the walk and talk the talk and are more a part of the fabric of life here. I feel blessed to have experienced Hawai'i when I did. A lot has changed. I do envy the closeness of the local families and their extended families. The whole camping at the beach thing. Swimming, fishing, sitting around the campfire playing music and singing. Just being out in nature in such a beautiful place called home. I suppose that's changing with our dependence on technology today, but what a great way to grow up. Even going up the mountain hunting, living off the land. All very cool." He paused. "I didn't have much of an extended family. I only met my grandparents one time, when I was twelve."

"I've never heard you talk so much."

"I know. I kind of have to. Otherwise, it's going to be a very short book."

Raoul laughed and nodded in agreement.

"I did enjoy the time I lived in Lahaina," Jon said.

"Early seventies?"

"Yeah. I had the bicycle shop. Myself, my business partner, his girlfriend, *and* their dog all lived in the shop. We weren't supposed to be living there but there was a parking lot in the back and a rear entrance, so it worked out. We built storage lofts above our work area, and slept there."

"And the dog?"

"Bear? He was mellow, no problem."

"Were these your friends in Hāli'imaile?"

"Actually it was the folks I picked puka shells with, although we did merge with Mike and Shay and took over their spot. I loved it. Every morning I would ride my bike out to Wahikuli beach park for a swim and shower. That's a cold shower, brah. Great way to start the day. Lahaina was mellow in the early morning."

"What happened to the shop?"

"Best laid plans. By the end of the summer, we were over it and bailed. When I think of it, Lahaina was a springboard for me. I made a lot of longtime friends and it was through meeting Kathleen that I ended up living up in Nāhiku."

The sun was now well above the West Maui Mountains and the day was becoming warm.

"Shall we cross over to the shady side?"

They headed back towards the car. Jon showed Raoul where his bicycle shop had been.

"Center of town," Raoul said.

"We had this big entranceway. Great for ventilation and you could walk right in. I painted a mural with our name Lahaina Cyclery over a backdrop of the universe, sky, clouds, and mountains. At the bottom of the painting was the road to Hāna."

"It's bigger than I thought it would be."

"Not bad, yeah? We scavenged weathered wood from the Lahaina dump and built a rustic wall to divide the front from the back of the shop. In the front were the rental bikes. They were these strange folding bikes. We even had a tandem bike that we rented. Also had used bikes for sale. We would buy junkers, fix them up, and sell them. In the back was our workspace, sleeping lofts, a mini fridge, and a hot plate. Our rustic wall had a long horizontal window cut into it, about chest high, so we could see when someone came in. Handy if we were working in the back or smoking a joint. Also, we had some good tunes. My partner would order cassette tapes through the mail, using a fictitious name, and then wouldn't pay for them. He could be a bit of a monkey."

Farther down the street, Jon pointed to a plaque on a shop wall commemorating the location of the Yamamoto Store.

Jon and Raoul sat at the harbor watching the people and boats coming and going, for a bit, then climbed into the rental car and headed north. Jon drove slowly down Front Street. Near the Mala Wharf he turned onto a side street and parked outside of the Lahaina Jodo Mission. Within the Mission compound was a Buddhist temple, a ninety foot tall multitiered pagoda, a heavy temple bell hanging in its own small pavilion, and a twelve foot high Buddha. The grounds in this dry beach area were simple and clean. Jon slipped some money into the donation box at the bottom of the steps that lead up to the platform where the large Buddha has been peacefully sitting since 1968.

"Any stories?" Raoul queried.

"Not really, but . . . when we were pineapple pickers, Paul and I came to a Bon dance here. We were eighteen years old. Not really the kind of dances we were used to. I don't remember much about it except it was crowded. The courtyard here was packed with people."

"So, what is a Bon dance?"

"It's to honor one's ancestors. Incense, lights, music, and dance. Specific choreography. I don't really know that much about it."

As they were leaving Jon nodded across the street to where an old graveyard lay in the sand among the kiawe trees.

Jon took the highway instead of the beach road so they could hit the Maui Brewing Company. Along the way were businesses, shopping areas, and strip malls mixed with condominiums, hotels, and apartments.

"Welcome to Southern California. They've never stopped building in West Maui," Jon lamented.

At the Maui Brewing Company, they settled into a table and ordered a couple of IPAs.

"Buddhists believe in reincarnation, right?"

"Right." Jon said. "As do the Hindus. And, well, Christians, whereas they don't subscribe to reincarnation, they do believe in an afterlife."

"What do you think Jon? Yea or nay?"

"Well . . ."

The waitress brought their lunch. "For you, sir, the fish tacos and for you a veggie burger with fries."

"Thank you."

"This looks good enough to eat."

"Got that right."

"Reincarnation."

"For many years I've been on board with reincarnation, but who knows. Death seems rather permanent. At this point in my life, I'm just hoping for the best." Jon's eyes wandered about the room. He turned back to Raoul. "Good fries. I've been thinking about reincarnation recently. I mean, you know on the one hand, reincarnation kind of lets you put things off. I'll do it later, next time, next life. Whereas if *this is it,* right now, limited-time-offer, then you need to make it count. Time is of the essence."

"With that in mind, Jon, are you going to be wanting another beer?"

22 | ON THE ROAD AGAIN

"Thanks for the ride. Have a nice day."

Jon was standing in front of the famed banyan tree in Lahaina. He walked along Front Street to Kat and Jenn's clothing boutique, Maui Ragtime.

Jenn was surprised to see Jon, and gave him a big hug. "Hey, poetry man. Come over for some fun in the sun?"

"Something like that. Oh, I like that top. It's beautiful. With all that lace, it has built-in air conditioning."

"It's cutwork from Bali. There are a lot of pukas but the embroidered flowers are strategically placed so I probably won't get arrested. Besides, I have on a bra. You see more at the beach. Anyway . . . how about that Kolohe disappearing?"

"Yeeaah." Jon wasn't sure what else to say; his feelings on the matter were too heavy for a casual chat.

"What can you do? Some things we can't control," she said. "Did you hear we have to move? They're going to tear down our Nāpili house and build a big hotel."

"I did hear that. Coconut wireless."

"Just like the song, they're going to pave paradise," she sighed. "Hey, I made you something. I'll be right back." She went upstairs to the sewing loft, and returned with something behind her back. She swung it around and handed it to him proudly—a shoulder bag Jenn had sewn from handmade Peruvian material. "Do you like it?"

"It's beautiful. So cool. Thank you. I love it."

"Good. I thought you might be able to use something like this."

"Absolutely."

"It's almost closing time. I'll be heading to Nāpili in a bit, if you'd like to come with."

Jon hung out in the shop.

"Did you see that lady's boobs?" Jenn asked, referring to a customer who had just left.

"Ah, yeah. Pretty hard to miss."

"I heard it was a silicone job gone bad and that they're hard as rocks." Jon laughed.

"She's one of our regulars."

Jenn took a phone call. "Okay. I'll close up and come right away." She had a concerned look. "Well, we're closing a little early. Paco is going berserk and breaking things at the house. He was gone for a few days. Kathleen and I did some rearranging and moved some of his stuff. Took some of his paintings off the wall. He's upset."

It was getting dark when they pulled up to the house. Elizabeth was standing next to her car in the driveway.

"I called the cops," she said.

"You called the cops?" Jenn repeated calmly.

"I got scared. I didn't know what to do."

"Jon, will you go in?" Jenn asked. "He's mad at me. I don't want to go in there. I'm the last person he wants to see right now. Well, except for maybe Elizabeth."

"Yeah, okay."

"It's been quiet for a while," Elizabeth said. "Jerry's in there too."

Jon found Paco and Jerry sitting at the large round dining room table.

"Hey Paco," Jon said, nodding to Jerry.

"What's up, Jon?" Paco said.

"Not much."

"Can you roll me a joint? I need to smoke a joint." Paco tossed a baggie on the table in front of where Jon was standing. The baggie contained a little pot and some rolling papers.

"Ah," Jon said, "apparently the cops are coming."

"What?"

"I guess Elizabeth called the cops."

"That bitch! I don't care. Roll me a joint."

Jon rolled the joint. Paco smoked. Jerry had a couple of hits. Jon didn't want any.

With pot smoke still lingering in the air, the Maui police drove up. They parked with their headlights and spotlights directed on the house. They began to speak on a bullhorn.

"Come out with your hands in the air," they repeated.

"I'm not going out there. If they want to talk to me, they'll have to come inside." Paco was defiant.

"I'm not going out there," Jon said.

"I'll go," Jerry said. "I'll go talk to them." As Jerry turned to leave, he asked, "Do you think I really need my hands up?"

"Might be a good idea," Jon said.

"I can't believe that bitch called the cops," Paco said, shaking his head and looking across the table at Jon, who was still standing. "Jenn and Kathleen waited until I was gone to move my art out of here. If they don't want my work here, I'll get rid of it. It pissed me off. I lost it. I'm okay now. I'm okay."

Two officers slowly entered the room with their guns drawn. They quickly appraised the situation and holstered their weapons.

"So, what happened here?" one of the officers asked.

"I just got mad, that's all. I'm okay now," Paco said. "Everything is okay."

"What made you so mad? We had a report that you were breaking things."

"I only broke my stuff, my own property."

"The girl said she got hit by some flying debris."

"Sorry about that. That was an accident. I didn't mean for that to happen. I apologize for that."

"Sometimes when folks get mad, things happen that they didn't intend to happen," said one officer.

"We see it all the time," the other officer added. "But you need to watch yourself. You were scaring people."

"Hey, I apologized for that. She doesn't even live here. This is my house, and you are trespassing. You need to leave." Paco was beginning to raise his voice.

The officers looked at each other. "We'll leave when we're ready to leave."

"Paco, you need to mellow out man," Jon said.

Jerry came back in.

"I was breaking my own stuff," Paco repeated. "I don't think that's against the law. Either arrest me or leave."

"Are you going to be causing any more trouble?"

"No. I'm okay now. I just got mad."

"Alright. We're going to go but we don't want to be getting any more phone calls. We don't want to be coming back here."

The cops left.

Paco got up and walked to the studio. As he left the room he said, "Jon, you're just a yes man."

Jon and Jerry were left standing in the dining room. A few minutes later they heard Paco leaving in his Jeep.

"That was crazy," Jerry said. "The cops didn't even mention the pot. I could still smell it when I came back in."

"I know. Maui cops can be cool sometimes."

"Hey some folks I met at the Tree House invited me to come have dinner on their sailboat tomorrow night," Jerry said. "They said I could bring another person. You want to go?"

"Sounds interesting. Sure."

"The boat is anchored offshore. We have to be at the harbor a little before sunset. The guy will pick us up in his dinghy."

"Cool."

"I can borrow my mom's truck. She's off island for a couple of days."

JON MET JERRY AT THE HOUSE the next day. They cruised into Lahaina. Jerry stopped at Nagasako Store in Lahaina for a six-pack of Primo. They parked near Maui Ragtime and walked to the harbor. As they rounded the corner by the library, they heard chanting.

"Hari Krishna, Hari Krishna, Krishna, Krishna, Hari Hari . . ."

They paused. The Hari Krishnas were set up in their usual Friday night spot. There were people sitting on the rock wall next to the ocean and on the grass, eating Indian food.

"They're good cooks," Jerry said. "Good grinds. Spicy but 'ono and the price is right—free. Have you tried it?"

"No, never have. I've seen them, but . . . no."

They continued walking and ran into a girl Jerry knew.

"Hey Connie."

"Hi Jerry."

"Jon, this is Connie. She works at the Tree House with me."

"I'm on my way to work. Just grabbed a shower at the harbor," Connie said. "I'll see you down there?"

"I've got the night off."

Connie looked at Jon seriously and said, "Jerry's the best. He saved my life." Then she waved and turned to keep on walking.

"Hey. You have a good one," Jerry said. As the they walked past the Pioneer Inn, Jon asked, "You saved her life? What was that?"

"Nothing really. She came over from the mainland on a one-way ticket. She didn't have much money, and no place to stay. I told her she could sleep at the restaurant up in the treehouse while she saves up her money. After we close she goes up and crashes. She has to get up early every morning though, and slip out." Jerry shook his head. "I wouldn't want to do it."

Jerry is a good guy when he wants to be, Jon thought.

As they walked onto the dock landing, Jerry motioned towards the water. "This looks like our ride."

Rowing up to the dock was a tanned man with short hair and a neatly trimmed beard.

"Hey Jerry."

"Howard, this is Jon."

"Aloha," Howard smiled. "Watch your step, this thing moves."

They slowly pulled away from the dock. Howard's rowing was steady and even. The harbor receded as they made their way out to where his sailboat was anchored.

"Going to be a good one," Jerry said, looking at the sky.

The setting sun was beginning to touch the clouds with colorful highlights.

"We get a lot of good ones," Howard replied.

Once close to the sailboat, Howard threw a rope to a tall, trim, blonde who quickly tied it off. She was a few years younger than Howard. He held out an oar, and she grabbed the end and pulled the dinghy alongside.

"Hi guys," she said. "I'm Stephanie. Welcome aboard."

Howard gave Jerry and Jon a quick tour, and then they settled in topside.

"All the comforts of home," Stephanie said. "We even have a hot shower."

"That's more than I can say," Jon said.

"I've got to go below and work on dinner," Stephanie said. "Would you like some red wine?"

"Sure," Jon said.

"I brought some beer," Jerry said, holding up the paper bag.

"Great. Would you prefer beer?" she asked.

"Yeah, I'm kind of a beer guy."

"Just relax and enjoy the sunset," she said as she ducked below.

"Stephanie is cooking a mahi-mahi that we caught trolling yesterday. We had a sailing charter and threw some lines out. Sometimes you get lucky. I'm going to go give her a hand."

"Did you see the moon?" Jon asked Jerry, pointing up. It was a half moon, just overhead.

"Oh yeah. There it is."

Jon sipped his wine while enjoying the view. The lights of the town were coming on. He felt a calm that was accentuated by the gentle rocking of the boat. Darkness fell as the last tinges of color faded from the clouds and sky.

"This is a nice contrast compared to last night," Jon said.

"For real," Jerry laughed loudly. "Now that was some drama. Whatever. It's all good. This is nice."

Howard and Stephanie brought the dinner up from the galley.

"Mahalo. This is a treat," Jerry said. "And I didn't have to cook it myself," he chuckled.

"Yes, thank you," Jon added. "One gets a different perspective from out here. It's great."

"The wind is shifting," Howard noted. "It's that time of day."

"Time to eat," Jerry said. "Personally, one of my favorite times of day."

"This fish is delicious."

"Good salad too."

"I made the salad," Howard said between bites. "I had a restaurant in Marina Del Rey, near LA, for five years. It was successful but I got to the point where I was ready to do something else with my life. I sold it."

"I was working for Howard when we started dating," Stephanie said.

"I told Steph that the restaurant had been sold and I would soon be, literally, sailing off into the sunset. I told her that I would love to have her come along. She had three weeks to be ready."

"Well," she smiled, "sailing off to Hawai'i no less. It took some doing but I got it together and was ready to go three weeks later."

"And the rest, as they say, is history." Howard leaned over and gave Stephanie a kiss.

"Are you married, Jon?"

He shook his head to say *no.*

"Girlfriend? Kids?"

He shook his head again. "I had a dog, but . . . ." He stopped. "Sad story."

Stephanie looked at him with sympathy in her eyes. Mercifully, she changed the subject.

"David Crosby's schooner, The Mayan, is anchored out here," Stephanie said.

"David Crosby, like Crosby, Stills, Nash and Young—that David Crosby?" Jerry asked.

"Yep," she said.

"Aren't they the ones who sing the Lahaina song?" Jon asked.

"Oh no. That's Loggins and Messina."

"Shows you what I know."

Howard sang a few of the familiar lyrics.

"I love that," Jon said. "Centipedes and all."

"The Tatoosh, Peter Fonda's ketch, is anchored off Mala Wharf. Beautiful ship."

"Great name."

The evening passed, and soon Howard was ferrying Jerry and Jon back to land.

The next day Jon got an early start. Paco was back. Jon caught a ride into Lahaina with him.

Outside of Lahaina, Paulo and Dawn picked him up. They had Anna with them. Everyone squeezed into the front seat of Paulo's big truck, Anna on Dawn's lap.

"Jon, did you get your hair cut?" Dawn asked.

"I had a dream that I cut my hair then a week later, I did!" Jon said.

"Your cut your own hair?"

"Um-hmm. Took about four inches off."

"Wild. Hey, we're going to Makawao but we can drop you off in Pāʻia and go the back way to Makawao, up Baldwin Ave.," Dawn said. "Right honey?"

"Not a problem. Jon, we're going to be on the mainland for most of next month. Leaving next week. You can hang out at our place if you want. It would be good for us to have someone there."

"I can't stay the whole time."

"That's fine. Come and go."

"Sure, I can do that."

A blue and white airplane was flying overhead. "You see that? Small Cessna," Paulo pointed. "That's the police airplane. That's the Man."

Jon had seen the plane around the island lately. *Hope they're not flying too close to my place.*

He got out in Pāʻia.

"If we don't see you before we leave," Paulo said out the window, "come on out and make yourself at home."

Jon got a ride taking him several miles, then waited forty-five minutes until another car pulled over. Waiting was much less fun without Kolohe at his side.

"Thanks for stopping," Jon said as he got in. The man was older than Jon and had his hair in a braided ponytail. His beard was short and scruffy.

"You live out this way?" he asked.

"Yeah. Out by Hāna."

"My name's Willie."

"Alright. Nice to meet you. I'm Jon."

The road narrowed and began weaving its way to Hāna. "How long you been out here?"

"About two years."

"Sure is beautiful. Hey, you want to smoke a joint?"

"Sure."

Willie pulled a joint out of his shirt pocket. "I twisted this up for the ride. I sometimes keep a joint behind my ear but that's a bad habit. One time I went through the airport with a joint behind my ear. Didn't realize I'd done that until I discovered it later. This stuff isn't all that good but it's all I got," Willie said. "I've already been out in Hāna. They gave us a huge ol' car. Way too big for this narrow road. I drove it back to the airport and switched. Got this one."

The two passed the joint between them.

"You know if there's any good smoke around?"

"Ah, not really," Jon said. "Fairly soon there should be some good stuff."

"That's what I keep hearing."

The road became narrower and the curves more plentiful. The blind corners and sheer cliffs dictated a slow and conscientious drive.

"What do you do?" Jon asked.

"I play music. I have a band. They're here with me on this trip, along with some of my family."

"What's your band called?"

"Willie and Family. We're tight. We're family. Jon, do you play any music?"

"Not really. You know. I have a bamboo flute I play around on and a harmonica. Nothing really. I like to draw and paint."

"An artist. How about radio? Get any radio out here?"

"There is a station I can pick up at night, out of Hilo. They play mostly acid rock. Heavy metal kind of stuff. What kind of music do you guys play?"

"Country."

The road to Hāna continued to snake through Maui's densely forested north coast. "What's this area called?"

"Ke'anae Peninsula."

"Looks like what you'd expect Hawai'i to look like," Willie said. "It's beautiful. It's all about the journey, ain't it?"

"Yeah."

"You know, I would like to get a coconut. Take a coconut or two back to the house where we're staying."

"There're some coconut trees next to where I live. I should be able to rustle up a couple for you. There're usually some good ones."

"Maybe you know a guy named Red? He's renting a house in Hāna. That's where we're staying. We're going to have a little party Saturday night. Play some music. You would be welcome to come."

"Thank you. Yeah, maybe."

They continued winding in and out of valleys and past waterfalls, finally arriving at Jon's house. Jon saw Sandy's truck, and an unfamiliar station wagon.

"Shouldn't take too long, ten or fifteen minutes," Jon said. "Come on in if you want."

"Okay. I'll come in, give me a minute."

Jon went inside.

"Hey Jon," Sandy said.

"Hi guys. Sean, is that your station wagon?"

"Yep. Wheels brah. And check this out."

There was a telephone on the wall.

"What? No way. Does it work?"

"Oh yeah. It works."

"Far out. Right now I'm going to find a couple of coconuts for the guy who gave me a ride. He'll probably come in," Jon said, slipping on his rubber boots.

Jon tromped through the brush next to the house. The coconut palms were close. Jon began picking up coconuts and shaking them. He found two with plenty of coconut water and dry around the top. From the house he heard voices and laughter. Apparently Willie had come in, and they were all getting along just fine.

Recently Skip had shown Jon how to husk a dry coconut. Previously Jon had used his machete, which did not work well, took precious time, and was dangerous. Skip showed Jon how to use leverage. At Skip's place, a metal spike was driven into the ground. The husk of the coconut was jammed onto it, then twisted—tearing off large sections of husk at a time. Quick and easy. In lieu of a spike, Jon used a pick imbedded in the ground, with the pointed end up. It worked well. Jon was thankful for the tip. Being a dumb haole wasn't always easy.

Willie was happy to receive his husked coconuts and continued on his way.

"Do you know who that was?" Sean asked Jon.

"Yeah, he told me his name. Willie."

Sean and Sandy looked at each other in astonishment. They laughed.

"That's Willie Nelson. He's the number one country singer in the country," Sean said.

"In the world," Sandy added.

"He's like really famous."

"That's cool," Jon said. "Nice guy."

"You're hopeless," Sandy said.

"Sandy is going to try to hook him up with some good da kine."

SEAN STAYED A COUPLE MORE DAYS.

Standing in their big patch, they marveled at how well the plants were growing, now dark green and head high.

"The days are getting shorter. It won't be long before they start declaring, male or female," Sean said. "Probably get some hermaphrodites. Got to pull those too."

"Yeah, I know. Sensimilla. I'll keep an eye on them."

"Can you dry it in the attic?"

"I checked it out. It's really hot up there when the sun's out. I dried some leaf. Nothing to write home about but it should work fine."

"It's going to get better and better."

"Sean, look here. I pinched the ends on these ones, and they've doubled. That was a good idea."

"Fantastic, man. The more the merrier," Sean said. "And now I can call and let you know when I'm coming. This trip I'm flying out of Kahului so I'm going to drop my car at Jaime's, in Pukalani. You know Jaime yeah? Next trip I'll try to fly out of Hāna so I can leave you the station wagon."

JON SPENT MUCH OF THE NEXT month at Paulo and Dawn's shack in Kīpahulu. He happily embraced the chance to experience this remote area of Maui that he had long cherished for its magnificent natural beauty.

They had left some oatmeal, brown rice, tahini, and spaghetti noodles. Their stove was similar to his, a Coleman white gas camp stove. They also had a white gas lantern. It was bright but noisy. Jon didn't use it.

The outhouse experience was quite different here. At home the out-house was tucked away, down a walk and surrounded by plants and trees. Paulo's outhouse was a toilet sitting on a grassy hillside looking out to the ocean. The toilet was mounted on plywood that covered the hole. After seeing Paulo's questionable carpentry skills on display in his shack, Jon didn't fully trust the plywood. He envisioned the whole thing collapsing, so was always glad to walk away unscathed. One good thing though—no mosquitoes.

Jon read, worked on some small paintings, and explored the area. He walked along the road. One direction took you to the Seven Sacred Pools and the other direction wound through luxuriant jungle, past waterfalls, and spectacular vistas. It was a win/win either way. There was little traffic. The morning walks were peaceful. It was just Jon and the birds. He stood on old one-lane concrete bridges where streams hurried underneath and fell away dramatically.

The cabin faced the east. The sun rose directly from the ocean in beautiful sunrise colors. The mountaintops of the Big Island were often visible to the southeast. All Jon saw was ocean. He didn't know where his life was headed, or who he was meant to travel alongside. But with the sun, clouds, rain, and at night, the stars, all floating towards him, he felt like he was on the bow of a ship moving through the universe. *Starship Maui.*

23 | ENCHANTED FOREST

Months passed, and the pakalōlō plants grew into small trees. They were six to eight feet high and fat with buds. It was a veritable forest.

The male plants along with the hermaphrodites had been culled. Sometimes Jon discovered them only after the small pods of pollen were open and comingling with the "girls." Some of the plants would bear seeds.

He scanned the patch with satisfaction. He was hunting grasshoppers. The marijuana-munching critters had become the enemy. These jungle grasshoppers were bright green and large, different from the big brown ones he knew as a child, in San Diego. When he found a grasshopper in the patch, Jon would quickly grab the offender between his thumb and forefinger, violently throw them to the ground and step on them. He did not relish the job. Once they were onto the fact that he was stalking them, they would fly to the other side of the patch upon his approach. Jon chased them from side to side. He wondered about the cognitive abilities of these insects. It seemed to be more than fight-or-flight. They had lives.

Another insect pest he looked for were the small green caterpillars. Their presence was indicated by areas where the buds and leaves were stuck together. Jon separated the matted bud to find them. Left unchecked, they would ruin a section of bud. He wasn't sure what flying insect, moth, or butterfly was responsible.

He cut several fat buds and set them into a well-worn paper grocery bag.

The work that they had put in was beginning to pay dividends in terms of money and some good smoke. Sean had made several trips back and forth to O'ahu. It was good, as Jon had hit bottom financially and had been flat broke for over a month. It felt good to have a few hundred dollar bills in his desk, and a stash.

For three months Jon had been receiving food stamps. He didn't like reporting to the government for a handout. He told his caseworker that he had sold some paintings and no longer needed the food stamps.

Back at the house, Jon trimmed the buds. When trimmed fresh, the leaves would shrink into the bud as it dried. It made for an attractive product. One could of course trim the leaves after the bud dried. It made them a little heavier, but the presentation wasn't as nice. His secret drying area was accessible through the middle bedroom. He removed the sheets and blankets Kathleen had left on the built-in corner shelves. Using a dining room chair, he climbed the shelves, reaching to the ceiling to open the attic access. He hoisted himself up and in. Inside the attic there was just enough room to sit up. It was hot and humid up there. A pungent earthy odor filled the still air.

He reached for the flashlight he had left. There were miscellaneous piles of leaf that filled shallow cardboard boxes. Buds hung like laundry from a string line tacked along the bottom of the rafters. He dumped his bag of goods onto a piece of cardboard and found places for the newcomers. On sunny days the leaf dried quickly. The buds, depending on their size, would take three or four days. Prolonged rain told a different story.

Jon was sweating as he climbed down into the bedroom. He carefully replaced the blankets and sheets onto the corner shelf. The phone rang.

"Hello?"

"Aloha, poetry man." It was Jenn. "How are ya? Getting any rain?"

"I'm good. We're always getting some rain. If it goes a week without rain here, people start talking drought."

"We're going up to Polipoli Park this Friday night. Would you like to come along? You can meet my traveling companion, Daniel. He's the one I traveled with in South America."

"I heard he was coming and I would love to see Polipoli again. I stayed overnight in the cabin, with some friends, three or four years ago. There's an awesome forest up there."

"Danny's brother and sister are here too, so they'll be coming. Danny's got a big truck but some of us will have to ride in the back. I have to work Friday morning, so we'll be leaving in the afternoon," Jenn said. "You know we're in Spreckelsville now, yeah?"

"Kathleen showed me where the house is. I'll hitchhike over Friday morning. Ah . . . what day is it today?"

"Wednesday. Jon, you've been in the jungle too long."

"Yeah, maybe."

"Do you know what month it is?" she asked.

"The month? Sure I know what month it is. It's . . . I'm thinking October."

"Right."

"1976."

"Very good. I'm just giving you a hard time."

"I know."

"Okay sweetie. See you then."

On Friday morning Jon hitchhiked to Spreckelsville. After being dropped off on the highway, he walked the beach road to the house. It was a half mile in.

The house was on Campbell Estate property and had a fancy six foot high metal fence fronting the road. There were several other homes within the compound. They were near the ocean but also close to the Kahului airport. Commercial airlines could be heard arriving and departing, with jets roaring overhead.

Jenn introduced Jon to her boyfriend, Daniel, his younger brother David, and his sister Elaine. Daniel was an ex-gymnast. He had a compact body, short dark hair, and a neatly trimmed beard. David was in his early twenties, and leaner than his brother. Elaine was the baby of the family. She graduated early from high school and was now studying at UC Berkeley.

They were soon on their way, Daniel and Jenn in the cab of the truck and Jon, David, and Elaine in the bed. They sat with their backs against the cab. Driving past Pukalani and through Kula they came to the Polipoli access road. It was narrow, one lane, and the pavement quickly turned to dirt as it snaked up the mountain in a series of switchbacks. Many sections of road were rutted and gouged from erosion. Slowly they crossed several cattle guards that were flanked by old rock walls. It would be a long ten miles to the cabin. The landscape was arid, punctuated by fields of tall grass, scrub brush, and scattered small trees. As they climbed, they caught sweeping views. The West Maui Mountains loomed in the distance. Below, poised on the blue Pacific, were the islands of Kaho'olawe, the small crescent-shaped Molokini, and farther, Lāna'i. Each turn pointed them in a different direction and offered a new vista. Around one corner they glimpsed a beautiful pheasant as it scampered into the grass. The western sky began to display vibrant sunset colors. Elaine suddenly pointed towards the mountain. Jon looked and was surprised to see the full moon rising over the ridge of Haleakalā. The moon was huge.

"You see the moon?" Jenn shouted from the cab.

Everyone looked from the setting sun in the west to the moon rising in the east.

Jon felt strangely connected to the universe. *Unreal.*

The air was becoming cooler. Jon noticed thick clouds ahead, hugging the mountain. Soon they entered the cloud bank. Maui and the world around them suddenly disappeared in the mist. Daniel stopped so Elaine could climb into the front. Jon put on his long-sleeved flannel shirt.

"I don't think it's much farther," Jenn shouted out her window.

"We're okay," David answered.

Jon unrolled his sleeping bag and he and David draped it over their legs.

They emerged from the clouds into another world. They were in a mountain forest, surrounded by tall trees. A roadside sign read *ELEVATION 6,400 ft.* Night was closing in fast as they arrived at the cabin. The moon had risen higher and looking west, beyond a carpet of cloud tops, the sunset colors were now muted shades of pastel pinks and purples.

"Magical," Jenn said.

"Truly. How's that moon?"

"Boy, it's nippy up here," Daniel said.

"This doesn't even look like Hawai'i," Elaine commented.

"It's cool, so cool," Jon said, looking around.

"Beyond cool, it's cold," David added.

"Yeah, that too."

"Hon, can you get a fire started?" Jenn asked Jon.

"Oh sure."

The cabin had a cast-iron woodburning stove in the living room. There were Presto logs and a small stack of newspaper beside it. Jon easily got the fire going.

Jenn had brought dinner. Spaghetti, salad, and a side of garlic bread. Jon was thankful she had made a vegetarian marinara sauce and kept the meatballs separate.

"This is really good Jenn," said Elaine.

"Yeah, great. Thank you." Jon said.

"The bread's a little soggy," Jenn admitted, "but overall, pretty good."

"I like the meatballs," said Daniel.

"I knew you would. That's why I made them," Jenn smiled. "So, Jon you've been up here before?"

"Yeah. It was a while ago. I came up with my friend Jeff. Some surfer dudes we knew from high school had rented the cabin. I have a story from that trip. There were six of us, including myself and my friend. We all did our own thing during the day. That evening, as it's getting dark, one of the guys hadn't come back yet. He had gone hiking by himself to spend the day taking photos. It was eventually revealed that he also had taken some acid—LSD."

"The plot thickens," said Daniel.

"It got dark and cold. There wasn't a big moon like tonight. It was totally dark. We drove the roadside, honking, flashing the headlights and calling his name."

"That's a nice fire. Thanks Jon," said Jenn.

"It feels good." Jon continued. "It was decided that a couple of us needed to hike the trail with the Coleman lamp and flashlights to see if we could find him. He certainly wasn't dressed for the cold night. Most of the guys were reluctant to go out because they were afraid of spirits. I couldn't believe it. Anyway, I volunteered to go search, with one other guy. On the trail we could only see a small area directly in front of us. We called his name as we walked. After fifteen minutes on the trail, he answered back. He explained that it had gotten dark before he could reach the cabin. He hiked until he could no longer tell where the path was and just hunkered down. He had been stuffing pine needles into his clothes for insulation from the cold."

"He must have been happy to see you," said Daniel.

"He was."

"That's a good story. I wouldn't want to be lost in this forest." Jenn offered Jon a homemade chocolate-chip cookie.

Jon nodded, and appropriately withheld the other story he recalled from that trip—when two of the surfers were lighting their own farts like mini blowtorches.

"Jon, you will find this interesting," Jenn said. "David is studying yoga in India."

"Far out," Jon said looking over to David. "What kind of yoga is it?"

"It's a comprehensive approach of asana, pranayama, chanting, and meditation. Physical, mental, *and* spiritual."

"Got the bases covered."

"In practice there's an emphasis on the individual. We all have a unique set of conditions, needs, and interests. It's yoga for health, healing, and personal transformation."

"That sounds good." Jon reasoned that knowing what you truly want was an essential part of getting there. *Where am I going? What do I want?*

That night Jon slept in the living room. He placed a mattress from one of the bedrooms on the floor next to the fireplace. He slept well and woke with the dawn. He could just barely see the setting moon through the thick condensation that had formed on the window. He set about to restart the fire, pulling a newspaper from the pile. Before he could crumple it, a headline caught his eye. *Hawaiians Occupy Kaho'olawe.* In the dim light, Jon scanned to the top of the page. It was a newspaper from earlier in the year. Jon read: *Eight Hawaiians occupied the island of Kaho'olawe to protest the Navy's ongoing use of the island as a bombing target. The protesters feel a deep cultural connection with the island and wish to preserve it as a place of spiritual and cultural significance.*

The article contained an eloquent quote from Hawaiian activist and musician George Helm expressing his love of the 'āina. Jon agreed with the sentiment that the Earth is sacred and deserving of our respect and care. Jon recalled seeing flashes of light from the bombs exploding on Kaho'olawe a couple of years back, when he and his friend Jeff were on their way home from dinner at the Silversword Inn, in Kula. It was Saturday, Mexican plate night. Jeff pointed out the distant flashes in the night sky. The image had stayed with Jon. It seemed so wrong to be using a Hawaiian island for bombing practice. He buried the newspaper back into the stack and used another one to start the fire.

THE MORNING WAS CLEAR AND BEAUTIFUL, with the forest birds heralding the new day. After a breakfast of granola and fresh banana, Jon ventured out. Inside his shoulder bag he carried a drawing tablet and charcoal pencils. It wasn't long before he took off his flannel shirt and tied it around his waist.

Polipoli was a cloud forest. The trees were sustained by the frequent afternoon cloud cover. It is said that the area was originally home to thick groves of koa, māmane, and 'ōhi'a, but was devoid of trees at the time of reforestation. Jon assumed the land had been logged and cleared for cattle. Reforested in the 1930s, it now contained dense stands of cypress, cedar, eucalyptus, pine, and even coastal redwood. In the understory there were hydrangea bushes with plate-sized pale pink flowers, and clumps of fuchsias that were as tall as Jon. The fuchsia plants had delicate cascading flowers of hot pink and purple.

Jon stopped at several spots along the way to draw. Coming to an area thick with trees, he looked for a place to sit. A fallen pine bordered the path, but the trunk was covered in moss. The trail here was a thick carpet of pine needles. Jon folded his flannel shirt, placed it on the trail, and sat on it. Filtered sunlight fell softly through the canopy. Everything felt clean and fresh. Jon took several deep breaths. The forest air was sweet and fragrant. He wrote in his drawing tablet beneath one of the sketches:

> *I stopped*
> *without stopping*
> *Sat*
> *without sitting*
> *Breathing in*
> *soft coolness*
> *Nowhere to go.*

He sat quietly, enjoying the surroundings.

"Beep beep."

Jon turned to see Jenn and Daniel coming down the trail.

"Hey Jon," Jenn said. "It's special, isn't it?"

"Yeah."

Jenn, Daniel, and Jon hiked together back to the cabin.

All too soon it was time to head down the hill. Jon asked to be dropped at the Hāli'imaile turn-off, but was happy when Daniel insisted on taking him all the way to his friend's house. It would have been a long walk.

"That was fun," Jon said, jumping out of the back of the truck at Mike and Shays' driveway. "Thanks."

"Sure thing. See you around, brother," Jenn said.

"Bye guys."

Mike was in his driveway, standing with a local guy. They were looking at a shiny souped-up car.

"Jon," Mike said. "This is Lawrence."

"Howzit brah?"

"I'm good. What you guys doing?"

"Lawrence is getting his car pinstriped."

Mike had a small table with his painting supplies. He grabbed a roll of masking tape and ran some strips along the sides and on the hood and trunk.

"The tape is just a visual guide," Mike explained, "I don't actually use it to paint along. Lawrence, I'm going to show you some different possibilities, a sample of different styles. Check them out and tell me which one you want."

Mike painted some pinstripes on the trunk.

"Solid," Lawrence said.

"Freehand," Jon said. "That's amazing."

"There's one," Mike said. "It dries quick. Can't leave it too long. Lacquer paint." Mike soaked a rag in lacquer thinner and wiped the pinstripe off.

Jon and Lawrence were shocked that he would do this as it had looked great.

"Here's another style," Mike said as he started painting.

"That takes a steady hand," Jon said.

"I've been doing this for many years. But, yeah, it does take a steady hand."

"I don't know. They're all good," Lawrence said. "Shoots brah. Let's go with this one."

They were quiet while Mike pinstriped the car. Lawrence drove away happy.

"Main thing is to have the right brush. I got paid two hundred bucks for that," Mike smiled. "Not bad for a half hour's work."

After putting away his painting materials, Mike and Jon went into the house and sat in the living room.

"I brought you something." From his shoulder bag, Jon pulled out a ziplock with bud in it.

"Alright Jon," Mike said. "This is yours? You grew this?"

"Yep."

"It looks good. This for me? It's a good day. Let's try it out."

Shay came home and made dinner, and Jon had a hot shower. The next day he borrowed their bright yellow VW convertible bug to drive to the laundromat in Kahului. He washed his sleeping bag and a few clothes. The laundromat always made for some interesting people-watching, mostly women.

After finishing at the laundromat Jon drove through Kahului. He had the convertible top down to enjoy the beautiful day. As he passed the shopping center and Ah Fook Market, Jon saw, up ahead, a girl hitchhiking. This was right before the road made a 90° turn. Jon was in the left-hand lane. He sped up to pass the car on his right, swerved over to the curb and stopped abruptly in front of her.

She was wearing light blue corduroy short shorts, a white top, a floppy hat, and sunglasses. Her shoulder-length blonde hair was tied back in a ponytail.

"Hi. I'm going to Pā'ia."

"Perfect. I can drop you off."

She got in, carrying a small daypack. Jon started off, and almost immediately pulled over again.

"Short ride," she said.

"Right? I forgot I was going to stop here at Hopaco. Do you mind? Shouldn't take long."

"That's fine. What are you getting here?"

"I'm going to look at the Rapidograph pens, for drawing. Check them out."

"I'd like to look at them too."

"What's your name?"

"Ellen."

"I'm Jon."

"Are you an artist?"

"Mostly I paint but I like to draw too."

"I like to draw," she smiled.

Inside the store Jon said, "They cost more than I thought they would. I'm going to think about it."

Ellen bought a Rapidograph pen, ink, and several tips. No sooner than they had climbed back in the car, they were approached by a young man with a backpack.

"Hey man. I gotta get to the airport. Can you give me a ride? It's not that far. I gotta catch an airplane."

Jon and Ellen looked at each other.

"Please," the young man said, looking desperate.

Ellen said, "It's okay with me if it's okay with you."

"Okay. Hop in."

"Thank you. Thank you so much. I don't want to miss my flight."

Jon and Ellen exchanged glances and smiled at each other.

"The scenic route to Pā'ia," Jon joked.

After dropping the guy off at the airport, they continued toward Pā'ia.

"Nice car."

"I know. It's not mine," Jon explained. "My friends let me borrow it when I come to town."

"Those are some good friends."

"They're really good to me."

"Where do you live?"

"Out near Hāna."

"I haven't been there yet. I want to. I hear it's beautiful."

"It is. Just the drive out there is gorgeous, and out past Hāna is incredible."

"What sign are you?" Ellen asked.

"Taurus. How about you? What sign are you?"

"Scorpio."

"Ah," Jon said. He'd known some Scorpios—intense, passionate people. "Where in Pāʻia are you going?"

"The health food store. I'd like to come to Hāna sometime soon."

"I've got a three-bedroom house, so there's plenty of room if you want to come stay over. I don't own it. I'm the caretaker. Beautiful area though."

"Do you have a phone?" she asked.

"Yeah."

"Give me your number. I'll call to tell you if I'm coming and to get directions. Nice meeting you."

Jon found himself smiling for quite some time after Ellen left the car. He drove up Baldwin Avenue to Hāiliʻimaile and returned the VW, then hitchhiked home to Nāhiku. His last ride was from a young schoolteacher from Seattle driving a rental car. At the house, she came in to see Jon's paintings. As she left she paused in the doorway, looked him in the eye, and told him, "I know right now you're just living it, but someday you'll be somewhere else, doing something else. You'll look back at this period of your life and think—*now that was a special time.*"

24 | KINDRED SPIRITS

"Hello."

"Is this Jon?"

"Yes."

"This is Ellen. Do you know who I am?"

"I picked you up hitchhiking the other day."

"Yes. You remember me. I'd like to come out to Hāna. Can I stay at your house? It will just be for a couple of days."

"Sure that's fine. I have plenty of room."

"I'll be hitchhiking, so I don't know how long it will take to get there."

"No problem. I'll be here."

Jon gave Ellen directions. After hanging up, he went down to care for his marijuana plants. He picked some buds that were ready and brought them up to the house. Jon hung the buds in the attic and bagged some that were dry. Everything would be good for a few days.

Morning turned into afternoon and the afternoon had begun to stretch towards evening. He had all but given up on Ellen when she arrived.

"I wasn't sure if you were going to make it."

"Here I am. I got out at the wrong spot. At the first place I got out there was a driveway, so I walked down to a house. No one was home.

An artist lived there. I looked in one of the windows and there was a painting on an easel that they were working on. But I knew it wasn't your work."

"Really?"

"I just knew. Anyway, then I remembered what you told me about the mile marker numbers starting over and not to get off at the first twenty-two mile marker but to keep going. I think I was just anxious to get here."

"Well, I'm glad you figured it out. Welcome."

"Do you have electricity?" she asked, eyeing the kerosene lamp and candles on the dining room table.

"No. No electricity. You can stay in this end room. It's the nicest one as far as the view goes. Come on, let me show you where the outhouse is. Watch your head on this doorway."

"A two-seater," Ellen said, laughing.

"Yeah. Not sure what that's all about. Lots of mosquitoes down here."

Upstairs they sat at the dining room table.

"I brought my Rapidograph pen." She pulled it out of her small day pack. "Check it out."

Jon opened a drawing tablet that was lying on the table.

"It makes a nice line," he said.

"I like it. This is the best point."

"How long have you been on Maui now?"

"Two months."

"I'm from Maine. Born and raised. How about you?"

"Wow, you're far from home. I'm originally from San Diego. I've been on Maui going on three years, this time. First came over in 1969."

"That's the year I graduated from high school."

"Yeah, me too. Would you like to smoke a joint?"

"Sure."

He rolled a joint. They quietly passed it back and forth.

"I saw a bamboo flute in your room. I have one, but I can't really play it. Do you play?"

"More or less. It takes practice. I couldn't play either, in the beginning."

"Can you play me something?"

"Okay." Jon grabbed his flute from his room.

She watched as he brought the flute to his lips.

"Pressure," he said nervously. He played.

"I'm impressed."

"Thanks. Hey, I should cook us up something to eat. I picked a handful of green beans and two beets. I'll cook some brown rice to go with it."

Darkness fell. They ate by the light of the kerosene lamp and a candle. That night, they slept in their respective bedrooms.

In the morning Jon took Ellen on a papaya run. Along the way, she asked, "What are those flowers? Is that what I smell?"

"Yellow ginger mostly, and some white ginger. They're very fragrant."

Farther down the road, she pointed and asked, "Are those the papayas we're picking?"

"No. That's a private field. Ours are wild ones, and not nearly as nice."

"Does somebody pick them? I see a lot of yellow ones."

"I think so, although I've never seen anyone there."

At the jeep road Jon fetched his papaya picking stick out of the brush.

"Can you eat these berries?"

"Yep. They're good. Thimbleberries."

"They do look like thimbles." She put a berry in her mouth.

Jon was enjoying Ellen's spirit of curiosity. It was fun for him to share his world with someone. He poked a papaya down and caught it.

"You've done this before," she said as he handed her the papaya.

"A few times," he said, smiling.

They returned to the house with their haul. Jon lined the kitchen window sills with papaya. He sliced one open for their breakfast.

"How far is the town of Hāna? I'm going to hitchhike in and check it out."

"About five miles. Do you want company?"

"No, I'm good. I'll be back."

While she was gone, Jon worked around the house and in the garden. He cut a large bunch of Cuban red bananas and hung them beneath the house on a rope.

She returned that afternoon.

"How was Hāna?"

"It's a cute little town. There's even an old movie theater."

"I know. How cool is that?"

"Do you ever go to the movies?" she said as she pulled her hair-tie from her hair, letting her blonde hair fall about her shoulders.

"No, not really. Kind of hard without a car."

"I brought you an orange."

"Thank you. I say we eat it now." Jon started peeling. "Would you like some?"

"Yes, I would." She brushed her hair. "There was this kid, I'm not sure how old, maybe early teens. He's a bit slow. He was standing by the road, selling Aloha Week buttons. He was sweet, and a good salesman."

"Yeah, I've seen him flagging down cars. How much were the buttons?"

"One dollar. I bought two. Then I went down and sat at the bay. I watched people come and go. There were some guys setting up a huge tent. A lady told me it was for the lū'au tomorrow night. Part of Aloha Week."

It began to rain. That evening Jon cooked lentils. Kathleen had left curry powder, which he used for seasoning. He added carrots from the garden. They sat in the soft light of the kerosene lamp and soon retired to their bedrooms. The rain continued off and on throughout the night.

"What a beautiful morning. I slept well, listening to the rain last night," Ellen said, looking out the window. "Oh, looks like someone's here."

Jon looked out. "It's Peter, Georgia's son, and his wife. They live in Huelo."

"Hey guys," Jon said.

"Hey Jon. Is it okay if we stay the night?"

"Yeah, for sure."

As they went to their car, Jon asked Ellen if she would mind moving into the middle room.

"I'll put my stuff in your room," she said. "For now."

"Oh, okay." Sharing space with Ellen was definitely fine with Jon, but he wasn't sure if he should read anything into the situation.

Peter and Pat came in and everyone was introduced. Peter was a big guy, and loud.

"Jon, you got to try this bud I grew. It's the coughing kine," Peter said.

"Coughing kine?"

"If you take a big hit, you can't hold it in. It makes you cough. It's some good shit. Check it out."

They all sat on the floor in the bedroom and smoked a joint. Peter was right, it was the coughing kine.

"Best bud I've ever smoked," Peter said. "Even if I do say so myself."

"It's good," Jon agreed. "Excellent."

Peter and Pat left to go exploring. They were looking for spots, in the area, to grow pot. They returned in two hours. Peter asked Jon about a nearby dirt road that went up the mountain.

"That road goes up to Piggery Sue's place," Jon said.

"We walked up a ways but didn't see a house or anything. How far does it go?"

"I don't really know. Never been up there."

"Jon, you know that little pasture around the corner?" Peter asked. "The cow pies are full of magic mushrooms."

"Oh?"

"We scarfed a bunch but there's still choke."

"We'll have to check that out," Ellen said, looking to Jon.

"We're going into Hāna in a while. There's a rodeo today," Pat said. "If you guys want a ride."

"That would great," Jon said. "Right now we have an appointment with some mushrooms. Shouldn't take long."

"No worries. We'll wait for you," Peter said. "Just don't take too long."

Jon and Ellen walked to the small pasture, climbed through the gate, and ate mushrooms from the cow pies.

"Earthy."

"Umm hmm," Jon said, making a face.

THE RODEO GROUNDS WERE PAST HĀNA, on the Kīpahulu side of town.

"Thanks for the ride, Pete."

"No sweat. We'll see you later, back at the house."

"I brought our Aloha Week buttons," Ellen announced proudly to Jon. The rodeo was free, but one needed to be wearing a button to get in. They both pinned their buttons on their jeans.

Jon and Ellen climbed the grassy hill that overlooked the arena. They sat with their backs against a large rock and surveyed the scene.

Calf roping was in progress. The announcer introduced the riders and standings. Crowds of people filled the bleachers and stood along the fence, close to the action.

"I don't think I've ever seen this many people in Hāna, all in one place," Jon said.

The crowd cheered and clapped for their favorites.

"Are you feeling the mushrooms?" Ellen asked. "I am."

"Yep."

"I have to pee," she said, pointing to the restrooms down below, next to the arena. "Want to come?"

"I'll wait here," Jon said even though he had to pee. Navigating the throng of locals near the arena, while high on mushrooms, was outside of his comfort zone.

He watched Ellen as she made her way down the hillside, moved through the crowd, and disappeared into the bathroom. His eyes alternated between the calf roping and the bathroom door. After a few minutes, Ellen emerged and made her way back to Jon. He watched her. She smiled at him as she approached. They grew tired of the rodeo and left, walking to nearby Koki Beach. The beautiful beach was framed with ironwood trees, with a backdrop of steep cliffs. The stretch of sand was accentuated with rocky outcroppings on either end.

They sat watching the waves and the large graceful sea birds sailing above.

"I love the ocean," she said. "Living in Portland, Maine, we were near the water and always had a small boat of some kind. Portland is a big fishing and boating town."

"When I was little, in San Diego, I would go fishing with my dad in Mission Bay. He says I would curl up in the bow and nap. I surfed for years, too. Junior high and high school. We didn't live on the ocean, but it wasn't far. In college, my dad had a twelve-foot aluminum boat that we could carry on top of the car. It was great. We would cruise around the bay. Good memories."

"San Diego is known for good weather, right?"

"Good weather and nice beaches."

"The Maine coast is rugged, and we get some brutal winters. Bitter cold."

"Snow?"

"Uh-huh."

"Does the snow go all the way to the ocean?"

"Yes. And good luck finding any fresh fruit in winter. I couldn't take it any longer. I mean, it's beautiful and all, but twenty-four years was long enough."

Late in the day, they stood in front of the lū'au tent, at Hāna Bay. The Hawaiian band was warming up and lots of people were going inside.

"Probably not going to be much we want to eat," Jon said. "Ten bucks, that's a lot."

"I've never been to a lū'au, have you?"

"Ah, once. When we were pineapple pickers, we befriended a pig, who we named Arnold. We used to go by on our way to the beach and give him treats. One day he was gone. We thought they must have moved him. After all, his pen was pretty small." He paused. "That night was the lū'au."

"Oh no."

"During the lū'au, one of us figured out that Arnold was the guest of honor."

"Jon, what do you think? Shall we go in?"

The food servers were appalled that Jon and Ellen were accepting so little of the food. Jon had the salad—iceberg lettuce with a token tomato here and there, white rice, and a small tub of poi. Ellen took salad. They carried their paper plates and sat next to each other at the end of one of the long tables. A couple of young haole guys sat across from them.

"Are you on a diet?" the guy across from Ellen asked. "You don't need to be, you look perfect."

"I don't eat meat," she said.

"You're vegetarian and you come to a lū'au? You're missing out. This is really good." He was clean cut, good looking, and confident. He continued to engage her in friendly banter.

Ellen had an ease about her. A natural unpretentious charm. The young man seemed encouraged when she asked him what sign he was. Jon noticed himself growing jealous, and realized that he was becoming attached to Ellen.

As the band turned up their volume, Ellen moved her attention to the stage. The guys across the table spoke amongst themselves. Good at eavesdropping, Jon listened in on the conversation, while looking toward the band. The music was a good cover.

"She's going to come home with me."

"What? Nah."

"Yeah. I can tell. She'll come home with me. I'll bet you ten bucks."

"You're on."

They shook on it.

Jon discretely told Ellen. "He bet his friend ten bucks that you'd be going home with him."

She briefly looked at the guy, then back to Jon. "Sagittarius, not a chance."

Jon smiled. He felt better. After a short while he said, "I'm ready to go. You ready?"

"Yes. Let's go."

Jon felt a certain satisfaction as they walked out. It was dusk and the day was fading. They walked to the corner above the bay and started hitchhiking. Jon stood behind Ellen. He massaged her shoulders.

"That feels good." She moved her hair away from her neck, as if offering it to him. He kissed her there. "You should be careful doing that. That turns me on."

"That's okay with me," he said, as he kissed her again on her neck, and then moved to her ear. She giggled.

"Stop it some more?" Jon laughed.

"Yeah, stop it some more," she said as she turned to give Jon a passionate kiss.

Thanks to all the people in town for the festivities, they caught a ride quickly.

Back at the house, Peter and Pat were in their room playing cards. They had the kerosene lamp. Jon lit a candle and brought it into his room. They climbed onto Jon's sleeping bag, which was unzipped all the way. Jon blew out the candle. It became very dark.

"New moon," Jon said. "Do you always sleep naked?"

"Yeah."

"Me too."

"You like to use your hands, don't you?" she said.

"I work with my hands a lot." He immediately felt stupid for having said that.

"Slow down," she said gently. "Not so fast. Slow down or you're never going to get there."

He had to relax and back off. They fell asleep. The early morning light found the two in each other's arms, making love. They heard Peter and Pat preparing to leave, going back and forth to their car. Jon's bedroom door was open a crack and looked directly onto the bed.

"They can see in. Should I close the door?" he asked. They had no blankets covering them.

"It's okay."

"I should get up and tell them goodbye."

"They're big kids. They'll be fine."

He ignored her advice, kissed her, and got up to tell Peter and Pat goodbye. He assumed she would wait for him in bed but when he returned, she was in the kitchen slicing a papaya.

"It's a nice morning," Jon said. "We can hike down the property to the ocean. There are waterfalls and pools we can swim in. It's a gorgeous area."

"Do I need a swimsuit?"

"Nah."

Before heading out, they smoked a joint.

At Blue Pond, naked, they waded into the cool water.

"Wow. It's beautiful," she exclaimed.

"Yeah, I know, right?"

The waterfall was flowing and the setting magical. They swam underwater and surfaced in the deeper water, next to the waterfall. After getting out they put their clothes on and continued toward the beach.

"That felt good," Ellen said, reaching out and taking Jon's hand. At the ocean, they paused to take it all in. Jon stood behind Ellen with his arms around her. They walked along the shore.

"Do you ever swim in the ocean here?"

"No, I haven't. It's usually pretty rough."

She followed him to Emerald Pond. They sat on the large rocks, taking their shirts off for some sun.

"I hope my tits don't get sunburned, not that I have much to burn."

"You have nice tits."

Thank you."

"If your tits get sunburned, I will personally massage—gently, mind you—some lotion on them."

"That's so thoughtful," she said smiling.

"Hey, even if they don't get sunburned . . ."

They sat quietly, enjoying the ambiance of the waterfall. The sound was mesmerizing and meditative.

That evening they smoked another joint and took turns drawing with Ellen's Rapidograph pen. Jon brought out his coloring book drawings, the ones that were finished, for her to see. They went to bed early, enjoying each other's company.

The next morning Ellen said, "You know what I want? I want to eat thimbleberries."

"We go."

At the jeep road they began to pick berries.

"Here's a big one," she said placing it in his palm.

"Thank you." After a minute he turned to her. "And here's a sweet one for you." He fed her a ripe thimbleberry.

In-between eating berries, she also picked some for later, putting them in a small ziplock. A vehicle was coming up the road—a Willys Jeep with a local man driving. He raised his hand in greeting and stopped next to Jon. He turned the engine off. The man looked to be in his mid-thirties, with dark skin and short curly hair.

"Hello. I'm Bully. I stay down Ulaino Road. Do you live up at the commune?"

"No. We're at the hui house, other side of Skip's. I'm Jon and this is Ellen."

"Oh. Okay. Where your property comes down to Ulaino Road, that's where I live, across from Blue Pond."

"The house in the jungle? The dogs sometimes bark."

"Yes, that's it."

Bully noticed Ellen's ziplock of thimbleberries.

"Those berries make a good jam."

"They're good to just eat fresh, too," she said.

"I'm on my way to work. Do you know the colonel? I'm doing some land clearing for him, for cattle. Bulldozing. Hey, good meeting you folks. Aloha."

"Have a nice day."

The afternoon was wet. Jon and Ellen were housebound.

"Is there a mirror here?"

"Just that one downstairs in the shower."

"You mean that broken one that's half missing, that you can barely see yourself in?"

"That's the one."

"I have a mirror," Ellen said. "A small one. I'm a girl."

"Yes, you are. I like that about you."

"Do you do yoga?" she asked. "Can you bend over and touch the floor?"

"I stretch every now and then."

"Let's see."

He could touch and briefly flatten his palms against the floor.

"Your turn."

She was flexible, and easily pressed her palms flat against the floor.

"Can you stand on your head?" she asked. "It's hard. I can't do it."

"A headstand. I used to be able to. Probably still can. There's a couple different ways."

"Show me."

"Let's go in where there's some carpet and more room."

Paco had brought out a scavenged carpet remnant for Kathleen's room.

"I'll do it against the wall."

"You can't use the wall. No cheating, Jonathan," she said playfully.

"Let me do it against the wall first, then I'll try the middle of the room."

"Okay, but I'm going to tickle you."

That evening, out of the blue Ellen said to Jon, "I've been thinking that I should go get the rest of my stuff in Makawao and move in with you. I don't have much. Would that be okay?"

"That would be more than okay."

"Jason, the guy I'm staying with, spends more time with his pot plants than with me. He probably hasn't even noticed that I'm gone. I can hitch over, stay one night at my girlfriend's, and come back the next day."

Jon was happy Ellen wanted to stay with him. But he was uneasy about one thing—he hadn't told her about his marijuana patches that were now themselves overdue for some attention. He thought it was best not to say anything just yet. While she was gone, he would tend to his crops.

When Ellen returned, Jon was overjoyed to see her walking through his front door. He felt like he had known her forever. They shared a passionate kiss, and when they finally pulled away from each other, he looked at the bundles at her feet. She was right, she didn't have a whole lot of stuff.

"Look what I brought." It was a large paperback book.

"*Survival into the 21ˢᵗ Century*," Jon read out loud. "Hmm. Looks interesting."

"And . . ." she said, "my bamboo flute. Play it."

"Say please."

"Pleeease."

Jon played a little. "Not bad. It's got a nice sound. I like mine better."

"Of course, you do, Mr. Taurus man. My friend Jason wasn't home, so I left him a note thanking him for letting me stay with him and everything. I ended with, 'Have a good life, love Ellen.'"

"Fair enough. You're an amazing girl, Miss Ellen."

She gave him a look that said tell me something I don't already know.

"I have my astrological chart. You have yours, right? We can check them out later."

He followed her into the bedroom.

"Miss me?" she asked.

"Every minute."

Their clothes fell to the floor.

The next morning, they sat comparing astrological charts.

"Someone's got a birthday coming up real soon."

"I do," she said. "Twenty-five."

"I turned twenty-five in May."

"I know. You're my elder."

"So, you have to do what I say. Respect your elders."

Ellen rolled her eyes, then held up the charts side-by-side. "We both have most of our planets in the top part of our charts."

"Not sure what that means," Jon said.

"Me neither, but I like that. I'm a triple Scorpio. My sun, moon, and rising are all in the sign of Scorpio."

"Oh yeah? Is that good or bad?"

"You tell me," she said. "Do you know what your moon is in?"

"Nah. I don't really know."

"Let's see if we can figure it out on your chart. Look here," Ellen showed Jon the chart. "Taurus is directly across the wheel from Scorpio. Do you know that Taurus is the best sign for Scorpio? I only get together with Taurus men. The signs across from each other are the best ones for relationships."

"Hmm, I didn't know that. Learn something new every day."

"Life is school."

"I thought I got out of school."

"Nope."

"Awww. Well, I guess I'm lucky you're my teacher."

"Everyone and everything are our teachers. Jon, what are those orange fruits on that tree out there? Tangerines?"

"No. They look like tangerines, even on the inside, nice and orange. But, they're really sour. Some kind of lemon or lime. Really juicy."

"The tree is loaded. Do you like hot lemon and honey tea?"

"Sure, I guess so."

"Is there any cayenne pepper?"

"A little. It's caked up from the moisture, but we can powder some. Hasegawa Store will have it for sure."

"Come on," she said, leading the way out the door. They picked a few fruits, heated water in a saucepan and made hot lemon and honey tea, with cayenne.

"This is good. Nice color too," Jon said. "The cayenne isn't bad, not too hot. Although the last sip will have some kick to it."

"Perfectly delicious."

"I agree."

It became their morning drink.

25 | PINEAPPLE DAZE

"**J**ON'S FINALLY GOT A GIRLFRIEND. I like it. You dog. I'm anxious to see where this is headed."

After lunch at the Maui Brewing Company, Jon and Raoul drove to Kapalua and sat on the porch of the Honolua Store. This was an area where pineapple once ruled the land.

"This was our company store when we picked pineapples. It was where we bought food and the gear we needed for picking; chaps, goggles, gloves, canteens, and kaukau bags. We sent Jim over a time or two to buy wine. He was the only one who had a decent beard and looked older. As far as food goes, we pretty much ate brown rice. Cooked before work and eaten cold in the field."

"Plain cold brown rice?"

"We added dry onion soup mix to it while cooking, for flavor. Not sure who figured that out, but it was a big improvement. We would freeze our canteens and have cold water as it melted. There was a full-on community here, a plantation town. See that brown building over there? That's one of the dorms we lived in. They store golf carts in it now. There was even a gymnasium/auditorium building. Above the dorms was a huge garage where they worked on the trucks and equipment. Farther up, there was a camp unto itself. It was a good-sized cluster of shacks where many workers lived. Across the street, that building was the pineapple company office. The ladies at the office were nice to us. One time they gave us two paper grocery bags filled with Haden mangos. Plenty of the plantation houses had mango and other fruit trees in their yards."

"Honolua Store was a bit of a hub."

"It was. The big pineapple trucks coming from the fields, full of pineapples, would come up through here. We could get a truck pass, from the office, and catch a ride to Lahaina. Riding in the cab with the driver was way cool. The pineapples were headed to the cannery in Kahului."

"How far are we from Lahaina?"

"About ten miles. The first time I went to Lahaina I went barefoot. Big mistake. Between the blazing hot pavement and the sharp little roadside stickers, it was torturous. Never did that again."

"Was picking pineapples hard work?"

"Here's the thing. We were a bunch of kids from the suburbs of San Diego, eighteen years old and on our own in Hawai'i. The beach was a short walk away. It was great." Jon paused. "As for picking pineapples, yes. We were working ten hour days, six days a week, and getting rained on often. All for minimum wage. You don't *even* want to know what minimum wage was at that time. On the flipside, we worked the night shift, so we had most of our days free."

"You picked at night? How did you see? You must have had lights."

"Yep. The haole crew worked from three in the afternoon until one o'clock at night. The boom, which was a conveyor belt type thing with short sides, had lights. The pineapple plants were around waist-high and planted in rows. Unless you were working a ratoon field—altogether a different story. Those were old fields, overgrown and tangled, with the rows indiscernible. Full of small trees and large cane spiders. Anyway, the boom hung out over the field. You would walk down your row, grab the pineapple, snap it off and toss it onto the boom where it would be transported down the line then up and into the truck. We're talking 10-ton trucks."

"What a trip."

"Yeah. We stuck to our same row positions every night. My friend Jim and I were out on the end."

"How many rows deep?"

"Eleven . . . I think. When one truck was full it would disconnect from the boom and another truck would back in to take its place. We were always hoping the next truck would be running late and we would get a break. Usually, the next truck was there waiting. We had nights when we filled ten trucks. We were jamming. Raoul do you want a latte or something? The store now has an espresso bar."

"Sounds good."

"One sure sign of progress in an area—the availability of expensive coffee drinks."

"And automatic opening glass doors."

"Don't get me started. They've ruined this place."

Jon and Raoul returned to the porch with lattes in hand.

"Did you guys make coffee in the morning?"

"No, not that I remember. I didn't start drinking coffee on a regular basis till I was, like, forty."

"I beat you by about twenty years. Working in an office it goes with the territory. Gets you through the day."

"For sure. One thing we did do when we got home from work at one o'clock in the morning was make coffee cakes. That was our treat. A giant pan of coffee cake, topped with brown sugar and hot out of the oven. We went through a lot of Bisquick flour mix. On occasion we would do caramel corn. Melted butter and brown sugar poured over popcorn. My friends Jim and Paul had brought their guitars so we would sit around listening to them sing and play. The dorms had bunk beds. We pulled in some extra mattresses. The mattresses were floppy, and we could fold them long-ways, part on the floor and part up the wall to form couches. Jim and Paul were both talented singer-songwriters who later had successful careers in music."

"I've seen Paul and Margie with their group, Golden Bough, play in San Francisco a couple of times."

"They're still doing it. They tour every year to Europe and all over." Jon had his hand on his chin and a distant look. He handed Raoul his phone. "Here's something I wrote recently commemorating that time period."

Fueled by double batches of Bisquick coffee cakes topped with copious amounts of brown sugar, friendship, and camaraderie, the sound of laughter, song, and guitar wafted through the wee hours of the Honolua morning . . .

"Did you do any painting that summer?"

"No. But my friend Dave painted a large silhouette of a naked woman meditating on one of the refrigerators, and that was quite nice. Shall we roll?"

They drove down the road towards the ocean. "This beach road used to keep going, paralleling the coastline. The resort blocked it off. Now you have to drive up to the highway and then drop back down. Which is what we'll do. To facilitate this detour, up above, they built a massive concrete bridge over a very wide ravine. Probably the largest structure of its kind on Maui."

"Guess they didn't want riff-raff driving through their multi-million dollar luxury development. Money talks."

"I know. Everything changes. Just sometimes I wonder."

Jon drove back up the hill on a road lined with Norfolk Pines.

"Another thing that seems odd is how Fleming Beach, which was well known, is now "Kapalua Beach." And the new "Fleming Beach" is down the road. That happened a while ago. I don't really know the details. Maybe it was all on the up and up. Just seemed a little strange. As pineapple pickers we hung out at both spots."

They drove past the Honolua Store to the highway then dropped down to Fleming Beach.

"Check this out." Jon led the way to the old church across the street from the beach. "We heard stories that the church was haunted. It was said that at night a headless woman in a dress floated among the trees. None of us ever saw anything."

They walked to the beach.

"There used to be some old stables at the upper end of the beach."

"Moloka'i?" Raoul asked, looking across the channel.

"Yep."

"I'm getting it."

"You are. Let's drive over to Honolua Bay."

Along the way Jon pointed to a beach trail, surrounded by cars. The beach was hidden from the road.

"That's Slaughterhouse. It's a small sandy beach flanked by cliffs. Apparently, there was a slaughterhouse here at one time. Good bodysurfing on the right swell, I've heard."

Jon pulled over on a cliff overlooking Honolua Bay. They got out and stood against the strong trade winds. A few boats were anchored in the bay, along with people snorkeling the reef.

Jon shook his head. "I've got too many stories man."

"That's why I'm here, right?"

"I can't even tell them all. I don't know." Jon hesitated. "Like—there was this guy named Peter who walked around Lahaina carrying a big wooden cross on his back. He was this big white dude with a shaved head; he was a self-proclaimed follower of Jesus. My friend Jeff and I passed him on Front Street one time. He had half a dozen people who trailed along behind him. They lived in a cave out here somewhere. There's a big cavern along here that you can walk to from the bay. One day Peter and his disciples were standing on a cliff, holding hands, and praying with their eyes closed. Suddenly Peter jumps off the cliff, taking the others with him. Several people were killed, including Peter. One of the survivors said there was no warning. They were standing, praying, and then they were falling."

"Looney Tunes."

"Maybe stories like that are best forgotten." Jon paused. "Hey, let's go down to the bay. I haven't been down there in years. We'll have to find a parking spot along the road. It's not like the old days when you could drive right in. As a surfer I was familiar with the name Honolua Bay. It's a legendary surf spot with some awesome waves in the winter, breaking out on the point. I remember after my first night of picking, coming home in the back of a truck. There were benches along either side, but I was standing with the breeze in my face. The Milky Way was clearly visible, scattered across the night sky. We were coming past here, and someone said, *that's Honolua Bay.* I'm like, *what? Honolua Bay? No way.* It was in our back yard."

A flood of memories filled Jon as they walked to the bay. He looked past the people, to the trees, palms, rocks, and out to the ocean. They sat next to the boat ramp.

"Honolua Bay has always been a special place for me. I'm not even sure why. There are certainly more beautiful spots. But still, it's one of my favorites."

"Your happy place."

"Something like that. The summer we were picking, the movie *The Hawaiians* was being filmed here on Maui. The film crew was hanging out in a trailer down here. They gave us a box of leftover donuts and pastries."

"A treat for you rice-eating pineapple pickers."

"It was. Also, down here we met an interesting long-haired, full-bearded guy named Rick. He made a quarter of a million manufacturing and selling roach clips."

"That was a lot of money back then."

"And a lot of roach clips. They were the little alligator clips with beads and stuff hanging from them. He marveled at how lucky we were to be experiencing what we were experiencing at such a young age. Dave and I stopped to see him later in Oakland where he lived. We sat around a big round wooden table, with a bunch of folks, smoking joints."

"I'm beginning to see a pattern."

Jon rolled his eyes.

"We had some good adventures. One time, the next year, my friend Mark and I were here on Maui. We heard that Joseph and a couple of other guys were living at Honolua Bay. We walked into their forest camp, back behind us here. Joseph had a mat rolled out and was doing yoga. I was like, *oh wow.* They had discovered a water line, a galvanized pipe, where they could get fresh water. Mark and I volunteered to fill the water jugs. We were instructed to not totally unscrew the cap on the end of the pipe. Of course, we unscrewed it too far and the cap came off. We quickly filled the water jugs and then tried to get the cap back on. Water was squirting everywhere. We alternated between horror and hysterical laughter. Of course, having just smoked a joint didn't help. After five minutes the water pressure dropped, and the cap went on easily. We went back to camp soaked."

"Would that have been an old-school pipe containing lead?"

"I suppose it was. But things were different then, all around. Joseph lived naked at Makena Beach for a couple of years."

"What a trip. Do I detect a bro-mance between you two?"

"Good guy. Good friend. We go way back. Junior High. Him and Boa were living in Berkeley for a while. They had a room on the second floor of an old building, with the toilet down the hall. They spent their time getting high, playing frisbee in empty parking lots, reading Zap Comix and going to yoga classes, among other things. As Boa once said, *We're so hip it hurts.* I remember being high on acid, standing in their shabby little bathroom taking a pee, looking up at the bare light bulb on the wall . . ." Jon stopped himself. "Ah, that's another time, another story. We must all go to our graves with untold stories."

"Are we going to drive around this west end?" Raoul asked.

"Not today. That's a gnarly road. We'll turn around at Honokōhau Valley. Maybe get you home in time for a nap."

"Look who's talking."

"I get up early."

"True."

"Speaking of Honokōhau, one time Dave and I hiked into the valley to stay overnight at a cabin. It was more of a shack than anything. We had to get permission from the pineapple company, and they even gave us a note. The folks who lived there were touchy about people going up into their valley. I'd heard that the drinking water for Lahaina came from up there, but I don't know if that's true. We started hiking along the far side of the stream, away from the houses. The stream was wide and flowing nicely but not deep. Tall trees formed a canopy overhead. We began seeing reddish-colored fruits, about the size of golf balls, scattered about. They were lychee."

"I've never had one."

"The flesh is kind of like a grape. There's a shell you peel off, and a big seed or two in the middle that you don't eat. We had never eaten lychee before either, but that didn't keep us from digging in. The ones out of the stream were chilled."

"Did you know they were lychee?"

"Dave thought that's what they were, but we weren't totally sure. There was someone across the stream, in the distance, yelling to us. We didn't want to get hassled so we just kept going, pretending not to hear them. We found a path and followed it. A pack of dogs came running up to us, barking wildly. They were wagging their tails as they barked so we continued cautiously and came to a house. An older woman came out. She told us her name was Hanah and asked us what we were doing and where we were going. We explained that we were pineapple pickers and once we showed her our note she warmed up and was sweet. Beyond her house the path disappeared, and civilization was left behind. We mostly walked on the boulders and rocks along the streambed. The valley was narrow with steep sides. We were surrounded by and immersed in a sea of green. It was amazing. The cabin was deep into the valley. We hiked for a long time. We were delighted to discover a trail above us, paralleling the stream. It was well-worn and took us up to the cabin. Some weeks earlier, Joseph and a couple others had stayed at the cabin. He told us they heard footsteps on the porch and knocking at the door at night. There was a big white cross painted on the door to keep the spirits out. That night Dave and I left the kerosene lamp burning. In the morning there was a ring of dead mosquitoes circling the lamp."

"Did you hear anything?"

"Nah, we never did. It was a magical place, though. We had our little Kodak Instamatic cameras with us, so I have pictures from the trip although they're fading with age."

"I hear that. Me too."

"Above the cabin, on the stream, was a small concrete dam. After a dip we decided to head out. Dave and I hiked the trail that we had found. The trail began to climb higher up on the side of the valley. Around one bend we were shocked to see the trail disappearing into a tunnel carved through the mountain. We could see light at the other end. It was straight. Not too tall though, maybe six feet give or take, and there were puddles on the floor. Dave didn't want to get his boots wet so he went barefoot. We walked with one hand above our head and the other out in front of us, moving slowly toward the light."

"How long was the tunnel?"

"Oh, I don't know. A hundred and fifty feet. Something like that."

"Indiana Jones."

"It was way cool, but there's more. We pop out the other end and keep hiking. Once again, the trail goes into another tunnel. So once again Dave takes his boots off. I think he tied the laces together and hung them around his neck. Again, we could see light from the other end and made our way through. This time the trail came out onto a suspension bridge that spanned a deep ravine. There were dramatic sheer cliffs with another tunnel on the far side of the bridge. We were blown away."

"I'll bet."

"I wouldn't believe it if I hadn't been there. On this third tunnel we couldn't see any light coming through. It was pitch black. It had a turn in it, or who knows what. We were standing there wondering what to do. We noticed a can with kerosene, some dry rags in a jar and some sticks. All the makings for torches. Luckily, we had some wooden matches. Lancer brand matches came in these cool little boxes, which also came in handy for stashing roaches. Anyway, we sloshed through this third tunnel with a flaming smoky torch. This was the longest tunnel yet. We came to an abrupt halt at the end of the tunnel. There was a metal grate with a big padlock."

"Shit."

"That's what we said. The bars were too close to fit through. Just by chance Dave touched one of the bars and it came off. We were able to slip through. We carefully replaced the bar behind us. Dave sat down to put on his boots. There was a leech attached to his foot."

"What?"

"Yeah. A leech. He pried it off. Pretty weird yeah? So we continued on the trail which led us along a ridge. Both sides had sharp drop-offs. I remember where the trail forked and headed back up the mountain in a different direction. I've always wondered where that went. The trails seemed to be used, maybe by hunters. We came out at the top of one of the upper pineapple fields and completely out of the valley. We wound our way back down to the highway following the pineapple roads. End of story."

"That's a good one. Speaking of endings, this Book One needs to be wrapping up. You know, it's the word count thing. I'll see you on the other side in Book Two. Right? Right Jon?"

"Absolutely. We both know that this adventure isn't over."

26 | SWEET MYSTERIES

JON ANSWERED THE PHONE.

"Hey Sean. Yeah, good. Some sunny days but still getting plenty of rain. They're looking good. Okay. I can put something together. Let me know. Bye."

Jon hung up the phone. He looked over to Ellen, who had been listening.

"That was Sean. He's one of the property owners here but lives on O'ahu. We're growing some weed together and he's ready for some more inventory. He'll be coming over."

"You never told me you were a pot grower."

"I'm sorry, I've been meaning to—but after your story about your friend, in Makawao, I thought maybe it was best not to say anything."

He was afraid she would get angry, but instead she looked curious. "I want to see them. You have to show me every plant."

He took her to the biggest patch.

"Holy shit, Jon. You have a plantation. Do we need to pick some for your friend?"

"Yeah. We can come back later. I'll bring my clippers and a trash bag. Let's go see the other patches."

"How many are there?"

"Three. This is the biggest."

"Do the other owners know you guys are growing weed out here?"

"No. No one knows."

Later, Ellen helped Jon harvest and trim bud. They worked at the dining room table on a trash bag, so they could close up shop in a hurry if need be.

"I'm learning a new skill," she said, holding her scissors in the air.

"Hey, life is school."

"Can we start sleeping in the nicer room?"

"Ah, yeah I guess we could. We'll just have to move back to my room when someone comes."

"There's more light in there, and it would be nice to wake up and see the ocean. How about those sheets? I see there's a stack of bedsheets, on the shelf in the middle room. Can we use them? I would like that."

"Kathleen brought those out for people to use. It should be okay."

Ellen got busy making their bed, a futon mattress, in their new room.

THE WEED TOOK A WEEK to dry. Sean was scheduled to fly into Kahului soon, and Jon was sweeping the floor.

"I want to pick some yellow ginger for the house."

"Are you in love with this guy, or what?" Ellen teased.

Jon laughed. "I just want the place to look nice. You know I don't pay any rent and, really, I don't do a whole lot to earn my keep."

They walked out to the road and climbed down into the yellow ginger.

"Jon, if you pick the younger ones, you don't have to pinch off the yucky flowers. They're nicer."

"Yeah, I know. But I feel bad picking young ones. I figure the older ones have had more time to live their lives."

"You're funny. I'm going to pick the young ones." She put her nose to the flowers. "They smell good."

"You pick young ones, I'll pick older ones. We only need a few."

SEAN ARRIVED AT THE HOUSE the next day. In the evening they watched him pack a box with the dried shake and bud.

"I'm flying out of Hāna, so I can leave my car for you."

"Far out. Thanks."

Sean had brought a box, large ziplocks, packing tape, and some girly-looking flowered wrapping paper. He even had ribbon, a bow, and small card. As Sean finished wrapping, Jon and Ellen were smiling and exchanging glances between themselves.

"Do you have a pen? Something to write with?"

After inscribing the card, Sean motioned to Jon, "Check it out."

"Happy Anniversary, Sweetheart. I love you." Jon read aloud. "Damn, Sean."

Sean asked Jon to drop him off at the airport. He was flying out on a small airplane operated by Royal Hawaiian. At the airport curb, he gave a wave and said, "Right on brother, thank you. See you soon. I'll give you a call."

Sean had on an aloha shirt, shorts, and slippers. He was traveling light—in his backpack were a few pieces of clothing and his lovely wrapped present.

"Alright Sean. Later man."

As Jon pulled away, Sean was already engaging the airport crew in friendly conversation. He spoke using his best pidgin accent, which was very good. Natural and unforced.

THE FOLLOWING MORNING WAS GREY and rainy. Jon stood at the window. He turned to Ellen and smiled. "Are you thinking what I'm thinking?"

"Road trip?"

"Road trip. Let's take advantage of having some wheels."

They grabbed some clothes. Jon cut a hand of ripe bananas from the bunch hanging under the house.

"These bananas," she said, "are orange inside."

"Cuban reds. Cool color. Got to be good for you."

"You are what you eat. Let's go find some sun."

Jon drove. The roadside waterfalls were flowing nicely. As they drove, patches of blue sky began to appear. The rain lightened, then stopped altogether.

In Pā'ia, they stopped at Charley's to share a papaya-banana smoothie. The owner, Jim, was leaving with his dog.

"Is he a Great Dane?" Ellen asked, petting him on the head.

"Yeah," Jim said. "This is Charley. He's a Harlequin Great Dane. He's a good boy."

"Small horse," Jon said.

"Check out those eyes," Ellen said. Charley had pale blue eyes.

"I remember Charley's Juice Stand in Lahaina," Jon told Jim.

"That was a while ago. What were you doing in Lahaina in 1969?" Jim asked.

"I was a pineapple picker out at Honolua."

"Oh, alright. That makes sense. I gotta run. See you guys."

"Bye," Ellen said. "Bye Charley."

"Cool dog."

Kathleen's in Spreckelsville was the next stop. She greeted them from the dining room table. She was drinking coffee and studying for her real estate license. Jon noticed a couple of cigarette butts in the lid of a jar she was using for an ashtray.

"I didn't pass the first time, but I can take it again. Messed up on some of the math questions. I have to study harder. I'll get it. Getting any rain in Nāhiku?"

"Quite a bit. We're heading over to the Lahaina side for some sun."

"I've been thinking about you. I'm going holo holo to the mainland next week and wanted to ask if you can watch Ruffus while I'm gone."

"Sure, we can do that," Ellen interjected. "Where are you going?"

"California. It's for a Swami Muktananda retreat. Ten days. Georgia is going too. This will be her second one. She's had her reservations for a while. I called last minute and they're squeezing me in. Luck of the Irish. Anyway, I leave next Sunday, the thirty-first. Halloween."

"The day after my birthday," Ellen said.

"That's better than having your birthday on Halloween. I can have Jerry bring Ruffus out, unless you're coming this way."

"We may be," Jon said. "I'll give you a call. We have a phone now, so that helps."

LAHAINA WAS WARM AND WELCOMING. JON drove down Front Street then out to Waikuli Beach Park. They changed into their swimsuits and spread an Indian print bedspread on the sand. Wading into the ocean up to their thighs, they dove under. The water felt good.

"Can you float on you back?" she asked.

"Sure," he demonstrated. This led to a back-floating contest, ending in a draw. It's hard to float on your back while laughing. They then tried floating on their backs and holding hands. That too proved to be a challenge. On the beach they enjoyed the sun, alternating between lying on their stomachs and their backs. Before leaving, they rinsed in the cold beach showers.

"We should have brought some shampoo," she said.

"We can stay at my friends in Hāli'imaile tonight."

She looked puzzled. Their eyes met.

"Hot showers," they said in unison.

Back in Lahaina town they stopped at the Nagasako Store and bought two apples and some almonds. Grabbing their paper bag of ripe bananas from the car, they walked to Maui Ragtime where Jon introduced Ellen to Jenn, who was working the shop.

"Would you like a Cuban red banana?"

"No thanks Jon, I'm good," Jenn said. "Aren't those cooking bananas?"

"They're good for eating fresh too."

Daniel, David, and Elaine popped in. They were on their way to the beach, at Kā'anapali. Jon hadn't seen them since their mountain adventure.

"Banana?" Jon offered, opening the paper bag.

David and Elaine tried one.

"Strange-looking bananas," Daniel said. "Are they from the property in Hāna?"

"Yes."

"They're good," Elaine said.

They were standing near the open door, facing Lahainaluna Street. Pancho, in his long black coat and hat, festooned with slogan buttons, came shuffling by. Jon nodded hello to Pancho as he passed. Jon and Ellen continued down Front Street. As they walked, she took his hand.

"You're not comfortable with PDA, are you?" she said.

"With what?"

"Public displays of affection."

"Ah, hmm. I guess not."

"No, you're not," she said. "I could tell from the way your energy shifted. That's okay. A lot of guys are like that. We don't have to hold hands."

Jon wondered what he'd done right to deserve this woman.

They sat on a rock wall, facing the Lahaina Harbor. With the sun to their backs, they began to eat their lunch. It was a typical Lahaina day, sparkling blue. Lāna'i lay across the channel with Moloka'i to the north. A few small clouds were suspended here and there in a vault of deep cobalt. A man around their age approached—a big man with broad shoulders, a full beard, and his dark hair pulled back in a ponytail.

"Hello, my name's Jake."

"Hi, Jake."

"This is beautiful. You guys live here?"

"Yeah. Well, not here in Lahaina but on the other side of the island. Just getting some sun."

"Me too. I've been working the pipeline up in Alaska. After a while you have to get away. Especially this time of year, it's cold and dark. You know, short days."

"The pay must be good."

"It is exceptionally good."

"Would you like to try a Cuban red banana?"

"Sure," Jake said. "Wow. I thought I'd seen everything."

"Hawai'i seems like a long way from Alaska."

"Opposites. But a lot of guys work for a few months, then come to Hawai'i for a month. Back and forth."

"What do you do? Do you work outside in the cold?" Ellen asked.

"I'm lucky. I have an inside job. There are so many guys up there working, mostly guys, they have a whole support system in place. It's a little town."

Jake winced slightly. It hadn't escaped his attention that Jon and Ellen were eating apples, bananas, and almonds for lunch. "I'm a butcher."

"A butcher?" she repeated.

"The guys have to eat," he said. "It's a service. Are you vegetarians?"

"Yes."

"I know being a butcher is not the most popular thing to be these days. But I take my job seriously and try to provide the best meat and cuts possible. And I do it in a respectful way. Every animal I work with, I thank them for giving their lives for us so that we may live. I say a prayer for their souls or spirits."

"Like the Native Americans," Ellen said. "Everything is Spirit, and everything is sacred."

"That's it exactly," Jake said nodding his head.

"It's all God," Jon said. "All of creation."

"A spiritual butcher," Ellen mused.

Jake laughed.

"I guess it's better to be a spiritual butcher than an unspiritual vegetarian," she said.

"I think so," Jake agreed. "It's just like anything. You can do it conscientiously and consciously, or not."

"True."

"You guys seem like you've been together for a long time."

They affectionately glanced at each other. "No, not that long. But it does seem that way."

The three of them sat and talked a while. After a round of hugs, Jake went on his way. Jon and Ellen walked out along the wooden plank skirt of the harbor, admiring the sailboats.

"I love the harbor," Ellen reflected. "The sights, sounds, and the smell of the sea. Joni Mitchell sings about the harbor and her dream of love and a longing to be free. She's a Scorpio too."

"I did not know that."

They drove to the cannery, where Ellen met Mike.

"I'll call the old lady and let her know you're coming to stay the night." Mike smiled. "Shay is working at the radio station now."

"She's a DJ?"

"Yep. They got her on during the day. That will change. She's a natural."

"He's nice," Ellen said, as they drove off.

"Yeah, Mike is cool. Interesting dude. Ex-biker. Hells Angels type, for years."

That night Shay made eggplant parmesan, garlic bread, and steamed broccoli. They all sat around their tiny table in the kitchen.

"It's all vegetarian."

"Thank you," Jon said. "How's your new job being a DJ?"

"It's a gas. I love it," Shay said. "I got lucky. The lady in charge likes me. Sweet Japanese lady. She let me slide on some of the educational requirements for getting my broadcaster's license."

"This is really good," Ellen said.

"I'm glad you like it."

"I love broccoli," Jon added. "When I was living at my dad's, sometimes I would cook myself broccoli for dinner, or cauliflower. That's good too, with a little butter on it."

"You're weird, Jon," Shay said. "You guys, feel free to take showers. There are clean towels on your bed."

"Thanks, Shay."

After hot showers, Jon and Ellen joined Mike in the living room. Shay had retired to their bedroom.

"Feel good?"

"Oh yeah. I mean, you get used to cold showers, but still."

"I'll bet. Good smoke, Jon," Mike said as he handed the joint back to Jon. "How are you selling it?"

"Sean is selling it over on O'ahu."

"Good. You don't have to deal with it, no pun intended. Back in the day . . . ." he gave a quick glance toward the bedroom, "back in the day, I saw a lot of deals go down. Not just weed but also speed and downers. At one point," Mike said, quietly, "the club was selling a lot of speed. The guy selling it would sit at this big round table. On the table was a big pile of speed, some stacks of money, and a gun. People were coming and going. This guy was flying. Eyes as big as saucers. Hadn't slept in days. As time went on, the pile of money kept getting bigger and the dude was getting more and more paranoid. It was a scene." Mike paused.

"So, what happened?" Ellen leaned forward in anticipation.

"He finally crashed, so nobody got shot."

"I'm going to shoot you if you don't stop telling those old stories," Shay said from the bedroom. Mike made a funny face and grinned, stroking his beard.

Shay came out of the bedroom. "Anyone want tea?" she asked. "I'm going to make some hot tea."

In the morning, after breakfast, Jon and Ellen drove into Makawao town. She had told him about an amazing kerosene lamp that burned with enough light to read by. One of her friends had one, and they were for sale at the Makawao Mercantile shop. The Aladdin lamp had a tall glass chimney and a circular wick with a mesh mantle. The mantle, once burned, became like ash, and would glow brightly. It was expensive—one hundred and twenty dollars plus ten bucks for the mantle, which was replaceable.

"Can't wait to try it." Jon said pulling his wallet out of his jeans pocket.

They made their way back to Nāhiku. Jon took advantage of the dry day and dropped down to his patches. He needed to be ready for Sean's next visit, which would be soon. Ellen went for a walk. She was back at the house, writing a letter to her mother, when Jon returned.

Ellen kept in close touch with her mom. Jon wrote to his mother, but he received more letters than he sent. He also kept in touch with his bohemian father, but more sporadically. He enjoyed sharing pieces of his life on Maui with them. The letters, as well as the envelopes, were always enhanced with drawings. Having a mailbox at the house was a blessing. Due to the wet weather, Jon's stamps and envelopes were always fused together. He often crafted his own envelopes and glued the stamps on.

As night fell, Jon anxiously fired up their new kerosene lamp. It lived up to its billing and put out significant light. He discovered the heat coming out the top of the glass chimney was perfect for lighting joints. They sat passing a joint between them.

"Listen," Jon said.

Rain moved through the trees, cutting through the dark night.

"You can hear the rain coming."

"Umm hum. Getting louder," he whispered. "It sounds like applause."

"You know, it does."

The sound of the rain grew louder and louder as it drew closer. Soon it engulfed the house with a roar.

Jon stood up. He glanced at Ellen.

"Why . . ." he said slowly for dramatic effect, "it's a standing ovation." He bowed formally towards the window, an amused smirk on his face.

Standing and wrapping her arms around him, Ellen said, "I love you."

It caught him off guard. In mere seconds his mind traveled to faraway universes and back. He realized he felt the same. "I love you too."

"I love you more."

They both laughed, as the rain applauded around them.

"Good morning, birthday girl." They lay in bed together. Jon lightly ran his fingers along Ellen's forearm. He loved the contrast of the blonde hairs against her tan skin.

Jon had never lived with a girlfriend before. He felt as if he was being initiated into a secret world. He was learning the steps of an ancient dance that moved as the ebb and flow of eternal tides.

"I once lived with a guy who would bring home other women," Ellen said.

"What? While you were there?"

"Yeah. They would be in the other room."

"That's crazy. Was he a Taurus?"

"He was. You wouldn't do that, would you Jon?"

"No. I mean, when you're already with the most beautiful girl on the planet . . . why would you do that?"

"Really? You think I'm the most beautiful girl on the planet?"

"In the universe."

"I'll bet you say that to all the girls."

"No," he shook his head. "Only the pretty ones," he teased.

The day was clear and sunny. Jon moved the Aladdin lamp from where they'd left it the night before, but he handled it too roughly and the mantle crumbled. He showed Ellen what had happened.

"Jonathan. I think you forgot what a special and magical gift this lamp is to us. It gives us light. It's not an ordinary thing. We have to be gentle, and take care of it."

Kind of like Ellen, Jon thought. *Gives light. Not an ordinary thing.*

He gave her a kiss. "You're right. Sorry. Guess we should have bought two mantles."

"Bull in a china shop." Ellen returned the kiss. "Can we go to that nice beach in Hāna today?"

"Koki? Sure."

At Koki, they walked along the white sand and sat on their towels at the far end. There were not many people at the beach, and nobody close by. She took off her bikini top. Jon raised his eyebrows. *So much for keeping a low profile.*

"Maybe they'll think I'm a boy."

"No. I don't think so. Your bikini bottoms will give you away."

"I'm French."

"Uh huh."

She went into the water without her top. The waves were rough and the current strong, so they didn't swim in too deep. Instead they returned to the beach to sunbathe. After soaking up some rays, they went to Hasegawa's for some coconut macaroons.

"Would you like to see the Seven Sacred Pools?" Jon asked. "Gorgeous drive, about ten miles. It's a national park."

Along the way, they stopped to admire roadside waterfalls. At the Seven Sacred Pools he parked off the road, just past 'Ohe'o Gulch. They stood on the concrete bridge overlooking the lower pools.

"Why are they called sacred?" she asked.

"Ah, well, apparently that's something someone came up with, a marketing thing to attract tourists to the area. I guess it just sounded good. There aren't seven pools, either. But it is a special place."

Jon noticed two young men standing nearby. They were contemplating jumping off the bridge to the stream below.

"These guys are talking about jumping off the bridge."

Ellen looked over the bridge railing. "Really? They're crazy."

It was a long way down, and the landing zone was small.

"You have to hit it just right," one man said to his friend.

"I know," he replied.

"I will if you will."

"I'm going to do it." Standing on the short concrete rail, the man jumped.

Jon and Ellen were horrified as they watched him sail through the air and into the water. There was a tense moment until he surfaced. With a big smile, he looked to the bridge and gave a thumbs-up.

The man's friend looked at them. "Here goes nothing."

He stood on the rail and jumped. Fortunately, he too landed in the small pocket of water and survived unscathed. The men made their way down through the lower pools.

Jon and Ellen were still on the bridge when a national park ranger truck pulled up. The ranger got out and walked towards them. He had a smile and was non-threatening.

"Hello."

"Hey."

"I heard a couple of guys jumped off the bridge." His gaze went downstream to where the two men were still visible.

"Yeah."

"Is that them?"

"Yep."

"It's dangerous." He looked Jon in the eye and extended his hand. "I'm Eddie. Eddie Pu," he smiled. "I'm a simple Hawaiian."

Eddie Pu was a humble man. This was his way of saying, "I'm no one special." Jon had heard of him and knew he was well respected in the Hāna community.

"Hey Eddie, I'm Jon."

"I'm Ellen."

"You live here on Maui?"

"Upper Nāhiku."

"Oh, okay." He looked back downstream. "I have to go talk to these guys. You folks have a nice day."

Eddie knew, as did Jon, that the men would exit through the adjacent designated camping area.

Jon and Ellen took the trail above the road, through the upper pastures where cows were grazing. It was the way to the bamboo forest and beyond to several waterfalls. They looked for psilocybin mushrooms along the way but found none.

As they walked, Jon was concentrating on his third eye, picturing himself in meditation.

"Don't be so serious." she said, noticing his withdrawn demeanor. "I'm not going anywhere."

Where the trail crossed the stream and disappeared into the bamboo forest, they turned around.

"Jon, for my birthday, I want to listen to Joni Mitchell. At the Spreckelsville house, I saw they have several of her albums.

"Tomorrow we can go pick up Ruffus and hang out. I'm easy."

"Sometimes . . . sometimes."

THE NEXT DAY THEY DROVE TO Spreckelsville, detouring briefly in Makawao to purchase two more mantles for the kerosene lantern.

It was Halloween. Kathleen had gone to her retreat in California. Jenn and her boyfriend, Daniel, were headed to Lahaina for Halloween. Halloween night in Lahaina was becoming quite the scene with everyone dressed in costumes, bar-hopping, and roaming Front Street. As she left the house, Jenn called out, "Cha Cha and Ruffus have been fed and there's homemade soup in the fridge. I made it last night. It's vegetarian."

"Great. Thank you."

She also left a bowl of mini candy bars in the unlikely event that any trick-or-treaters showed up. Jon wasn't sure where Jerry was; he may have been working. And Jon hadn't seen Paco in a while.

"Looks like we have the house to ourselves," Ellen said, grinning.

"Hey," Jon said, raising his hands as if he had something to do with it.

27 | BUSY BEING FREE

"Ruffus, you're amazing."

Jon and Ellen were back in Nāhiku. They were taking Ruffus for a walk to the ocean. The dog had just made his way across the lava bridge.

They continued down the steep trail to Blue Pond.

"Beautiful. Shall we?" Ellen said.

They stripped and waded in.

"It's chilly."

Jon dove under. As he surfaced, he heard Ellen say, "Hey look. That's so cool. Good boy."

Ruffus had entered the water and was dogpaddling toward them.

"He's a water dog."

"What kind of dog is Ruffus?"

"I'm not sure. Some kind of Lab or something. Golden Lab?"

After the swim, they dressed while Ruffus gave himself a good shake.

They walked along the dirt road, toward the ocean. Abruptly, Ellen stopped and turned to face Jon. "I'm pregnant."

"You're pregnant?" He tried to stay calm, taking a deep breath. *Is this happening?*

"What do you think about that? Are you scared?"

"I don't know. I guess. I haven't had time to think about it."

Ellen searched his face as if looking for clues. Then she gave him a small smile. "I'm not really pregnant. I just wanted to see how you might react."

"You're not pregnant?" He was confused.

"No. Although with all the sex we're having, it does take a lot of psychic energy to keep from getting pregnant."

Jon wasn't sure what psychic energy had to do with it.

"I do have something important to share with you," she said.

He waited, listening.

"I have a son. He's five."

"You have a son? Where is he? Where does he live? Doesn't he need his mom?"

"He's in Maine with his father. He's fine. He's a daddy's boy. He's happy. I got pregnant when I was eighteen. Babies having babies."

Ellen had kept a secret from him. He supposed he understood—she didn't want to be judged for the decisions she'd made.

The jungle receded as they neared the ocean. They stopped. An old Hawaiian man was standing alongside the brackish stream. He had long white hair, tied back, and a long white beard. He was draped in a wrap that hung diagonally across his body, leaving his brown shoulders and arms exposed. In one hand was a spear, a three-pronged harpoon, which he held upright. The man seemed to be from ancient times as he stood very still, quietly observing the water near where it disappeared beneath the shoreline rocks and sand.

"Fishing?" Ellen said quietly.

Jon nodded.

The man remained unmoving but acknowledged them with his eyes.

They turned toward the beach to avoid walking directly past the man and disturbing his fishing. Ruffus followed. They sat on the beach. The sky was heavily overcast, and on the horizon were ominous dark clouds.

"We should probably head back up the hill," Jon said.

As they left the beach, the fisherman stood looking out to the ocean.

Halfway home, the rain began. By the time they reached the house they were soaked. Downstairs they took off their clothes and hung them on a line. Ellen gave Ruffus a quick rub with a towel.

Upstairs, in the bedroom, one thing led to another. While making love, she asked, "Do you know what a kegel is?"

"A what?"

"Kegel."

"No. Not a clue."

"They're exercises. Push-ups for my pussy."

"Push-ups for . . ."

"Pussy push-ups. It's something they teach you after giving birth. You contract and relax the pelvic muscles. After having my son, I was so worried about being loose, I started doing kegels a bunch. I still do. Hold still. Can you feel that?"

"Yeah."

"Try and pull out."

"Really? Okay." Jon gently tried. He smiled, impressed.

After making love, she said, "You wet you pants again."

He didn't understand what she was trying to tell him.

"You're just a bay-bee. I'm going to call you Babycakes."

Jon frowned.

"You don't like me to call you Babycakes, do you?"

"Not really. It doesn't sound good."

"Okay Babycakes." She paused. "After I separated from my husband, I was working in a shop on the pier in Newport, you know, where I'm from. I met this guy from Maui. He was incredible. He was better than all of my other lovers put together."

"Is that why you moved here?"

"Yeah, maybe. That was part of it."

"Did you ever see him again?"

"No. Never did."

THE RAINY WEATHER CONTINUED. It WAS Sunday. They were now fasting on Sundays. Ellen kept track of the days. She made them a hot cup of lemon and honey. While Jon trimmed some bud, Ellen read aloud from *Survival into the 21ˢᵗ Century.*

"Did you see this? Biological superiority of women."

"Um-hmm."

"How tall are you?"

"Five-eight."

"I'm five-seven. I'm going to keep stretching until I'm five-eight. Then I will be the same height as you."

"Well, I'm going to stretch until I'm five-nine and I will still be an inch taller."

"We'll have a bet," she said.

On a piece of pater she wrote:

THE BET
ELLEN 5'8"   JON 5'9"

"If I win," she said, "I want . . . I'll write it down."

10 HARD APPLES (PRIMAS)
10 AVOCADOS (RIPE)
10 TOMATOES OR 3 BOXES OF SMALL TOMATOES

"Here Jon, write what you want if you win."

"Okay."

2 COCONUTS
12 BANANAS
4 AVOCADOS
3 APPLES
1 PINEAPPLE
12 DATES
12 FIGS—OR THEREABOUTS

Ellen took back the paper and added:

IF YOU LOSE + THIS MEANS YOU JON! YOU MUST DRINK
1 CUP OF RED PEPPER TEA WITH 7 PEPPERS! IN 24 HRS!
1 CUP WHISKEY FOR ELLEN

"So," Jon said. "If you lose, you have to drink one cup of whiskey."

"Maybe we should make that two cups."

"This is starting to sound like the Brer Rabbit and Brer Fox story. Whatever you do—don't throw me into the briar patch. I'm thinking you might like drinking some whiskey."

She let out a little giggle. "Maybe."

She went back to looking at *Survival into the 21ˢᵗ Century*, stopping at the section on iridology.

"I've heard," she said, "that if you look into someone's eyes with one person upside down, after a while it's like looking right-side up, regular."

"Hmm."

"Want to try it?"

She lay on the mattress, a pillow under her shoulders and her head hanging over the edge. Jon lay on the floor with his head cranked up. Their faces were very close. He studied her upside-down eyes.

"You have a golden sun around your pupils," Jon said. "Like a halo."

"I know. Not sure it's a good thing according to the iridology chart."

After a few minutes, he said, "Okay. I can see the effect. You have to look just into the eyes. Pretty cool."

The phone rang. It was Sean. He would be flying into Hāna airport as soon as Jon was ready with more pakalōlō. Jon needed a couple of sunny days to complete the drying process. Sean advised Jon that some better weather was in the forecast. That night it rained hard, but the next morning the sun danced brightly between large fluffy clouds.

In the afternoon an old beater pulled up. Jon looked out.

"Hey."

"Hey man." It was Paul Fingers.

"Come on in. How's it going?"

"Good." Paul said. "Although I got kicked out of my church in Kanaio. The cops showed up and gave me the boot."

Ellen came up the stairs. She was returning from a walk.

"Ellen this is Paul. Paul Fingers."

"My pleasure." Paul bowed. "Jon, I wanted to ask you if I could crash here tonight. I'm headed to Wailuku tomorrow."

"Sure, no problem. Shall we smoke a joint?"

"Thought you'd never ask." Paul smiled. "Praise the Lord."

"So, you got booted from your church?"

"Yep. You know, I was there for quite a while. It blew my mind one evening to see the cops pulling up. Can you believe that?"

"Kanaio is in the middle of nowhere."

"It is. They said they had a complaint." Paul sighed. "I had some pakalōlō plants growing in pots. The cops told me they were going to have to arrest me. Praise the Lord. Praise Jesus. Whatever they said I responded with *praise Jesus, praise the Lord*. The cops were nice and all. They could see that I was keeping the place clean and tidy. I considered myself the caretaker of God's house and I took my responsibility seriously. I told them to do whatever they had to do. Praise Jesus. After a while they just pulled up my plants and told me I had to leave the next day. Of course, I agreed to that. I praised the Lord out of that one. Praise the Lord."

"Good story," Ellen said. "Well, except that you had to move. At least you didn't get busted."

Jon turned to Ellen. "How far did you walk?" he asked.

"All the way to the ocean. The waterfall on the ocean was raging."

"Really? I've never seen it like that. It's always been super mellow."

"The waterfall was coming out almost to the ocean."

"Whoa."

"That Hawaiian man was down there again, standing on the beach. I could tell that he was watching me. It kind of creeped me out. Glad I had Ruffus with me. On the way back, I picked a stalk of bananas. They were in the banana patch on the dirt road. A couple of the top bananas were turning yellow, so I figured they were ready. I'm wondering if that's where the saying about the top banana comes from. Do the top bananas turn ripe first?"

"I'm not sure. That kind of makes sense though."

"I cut them down with your pocketknife."

"That must have been a chore."

"It took a while. I carried them as far as I could. They're heavy. Got them all the way up the steep part of the trail. That's where they are, by the broken-down shack."

Jon and Paul hiked down the property trail and fetched the bananas. Jon hung them under the house.

"You're incredible," he proudly told Ellen. "That is a nice bunch of bananas. I can't believe you carried them so far, they're heavy."

"Tell me about it," she said.

That night Paul played his bamboo flutes. It was a wonderful treat. If you didn't know he was playing a bamboo flute, you never would have guessed. The pure notes danced about the room and filled the night.

Paul left early the next morning. Later in the day, Harry came by to pick up the piano backboard. It was heavy, and Harry had two guys with him.

"I told you I would be back for it."

Jon hated to see it go. It had been fun to play around on, plucking and strumming the strings. He made an effort to make friendly conversation with Harry, to cut the tension between them.

"Ellen likes boats, and loves to be out on the ocean. Maybe someday you could take us out on your boat?"

Harry looked at Ellen. "Yeah, I could take her out on the boat."

He purposely left Jon out of the equation.

"You know," Harry said, "the waterline that runs from the river?" The line provided water to the shower under the house and sink in the kitchen. "That pipe cost me a lot of money, plus it was a lot of work to put in. If the hui wants to keep it, they need to pay me for the pipe. Otherwise, I'm going to come take it out. I can sell it."

Jon was happy to see him leave.

"Jon, does that bicycle downstairs work?" Ellen asked.

"It does indeed."

"Have you ever ridden to Hāna on it?"

He nodded. "Coming home is the hard part. Lots of uphill."

"I'm going to ride to town. Show me how the gears work. How far is it?"

"About five miles, one way."

She did a few practice runs, back and forth, in front of the house.

"That's it. You got it. Be careful." He felt protective and said a quick prayer that she'd be safe on the road.

While Ellen was out on her adventure, Jon and Ruffus walked along the highway to the jeep road to pick papaya and thimbleberries. A Jeep came up the hill. It was Bully.

"Howzit?"

"Good, good."

"Hey, tell your lady friend to be careful when the waterfall is rushing like that. It can be dangerous. Uncle Sol said she got pretty close. He was keeping an eye on her."

"Oh yeah. No. She's good. She knows. Thanks, though."

In the afternoon, Ellen arrived back at the house.

"How was it?" Jon asked. "Did you walk at all, on the way back?"

"I loved it. I rode the whole way." Jon was impressed.

"Kat's back in town. Her son Jerry's going to come pick up Ruffus tomorrow."

"Maybe we can hide Ruffus when Jerry comes. We could put him in the bed, under a blanket."

"With just his nose sticking out."

"Jon, kukui nuts are edible right?" She held one in her palm.

"They're said to be a natural laxative. So, yeah they are edible. I've heard you eat one and you walk to the toilet, eat two, and you run. Three and forget it. Guess they're really oily. The Hawaiians used them for candles."

"Have you ever eaten one?"

"Ah, no."

"I want to try one and see what they're like. They're a nut, so maybe they're good. There's a bunch on the ground by the outhouse."

"True."

"Will you help me crack some?"

He cracked the hard kukui nut shells with a hammer and picked out a few of the good kernels.

She ate one. "Not bad. Eat one," she coaxed. "Don't be a chicken. Come on."

"I don't know." He tried one. "Not bad."

"I'm going to have another one."

"You're crazy."

She ate three altogether. It wasn't long before she was headed to the outhouse. She came back upstairs and sat at the table, made a face, and got up to return to the outhouse.

The next morning Jerry came. "Okay big boy," Jerry said. "You ready to go home?"

Ellen gave Ruffus a big hug. "See you around, kiddo."

Jerry was driving Kathleen's truck. He gave Ruffus a boost to help him jump in. Jerry got in, and held up a beer. "Last one. I forgot how long it takes to get out here. I'll have to hit Hasegawa's."

They drove away. Ruffus with his head out the window.

"I'm going to miss that sweet boy," Ellen said.

"Jerry?"

"Nooo, silly. Ruffus."

"I know. I know. Me too." He thought of Kolohe, with a pang.

"Let's go to the ocean," Ellen suggested.

They hiked down the property.

"Time to trim the ferns again," Jon said. "Should have brought the machete, I guess."

"I know. I'm getting wet."

They crossed the lava bridge and were at the top of the narrow steep part of the trail, next to the cliff.

"Careful, it's slippery," Jon said.

"You know this is a bridge too, right?"

"What?"

"This is a bridge," Ellen repeated.

"What do you mean? Bridge? No way."

"There's a hole underneath here that goes all the way through, side to side. You don't believe me."

"It just seems so unlikely. It goes all the way through? How do you know?"

"I had a hunch, so I climbed down the other day to check. And sure enough . . ."

None of it made any sense to Jon. *You had a hunch.* "You climbed down there?"

He was looking down the opposite side from the cliff. It was steep but more gradual than the cliff side, which was a sheer drop. Jon had to see for himself. He gingerly climbed down. She waited, watching. He was surprised to see that it was indeed a bridge that the trail crossed over. A large opening went all the way through to the face of the cliff.

"Unreal," he said as he climbed back up. "I wouldn't have believed it if I hadn't seen it."

"Told you."

They continued down the trail, pausing at Blue Pond.

Blue Pond had many faces. Today the small waterfall was quiet, and the pool was the color of coffee with cream.

Upon reaching the ocean, they walked along the edge of the water.

"This cove is somewhat protected," she said. "Let's go in."

"Really?" He didn't much like the idea.

"I'm going in." She began to take off her clothes. "You coming?"

He didn't want her going in by herself. Besides, it seemed to be another double-dog-dare that he couldn't refuse. He took off his clothes and joined her. It got deep quickly. They stopped with the water to their shoulders, bobbling up and down with the swell. The murky water made Jon uncomfortable.

"I love this," she said.

He forced a smile. He was relieved when, after fifteen minutes, they got out.

As they walked back to the dirt road, Ellen pointed to the ground. "Do you know this sensitivity plant?"

He looked down to see a small plant that hugged the ground like a ground cover. "Hello plant. Pleased to meet you."

"Watch this." She touched the small plant that immediately recoiled, folding its leaves together.

"What a trip. I've never really noticed that. How long does it stay closed up?"

"Oh, a minute or two. But look here."

"Isn't that the same plant?"

"No. See, this one has yellow flowers. The one that closes up has purple flowers."

Jon experimented touching the two different plants. "This one with the yellow flowers has little thorns," he said. "Learn something new every day." *Especially with Ellen and her hunches.*

"Life is school."

"We should get going. Sean's flying into Hāna this afternoon. I still have a few things to do."

"Are you going to pick flowers for him?" she teased.

"No. I don't know, maybe. It does make the house smell good."

"I'm going to stay here and stretch a little."

"Okay. I'm going to head up to the house."

He starting walking back. After a minute, he had second thoughts and turned around. He was surprised to find her doing yoga on the beach, naked. She was doing the bow position, supported by her hands and feet with her pelvis thrust skyward.

"You're crazy. You know people do sometimes come down here."

"You came back for me," she said, grinning as she eased out of her pose. "Yeah, I know. Okay. I'm ready to go."

Jon picked up Sean at the airport that afternoon. Sean planned to hang out at Jamie's in Pukalani, pack up "the goods," and mail it to himself. He stayed just one night.

They watched as Sean pulled away the next morning. They were once again without a car.

"Nice while it lasted."

"Yeah," Jon said. "Shall we go for a walk?"

Walking along the road, they ran into Rainbow. He was at the bottom of the commune property, standing next to a car.

"Hey guys."

"Good morning, sir."

"Check this out." Rainbow opened a drawing tablet. "Best art I've done in years."

It was a replica of a safety sticker.

"Safety sticker," Rainbow said.

"Yeah. Yeah. It looks good."

"I just have to seal it real good and figure out the best way to stick it on the bumper. It's the only way this junker is going to pass the safety check."

"Where's Patchouli?" Jon asked. He was used to seeing them together.

"She's up at the house, baking some bread. We got one of those ovens that sits on top of a Coleman stove. Works pretty good. And speaking of having a bun in the oven . . . we're pregnant. Going to have a baby! I'm going to be a dad."

"Oh, wow. Congratulations." Jon glanced at Ellen, remembering what she'd revealed the other day, about her five-year-old son at home. It was easy to forget she had this whole other part of her life he'd never seen.

"It's a strange feeling," Rainbow reflected. "I'm going to be naming another human being. It's a trip."

"You'll figure it out," Ellen reassured him.

Ellen decided to hitchhike into Hāna to get honey, which they were low on. Jon was back at the house when she returned.

"Hey, honey," Jon said.

"Hey. I got a ride home with a nice Hawaiian guy."

"Oh yeah?"

"I was walking out of town on that upper road, you know where there are a few houses. Some guys were having a party in their carport. As I walked by, this guy asks me if I want a beer. I told him no thanks. He then asked if I needed a ride. I said, no I'm good and kept walking. A couple of minutes later he came by in his car and picked me up. Sweet guy. Good looking, too. He didn't know who you were, and thought no one lived here."

Jon laughed, "I'm not surprised." He looked away, feeling a bit threatened by this handsome stranger.

"You know you do this fake little laugh thing, when you're uncomfortable."

"Yeah . . . maybe. A lot of people do that," he said with a pained expression. He felt judged.

"True. A lot of people do that."

They looked to the window as a hard rain began to fall and sat quietly for a minute.

"Kathleen called," Jon said. "She invited us for Thanksgiving in Spreckelsville. We're in charge of the fruit salad."

"Perfect."

The day before Thanksgiving, Jon hitched to the other side. He met Ellen in Hāli'imaile at Mike and Shay's. Ellen had gone over early to see a girlfriend in Makawao. She was already there when Jon arrived, but Mike and Shay were out for the evening. Jon and Ellen made love on the carpeted living room floor.

The next morning they hitchhiked to Spreckelsville.

Kathleen was in the kitchen stuffing a big turkey. She owned Thanksgiving. It was her day to cook for everyone. Jerry walked out in his boxers and a T-shirt. He went straight to the coffee maker.

"Good morning sleepy head," Kathleen beamed.

"Hi," Jerry said while eyeing the turkey. "Will that big bastard even fit in the oven?"

"I checked it," Kathleen replied. "It fits."

Jon and Ellen borrowed Kat's truck to go to Ah Fooks Market in Kahului to buy fruit.

Upon returning from the store, Jon emptied two large paper grocery bags. Red apples, green apples, a cantaloupe, honeydew melon, papaya, a hand of ripe bananas, some golden raisins, and—last but not least—a coconut.

"I should be arrested for actually buying a coconut, but I wanted some crunch."

"I love coconut," Kathleen grinned.

"I can open it." Jon poked a hole in the eye of the coconut and drained the coconut water into a glass. "It's good."

He handed the glass to Ellen. Then he cracked the coconut on the concrete step in front of the house, and proceeded to pry pieces of coconut meat from the shell with a butter knife.

"Do you want me to make . . ." Jerry paused. A jet flew overhead. It was loud. No one paid any attention to it as it was a regular occurrence here, next to the Maui airport. ". . . the mashed potatoes?"

Jenn and Daniel came home with pumpkin and apple pies, and David and Elaine came later in the afternoon. Their parents had moved from the East Coast and were now living in Makawao. David had his girlfriend with him. Everyone enjoyed the Thanksgiving feast. Jon even ate some turkey.

After eating, Daniel took Jon and Ellen to look at some interesting bamboo growing on the property, close to the beach and not far from the house. Jon was surprised to see the bamboo growing out of the sand. It was a pale golden yellow with delicate green pinstripes.

"Is it growing here naturally?" Ellen asked.

"No. It was planted," Daniel said. "The caretaker guy keeps it trimmed and watered."

Daniel went back to the house. Jon and Ellen went for a walk along the shoreline.

That afternoon, they hitched up the hill to Mike and Shay's, in Hāli'imaile. They stayed over one night and made their way back home the next morning.

"I really like Mike," Ellen said. "I usually don't get along well with Leos."

"Mike's cool."

"But Shay. For a Taurus, she's pretty uptight."

A winter storm brought heavy rain. Jon played tag with the rain for several days, working his pakalōlō patches between downpours. Ellen left to stay with her girlfriend in Makawao for a couple of days. The storm passed and the days became hot and beautiful. Ellen returned. Jon rolled a joint while she made them a cup of peppermint tea. They sat at the small dining room table.

"I'm putting together another box for Sean. He wants me to send it to him on Royal Hawaiian, airfreight from the Hāna airport. Guess I will ride it down on the bike. Did one before like that. Kind of weird to be riding up on a bicycle with a box of weed to ship."

"I can do it. I don't mind," she said.

"Okay. Sure. How was your trip to the other side?"

"Good." Ellen paused, "But I've got to stop asking people their astrological sign. Going to get myself into trouble." She looked at Jon. "I need to be married. It grounds me."

He raised his eyebrows.

Quietly but firmly, she repeated to herself. "I need to be married."

"Yeah? Hmmm. Not sure I'm ready for that."

He knew he wasn't ready to marry Ellen, but he didn't want to hurt her feelings, or push her away. He changed the subject.

"I got a letter from my mom. She invited me to come for Christmas. It's been a while since I've been to the mainland. I'd like to go. She lives in Half Moon Bay, in California. It's a great place. We could both go. My mom would pay for the trip. And we could go see my dad in San Diego. It would be fun."

"I don't want to go backwards, Jon. I only want to go forward."

"Have you ever been to California?"

"No."

"So how is it going backwards?"

"California is your past. I just want to go forward." She got up, went to the living room and started sweeping the floor.

Jon could make out the words she was softly singing. *If you want to keep me, you gotta make me happy.*"

She was sweeping the kitchen now. "Someday, you need to get out and test yourself in the world. Not just hide out in the jungle. Strong spirits shine."

"But it's so beautiful here. I love it," he protested. "It's hard to get a place to live on Maui. It feels like such a blessing to have a house here in Hāna."

"Eventually, though, you have to leave it. You have to leave it all. When I left my marriage, I walked away with nothing. There were still paintings on the wall, everything. I let it all go."

"I'm not ready to leave this place. It's my dream. My Garden of Eden."

The days passed. Ellen rode Jon's bicycle to the airport to send the box to Sean. No problem.

Jon couldn't convince her to go to California with him. He made plans to go by himself.

On a sunny morning, Jon sat in the yard rolling bud joints and standing them up in a Planter's peanut can. The joints fit perfectly. He knew his friends in San Diego would enjoy sharing in this sunny-morning-in-Nāhiku infused smoke. He would mail them to himself so the stash would be there when he arrived.

Sean made another trip to Nāhiku to pick up more herb. "'Tis the season," Sean said with a smile. Business was good, and Sean knew Jon would be gone for two weeks on the mainland. He gave him several hundred-dollar bills, and left the car. When Jon flew to the mainland, he would leave the car at Jamie's in Pukalani. Jamie would give Jon a ride to the Kahului airport.

Days before Jon's trip to California, Ellen decided she wanted to go camping on the Lahaina-side. She borrowed one of Jon's small tents.

With mixed emotions, he drove her to Lahaina. They were almost there when Ellen revealed, "Jon, if you liked to eat girls as much as you liked to eat vegetables, I might not be leaving."

With a look of dismay, Jon bit his lip and his thoughts swirled. It hit him hard as he realized he hadn't given Ellen what she needed. He felt like pulling over, right then and there, to remedy the situation but didn't . . . quietly driving on.

Am I about to lose the woman I love because I'm an idiot? How could I have been so stupid, so selfish. Is that what this is really about or is she angry I told her I'm not ready to be married?

Jon sighed.

It was late afternoon when they arrived in Lahaina. Jon parked near the library next to the Pioneer Inn. He helped Ellen with her small backpack. They kissed. Leaning against the car, he watched as she walked away. When she was a short distance away, she twirled around, their eyes meeting briefly, a smile on her face. Completing the twirl, she walked on. Jon admired her spirit and her courage.

With a heavy heart, he drove to Spreckelsville. The sunset that day was a spectacular display of brilliant colors covering the entire sky in every direction. Jon cursed the beautiful sunset. He knew Ellen would take it as a sign—a sign of endings, of new beginnings. Maybe it was.

28 | FULL CIRCLE

Sitting in the dim morning light of his father's living room, Jon reflected on his journey up to this point in his young life. Maui had brought a multitude of lessons and some unexpected gifts. He was grateful. He realized how much he'd grown. *Life is school.*

Jon's father, Karl, lived in a modest house in East San Diego, on the same street where Jon grew up. After his parent's divorce, Jon lived with his dad throughout high school and college, first in La Mesa, then back to East San Diego. Over the years, the neighborhood had become sketchy, even dangerous. Once when Jon's sister, Bev, was visiting, her rental car was broken into. Karl learned the hard way not to leave his bicycle unattended in his yard after having a couple stolen. Another time, Karl heard a noise in the kitchen. Upon investigating he noticed the back door ajar, and the door to the freezer compartment of the refrigerator wide open. Two steaks were missing. Most alarmingly, late one night someone was murdered at the bus stop right in front of his house. Karl had slept through it all, only finding out the next day. *Maybe that's why he plays classical music throughout the house, 24-7. It makes him feel safe,* Jon thought. *I'm glad I don't have to worry about keeping my doors locked back on the island.*

Jon was a bit apprehensive now when he came to visit his dad but he tried not to let his unease show. His father, on the other hand, was happy to call this home. He had no intention of leaving the area. He knew many of his neighbors, the near-by shop owners called him by name, and he was a familiar sight riding through the neighborhood on his bicycle. Jon could understand the appeal of community. He was starting to build that for himself.

Jon's mother remarried and relocated to the Bay Area. As a teenager he spent holidays and summers with his mother and stepfather, Dean. He'd held a summer job working with Dean in the cable TV industry. It worked out well, as he was able to move between two worlds: San Diego was a conservative Navy town with wonderful beaches and great weather. San Francisco was, well, . . . *San Francisco*. It was the epicenter of the counterculture. To his San Diego friends, Jon was a Cheshire Cat who seemed to mysteriously disappear and reappear at will.

Jon picked up his drawing tablet and opened it to thoughts he had written for Ellen.

> *Here to share your love*
> *and beauty.*
> *Your light*
> *comes to all*
> *who move*
> *around you.*

The writing was separated into two parts by a drawing. The word OM was inside of a triangle which itself was inside of a circle. Lines radiated outward from the circumference of the circle. Clouds, a full moon, and stars lingered above a simple tree-line ridge.

> *Growing, flowing,*
> *beautiful flower*
> *of God,*
> *your aura*
> *fills my being*
> *with peace.*

He turned the page, and continued reading:

Ramblings

You engulf me
like the morning fog,
adorning the coastal mountains,
cool, healing, refreshing,
both magical and alluring.

You work me
like a pick-pocket
on a crowded bus.

My mind, like an eel
bites onto thoughts
of you
and won't let go.

You are my teacher,
guiding me
to hidden corners
of myself.

Quiet moments followed, as Jon's eyes wandered about the room. He grabbed his pen and turned to a blank page. He drew a mountain peak with the sun rising from behind. He heard his father emerge from his bedroom and duck into the bathroom.

Beneath the new drawing, Jon added words to himself.

If I follow her,
I lose her,
if I follow
the path
of love and light
I grow closer
to her.

See her
as an angel
who came
to show you
far off vistas.

"Good morning sunshine. How did you sleep?" Karl had on a long, well-worn terrycloth bathrobe.

"Hey Dad, and a good morning to you. I slept fine. The pad on the couch is firm. That works for me."

"Sorry your old bedroom is full of junk. I needed more room for my *Life* magazine collection. I have almost two complete sets. Got rid of your bed a while back."

"Not a problem." He knew all about his father's collections. It was best not to get into it.

"Let's take a look at our day," Karl said as he opened the heavy living room drapes, leaving the thin inner curtains that provided privacy from the street. "Gray and gloomy. Looks like it rained last night. I'm going to heat water for my coffee. Do you want tea or something? There's orange juice."

Jon requested peppermint tea. The two sipped their hot drinks in the living room, Karl in his customary position in his recliner. It was his throne and command center. Next to the chair on a small table lay the TV remote, a notepad and pen, several books, and a pair of reading glasses.

"I was hoping to get in some more tennis. That's not going to happen, not with this weather."

"Next time, Dad. Good thing we went when we did. My friend, Dave, is coming to pick me up. We're going to the beach."

"It's not a very good day for the beach."

"I know, but tomorrow I head back to Hawai'i, so . . ."

"I'm sorry to see you go but I sure appreciate you coming. I enjoyed our walks and tennis matches. And thanks for all the help cleaning up around here."

"Me too. It was fun." Cleaning brought its own satisfaction. Especially here where the transformation was so clearly evident. Jon was happy that he could help. He considered it to be quality time spent with Pops.

When Dave arrived, Karl answered the door. He was still in his bathrobe.

"Hi, Mr. Jon," Dave said, reviving an old nickname. "Good to see you."

"Likewise. Had I known you were coming I would have dressed for the occasion."

"He knew you were coming," Jon called out from the living room.

"Come on in, lad. Would you like some orange juice?"

"Ah, sure."

"Hey bro."

Dave had short dark hair, a full beard, and was wearing a baseball cap. He took a seat along with Jon on the couch. Karl brought Dave his orange juice, served in a soup can rather than a glass. Dave quickly glanced over to Jon, who was smiling.

"Your house looks . . . nice and neat," Dave said, attempting to deflect the awkwardness of the moment. "You change things around since I was here last?"

"On trash day," Jon related, "we had twelve trash bags lined up on the curb. Trust me, a lot of it was literally trash."

"I hate to throw anything away," Karl said, from his recliner. "Jonny is a good cleaner-upper. So Dave, what kind of work do you do?"

"I'm a potter. I make pottery. And I teach at Grossmont College where I'm head of the ceramics department. It's a blast. I get paid for doing what I love."

"You're one smart cookie. Making a living on pottery. Maybe some of that will rub off on Jon. I think he's living in the jungle on Maui, contemplating his navel. I taught him everything I know and he still doesn't know anything," Karl teased.

"Thanks Dad. I love you too."

"Mr. Jon, I like your ceramic incense holder. That's a nice design. I'm going to have to make some of those."

"I picked that up at the flea market for a buck. I can't resist a bargain."

"That Primo stick incense is the good stuff. Very sweet."

"Flea market." Karl leaned forward in his chair. "I'm going to let you in on a little secret I've discovered. Incense doesn't have to be burned to give off fragrance. It really doesn't. Just having a couple of sticks in the holder does the trick. I do burn them after they've been sitting out for a while but one stick can last me a week or more. It's an air freshener."

"You're a genius," Dave exclaimed.

Karl put his forefinger to his lips. "Shhh. Don't tell anyone." He paused. "But it's true, I'm smarter than I look. When I was a kid, our school gave us IQ tests. Out of everyone, I had the highest IQ and the lowest grades."

Jon had heard the story before. He threw out one of his dad's own quips. "Are you bragging or complaining?"

Karl ignored the comment, turning back to Dave. "Do you need any coupons? They can save you a lot of money. I have stacks of them. Everything from soup to nuts. And I go to one store that doubles the coupon value so they're practically paying me for my groceries."

"Hence the five boxes of laundry detergent in the garage," Jon added.

"I appreciate it Mr. Jon," Dave said. "I'm good for now."

"Alright Pops. We're going to be heading out. We'll see you later."

"Have fun. Don't do anything I wouldn't do."

Jon and Dave climbed into Dave's Morris Minor.

"I can't believe you still have this car."

"Purrs like a kitten. Unfortunately, it also has the horsepower of a kitten. She's been a good one though. Good on gas too. British. They don't even make them anymore. Getting parts is a challenge."

"I remember you driving on the sidewalk, chasing little kids in it. They'd be looking over their shoulders, thinking, *what the hell?* There you were, trailing along behind them in this tiny car. Then you would start honking the horn."

"Did I do that?"

"You know you did. And how about that time you basically made a U-turn on the freeway? It was late at night and we missed our exit, there by the high school. You cranked the car around and exited via the on-ramp."

"What can I say? We were drunk and the next exit was a good ways down. I was just being efficient."

"More like wild and crazy."

"We weren't even the wild ones."

"Oh, I think we *may* have been the wild ones."

"Speaking of wild, I've never been served orange juice in a soup can before. That was a first."

"He was just showing off."

"How was everything up north?"

"Good. I always enjoy seeing my mom and hanging out with my sister, nieces, and everyone. It's nice spending Christmas with family."

Where did Ellen spend Christmas? Who did she spend it with? Jon regretted she hadn't come with him to California. They both were stubborn.

"Shall we go the scenic way?" It was more of a comment than a question, as this was their usual route when not in a hurry to get somewhere. The road skirted the bay then passed through residential areas of Mission Beach and Pacific Beach, heading up the coast. Dave dropped down to La Jolla Shores and parked in the public parking lot. Getting out, they trudged through the soft white sand to the water's edge. The ocean was angry, with a confused jumble of winter swells rolling in, choppy and windblown. Dark grey storm clouds filled the sky, threatening rain. Few people were on the beach.

The beach had always been a place where Jon could walk, sit, reflect. Whatever was going on in his life, a stroll along the shore always seemed to help sort things out.

They walked towards Scripps Pier. The sand just above the waterline was compact and firm, although one had to keep an eye on the ebb and flow of the waves to avoid getting wet. An older woman walking her golden retriever was coming towards them. The dog ran up to the men for a pet.

"He loves attention," she called out.

"Don't we all," Dave returned.

Jon petted the dog on the head and gave him a little scratch behind the ears. He thought about Kolohe, his loyal furry-faced companion who had disappeared without a trace. It was a mystery. Jon still hung onto the hope Kolohe was somewhere on Maui living a happy life, possibly curled up on someone's couch, or stalking a mongoose. *I miss that rascal.*

Farther up the beach they discovered a long strand of kelp that had washed ashore. They stopped to appreciate this curiosity from another world. It had many branches of flat blades and a large bulbous hollow float as part of its thick stem. The color itself was unusual—a golden brown. The entire plant looked and felt like it had been made of rubber.

"It's so cool you've ended up in Hāna," Dave said. "Do you ever see Joseph?"

"Oh sure. I run into him at Hasegawa Store and here and there. He's good, living life."

They continued to the pier, walking underneath through the pilings to the north side. The winter waves had removed a lot of the sand, narrowing the beach and revealing rocky outcroppings. The sand would be back, come summer, when it would once again completely cover the rocks. This was an area they knew well from years of surfing here. They sat on a concrete wall, looking out to the ocean.

"Are you happy?"

The abrupt question surprised Jon. It wasn't something that people generally asked. Dave was a good friend.

"It depends on what time of day you ask me."

"I *hear* that. I think life is one of those things we're perpetually getting used to. It just keeps changing. Living itself is an art form. So, tell me about this woman you mentioned the other day. The one you've been living with."

"Ellen. My beautiful sweet girlfriend. No, right before I left Maui, to come here, we went our separate ways." Jon sighed. "She wasn't going to be happy living in the jungle. It just isn't her world. And I'm not ready to leave my Garden of Eden. I'm totally bummed but I'm okay. I'm headed in the right direction. You can love someone without having to possess them."

Dave nodded, letting Jon have a moment with his thoughts.

"She made me realize that I am capable of loving and being loved. And that I'm worthy of love, that I'm a real person."

"Someone had to do it."

"Yeah. Fuck you. Sometimes I think about that fateful day I picked her up hitchhiking. I find it intriguing how seemingly insignificant choices and random events can change the course of our lives. Timing. The variables are endless as are the outcomes, I suppose. Literally, one minute sooner or one minute later, a right turn instead of a left turn."

Dave and Jon sat quietly, watching the waves.

"I'm not sure what the future holds, but I'm ready to find out. I do love Maui and being in Hāna. I know now it's where I belong. It's where I fit into the universe. And, you know, somewhere along the way there's a beautiful soul waiting for me, to share the journey."

The wind picked up and a cold rain began to fall. Jon smiled. "Time to go."

GLOSSARY

'Āina – the land

Aloha – hello, goodbye, love

Buggah – person or thing

Chance um – try it, give it a shot

Choke – a lot

Church key – bottle opener

Cockaroach – to steal

Coconut wireless – heard on the grapevine

Da kine – all-purpose word substitute filler, literally anything

Grinds – food

Hala tree – distinctive indigenous tree with thick aerial roots

Hale – house

Haleakalā – Maui's dormant volcano

Haole – white person, foreigner

Hau tree – grows horizontal, forming thickets

Heiau – ancient temple

Hele – to go

Hōkūle'a – "Star of Gladness," Polynesian voyaging canoe

Holo holo – go out for leisure

Howzit – how are you? Hello

Hui – undivided ownership of a common property

'Io – Hawaiian hawk

Junk – not good
Kai – ocean
Kalo – taro
Kāne – man
Kapu – keep out, forbidden
Kaukau – food, to eat
Keiki – child, children
Kolohe – mischievous, rascal
Lauhala – art of weaving bowls, hats, etc. from the leaves of the hala
    tree
Lei – garland of flowers
Lo'i – paddy for water grown taro
Loulu – species of palm
Lū'au – Hawaiian party or feast
Mahalo – thank you
Mainland – continental U. S.
Makai – toward the ocean
Mana – spiritual power
Mauka – toward the mountain
Mauna – mountain
Nēnē – Hawaiian goose
Mongoose – small weasel-like animal
'Ohana – family
'Ōhi'a – native tree endemic to Hawaii
'Ōkole – butt
'Ono – delicious
'Ōpae 'ula – tiny red freshwater shrimp
'Opihi – Hawaiian limpet, cultural edible delicacy
Pakalōlō – marijuana
Pali – cliff
Pau – finished
Pau hana – after work
Poi – a traditional staple food made from taro
Poi dog – mixed breed
Pomelo – large, thick-skinned grapefruit
Puka – hole

Pūpū – appetizer

R&R – rest and relaxation

Shaka – hang loose hand sign

Shake – small remnants of bud and leaves from trimming marijuana

Shoots – okay

Snowbirds – seasonal tourists escaping cold weather

Talk story – conversation

Taro – also known as kalo, a Hawaiian food source with edible tuber and leaves

'Ulu – breadfruit

Wahine – woman

ACKNOWLEDGEMENTS

THANK YOU . . .

Mom and Dad for your love and support. When I was younger I didn't understand why authors often acknowledged their parents. I get it now. And a shout-out to my step-father, Dean, who always encouraged my creative endeavors.

Patricia, my wife, who has been an invaluable sounding board along the way. And thank you for patiently and steadfastly typing and retyping the manuscript. I am grateful.

To my children, my sister Bev, extended family and friends. You do make a difference in my life.

Elaina Ellis, my editor. My deep gratitude for your skilled and thoughtful edits.

Bob Paltrow, talented graphic artist and musician, for the beautiful cover and customized Maui map. You rock.

Dr. Zella Mansson for proof reading. I appreciate your diligent work on this project.

Melissa Vail Coffman, of Book House Publishing, for your conscientious formatting and interior layout. Well done.

Chloe Hovind, Jessica Moreland, Stephanie Dethlefs, Sean Kearney, Sophie Richmond, the crew of Village Books Publishing. Thank you for your commitment, support, and guidance on this publishing journey.

Ken Moorhouse, of K-Elements Design, website designer extraordinaire, for the "beyond my dreams" website. Mahalo!

Margaret Smith Pierce. Mahalo nui loa, my friend, for lending your eyes for a final proof read.

LAHAINA FIRE

OUR HEARTS ARE BROKEN. UNIMAGINABLE TRAGEDY struck Lahaina on August 8th, 2023. A fire, spread by extremely high winds, burned Lahaina to the ground. In this horrific nightmare, over 100 lives were lost. This vibrant and sparkling jewel of Maui is gone. Lahaina was a place I knew well, and loved. In my mind I still walk those familiar streets. We pray the strong spirit of Lahaina will rise from the ashes.

ABOUT THE AUTHOR

Richard Dux Missler was born in Seattle and grew up in San Diego. He first ventured to Maui in 1969, at the age of eighteen. The beauty of the Islands inspired and nurtured his creativity. He called Hawai'i home for forty-eight years. In addition to being a writer, Missler is also an artist who has had a successful career as a painter. He is a lover of nature and a passionate gardener. Missler is currently living in the Pacific Northwest with his wife, Patricia, who is also a writer and artist.

Visit the author's website:
richardduxmissler.com
starshipmaui.com

Stay tuned for *Starship Maui, Book II*

www.ingramcontent.com/pod-product-compliance
Lightning Source LLC
Chambersburg PA
CBHW040859010826
48978CB00013BA/1088